Rosa Vertner Jeffrey

Woodburn

Rosa Vertner Jeffrey

Woodburn

ISBN/EAN: 9783744641241

Printed in Europe, USA, Canada, Australia, Japan

Cover: Foto ©Andreas Hilbeck / pixelio.de

More available books at **www.hansebooks.com**

WOODBURN.

A Novel.

BY

ROSA VERTNER JEFFREY,

AUTHOR OF "POEMS BY ROSA."

NEW YORK:

SHELDON & COMPANY, PUBLISHERS,

335 BROADWAY, COR. WORTH STREET.

1864.

Stereotyped by
SMITH & McDOUGAL,
82 & 84 Beekman St.

Printed by
S. C. WESCOTT & CO.,
79 John-Street.

To

An Only, and Dear Sister,

Is this Volume

Affectionately Inscribed,

By the Author.

CONTENTS.

CONTENTS.

CHAPTER I.

OUR FAMILY AT WOODBURN.

"WELL! the new teacher will be here to-morrow," said my father—putting a letter into his pocket with one hand, while with the other he caught hold of my tangled curls—"and then, Miss Mad-cap, I fancy you will have some occupation besides fastening night-caps on old Towser, and tying strings and feathers to poor pussy's tail,—to say nothing of crowning your reverend father with laburnums"—and he touched gayly, I might say gallantly, the chaplet of golden spring flowers I had just fastened above his brow, over great masses of fine, wavy white hair—which, blown about by the mild Spring air, looked like spun glass—thinking how grand and royal he looked. My dear, noble father! And how much more deserving he was the title of king or emperor than the many wicked monarchs in history; and then his perfections were marshalled, in bright array, against legions of horrors committed by defunct royalty—my hasty list beginning with Caligula and Nero, and ending with Harry the Eighth—when he interrupted my soliloquy as above, and turning to my brother, continued. And you, Master Ralph, must go back to Latin and Greek, instead of riding races with that wild gypsy, Pearl Dunbar; for Zebra had the thumps when you returned from that scamper to the cliffs last night—and as to Ethel's beautiful Arabian, Fleet-foot, I only wonder she is alive, after your late hard usage of her. But all that is over now, for awhile. The saints be praised! And we—viz.:—dogs, cats, horses and self, will have some rest."

"What, father! said Ralph, laughing,—you don't mean to say that all the fun is up, when your old English dominie arrives,—are we to have no rides, no races, no walks, no anything like frolic, between school-hours? Are we all to sit up, and twist our thumbs, and look as demure as Miss Tabitha Tipps, when presiding over one of those solemn conclaves, (styled by out-siders) "a spinsters' tea-fight"?

Saying which, the handsome scamp drew down his mouth, twisted his thumbs, and looked as much like an antiquated spinster as such a radiant young face could be made to look.

"What do you say to such solemn proceedings, Miss Amy," he continued, glancing up at me. "Would it be within the range of possible events, for you to become such a pink of maidenly propriety as Miss Tabitha Tipps?"

"Very well," said my father, "laugh away while you can, enjoy your freedom to-day, you saucy rogues—for when Mr. Clifford arrives, there will be no time to give us snatches of burlesque acting from the private life of Miss Tipps, a most respectable person by the way, for then books—books—study—hard study will be the programme. A rather more difficult one, too, I imagine, than has lately been submitted for your consideration."

"Mr. Clifford!" I exclaimed, "what a pretty name! I was certain it would be Jones, or Jenkins, or Fitz-boodle, or some such horrid thing; but Mr. Clifford, sounds so soft and genteel, perhaps we shall like him after all, and at all events there's some consolation in having a tutor in place of a governess, ugh! I can see old Mrs. Blake now, looking (or rather pretending to look) as if petrified with horror, by the shock of an earthquake, or some other convulsion of nature—because of a blot on my composition; and then, I'd rather hear a cannon go off suddenly at any time, than be electrified by the shrill, sharp voice in which she used to snap out 'for shame, young ladies' —because Pearl, and myself stuffed our handkerchiefs in our mouths, to keep from laughing out at Ralph's fiendish faces, when we could see-him, and she could'nt. I detest a governess, at least if she is a type of the class—and am sure we shall like Mr. Clifford better."

"Like him, indeed!" shouted Ralph, "hoity-toity, Miss Sentiment, so you fancy the owner of a pretty name must needs be a pretty man too; a dapper little gentle-man, forsooth, with smooth face, sleek hair, pink cheeks, and polite as a French dancing master; don't console your little ladyship in that way, for I am quite sure, in spite of his fine sounding name, that this John Bull dominie is a perfect fright, and as cross as an old bear. Mrs. Blake's reign, will be looked back upon as the golden age of our school-room, in spite of her snapping voice, freezing white eyes, and thundering frown, when Clifford the First, takes his seat upon her vacant throne,—and when he de-parts this life, should we be duly informed of that melan-choly event, I venture to say his ci-devant scholars here-abouts, will never worship him as their tutelary saint; hear me describe this gentleman :—Short and thick, bald as a bat,—except a circle of grisly hair round the back of his head, which will stand up like porcupine quills—especially when he is angry ; little round green eyes, big nose, par-ticularly fat towards the end, and the color of a red cab-bage, frost-bitten at that,—English whiskers, wiry as hog bristles, and the biggest, ugliest mouth you ever saw, full of black tusks, ' to eat you up with the better, my dear,' and he made a spring towards me, so sudden, that I cried out—for his description had wrought me up to quite a pitch of nervous excitement, and my sister Ethel, said,—

" For shame, Ralph! why do you try to frighten poor Amy into believing her new teacher is a regular ogre ?"

" He cannot frighten me, sis, with such nonsense," I

answered,—rather upon my dignity, being past fifteen and fancying myself a woman—"for in the first place I am not quite baby enough to like 'dapper little men,' and don't imagine Mr. Clifford as either pretty or small; and in the second, I don't believe such ogres as he has depicted are very common. My idea of our new tutor is—a long, dangling man, who has false teeth and wears a wig and spectacles! What do you think, sis?" and I knelt before Ethel, resting my head on her lap.

And here let me sketch a word picture of the radiant woman, who had been more than sister, and even as the best of mothers to me, from an early period of motherless infancy. I hate regular descriptions of heroines—beauties especially—yet in spite of this, cannot resist the temptation of inflicting upon my readers (perhaps selfishly) the perusal of what might be a task to write, were the subject less dear.

Ethel Linton was the most superb beauty I ever saw. At that time past the bloom of early youth, being twenty-five, yet her loveliness had ripened,—matured,—losing not freshness, yet gaining depth and tenderness of expression, in its growth to full perfection. She was tall, and elegantly formed,—a wavy, graceful figure, yet so round, there were no harsh angles there to mar its stately symmetry; fair, very fair, with large, lustrous hazel eyes, into whose clear depths you might gaze long and earnestly, and while gazing, feel as well assured that the soul within was a temple of purity and truth: as in watching the stars, we know those blue steeps which they adorn are boundary lines to a world of angels. The features were regular, yet not with the severe perfection of a Grecian statue. And it was the ever-changing lights, and shades of expression that constituted Ethel's chief attraction; the glow, the beam of intellect, the bewitching smiles, or laugh of gayety,—at times almost childish in its ringing merriment, and then, a shadow of mournfulness flitting over her face, eclipsing its light, like wreaths of purple vapor, that some times start suddenly across the glory of a summer sky, breaking into shimmering gleams the glow of sunshine on some enchanting landscape; yet shading it so softly, so dreamily, that we know not which to deem most lovely; the living picture bathed in light, or shadowed by its veil of purple cloud. My sister's hair was her crowning beauty. Golden brown, silky and abundant, it rippled in shining waves over her white brow, and braided into a mass at the back of her regal head, shone like a halo,— illuminating her whole form.

There were five of us grouped together, on that balmy May evening, on the gallery of our luxurious southern home. It·was a fine old country-house, built in my grandfather's time, with high ceilings, wide hall and stair-case, large conservatories, etc.,—in fact, all the comforts, and elegancies, that fine taste could suggest, or wealth purchase. The house stood on a high, double terrace, with sodded steps, leading down to a wide gravel carriage-path, winding gracefully to the front gate through a grove of live oaks. To the right of the house—approaching it—and running far back, was the garden, hedged with myrtle, and cape-jasmines, terraced also, deep, wide terraces, made long ago, with borders of box so tall and wide, that they imparted to the beds that venerable look which great staunch trees impart to a forest; how I doted on these closely clipped box borders,—so thick, and smooth, and flat on top, that as a child I had often spread them for a fairy banquet, with acorn-cups and the scarlet bell-shaped caps of the pomegranate blossoms.

Oh, that fragrant, grand old garden! how I delighted to revel in its cool depths of shade, and ever since those halcyon days of happy innocence, the fresh aromatic odors of box has had a peculiar charm for me no matter where, or in what clime, whether springing up from some humble flower plot, on the murky out-skirts of a city, or stealing to me in the dusty crowded street, upon a sweet cool breath of country air,—it comes as a waif of that beloved spot, and by some subtle spell of memory makes the present vanish, and again I seem a child among those fragrant borders, in the garden at Woodburn. There was a mossy rustic temple too, built of gnarled vines and roots, and tapestried with festoons of white and yellow jasmines; which I selected as a favorite retreat, and when worried with my lessons, or stupid in writing my composition, to the summer-house would I fly—for the balmy, inexpressibly sweet atmosphere of that retired spot, where the fragrance of an infinite variety of flowers, from the royal magnolia to the modest sweet violet—each season presenting its own perfect bouquet of odors—never failed to soothe, cheer, and encourage me, and the memory of those hours, when weary and heated I rushed from the school-room and hid myself there to rest—or at twilight, when that strange hum of insect life which thrills the southern air as night steals on, making all space around seem haunted with mysterious sounds, would lure me there to dream of nature's mysteries, as children with such temperaments as mine are wont to dream—the stars,—the calm blue depths of sky,—the very home of God,—wonders to the wise men of earth,—it is scarcely strange they should fascinate the minds of thinking children, with their endless and inexplicable marvels! And then the dewy, moon-lit nights in that garden, beneath that bower, alone, or with my cousin Victor—or a whole merry party trooping through the walks, singing— laughing—happy, these times, these scenes, stand out as the bright, never changing pictures of memory, the fairest, dearest treasures of her store.

But in the mazes of the garden I am losing sight of our family circle, and must now return to them. To my sister Ethel you have been introduced—at least to her *personnel*—and as the next chapter will be devoted to a sketch of her early history, I will pass on to some of the other actors in this little life drama.

My father, whose name was Edward Percy, at the time my story begins might have been sixty, or a little past—florid, with the thickest suit of grey hair I ever saw, or rather white, for not a dark strand marred its silvery beauty. Of medium height, his face wore an expression of intelligence and firmness, yet mingled with a look of almost feminine tenderness, so winning, that his children and servants never feared, while they so fully respected him, and as father, master, friend, there never was a man more truly and perfectly revered and beloved.

My brother Ralph was handsome, talented, impetuous, and just eighteen.

Being a narrator of, rather than a conspicuous actor in the strange events I am about to relate, my appearance is of very little importance, and therefore let me pass on to the fifth party in this group—Rachel Thorn. An orphan niece of my father's, poor, and without a home, he had invited her to Woodburn just after Ethel's marriage, and with his usual noble delicacy of feelings, lest she might shrink from becoming dependent and feel herself a burden upon him, Rachel was requested to come and take charge of his motherless children, filling my sister's place—thus making it appear that she was conferring an obligation instead of receiving one. Her only brother, Basil Thorn, he had educated for a physician, and offered him the plantation practice, with his influence to procure that of our whole neighborhood, but Basil was dissipated and unprincipled, though a young man of good appearance, and quite clever at his profession. He fell violently in love with my sister upon his return from college, and pretending that her scorn had driven him to desperation, ran into all kind of excesses—gambled deeply, and ended by forging my father's name for several thousand dollars, which was not discovered until after the money had been paid, when with his usual generosity, and kindness of heart—not altogether unmixed with family pride—he hushed up the matter, and allowed Basil to keep his ill-gotten gold provided 'he would leave the country and give a solemn promise never to return. This promise was given, and young Thorn went off, no one knew whither, leaving his sister poor, and unprotected, and then it was my kind father offered her a home, which she gladly accepted.

Rachel Thorn was, perhaps, some three years younger than Ethel, and as *petite* as my sister was stately. She too was fair, but such a different type of fairness, you could not call them alike in complexion, as well compare the dead lustreless white of a detura to the dewy freshness of a pale tea-rose. Rachel's hair was very light, as were her brows and lashes, over-shadowing eyes of a cold, steel grey, almost cruel in their expression when lit by anger, and always having, even in her pleasantest moods, something in them, as had also her thin, sneering lips, disagreeable, one scarcely knew why, and never hidden—not even when she uttered honeyed flatteries—from those who knew the inner workings of her subtle nature.

I never liked Rachel Thorn; nay, I even disliked her from the first moment of our meeting; not because she came to fill the place of an almost idolized sister, for had she been lovable I should in time have learned to love her; but sometimes children, with the pure instincts springing from their perfect innocence, seem to shun with aversion their opposites, reading the characters of deep and dangerous people oftentimes with far more accuracy than those well versed in the ways of the world. It seems to me a strange divine kind of instinct, such as leads young birds and animals to know and avoid their natural enemies. Rachel's nature was imperious and domineering, and the year she ruled at Woodburn during Ethel's absence, was a sad trial to Ralph, myself, and the servants, for she proved exacting and tyrannical to all save my father, but invariably smiling, attentive and affectionate to him, she anticipated every wish, and exerted her really fine conversational powers for his amusement, sang his favorite songs, played his favorite games, and in short used all the arts that a smart, wily woman can use with such advantage to fascinate an old uncle, upon whose good opinion she depends for home, dress, position, every thing that such women prize with the intense selfishness of their ambitious and designing natures.

My father liked Rachel, because she interested and amused him, and when either Ralph or myself complained of her being unreasonable and domineering he would.fancy that regret at losing my sister's gentle government, prevented our judging her successor with any degree of impartiality, and therefore soothing us, as children are so apt to be soothed on such occasions, he would end by saying:

" Well, well, my little ones, you must try and love cousin Rachel, she is a smart, pleasant girl, and wants to do right. You cannot expect every one to be as perfect as Ethel."

So as time wore on we scarcely ever spoke of Rachel's faults to my father, looking upon her as a fixture in the house, avoiding her as much as possible, and laughing together over the sly, artful way, by which she kept herself in good repute with the master of Woodburn, where she ruled with a high hand until my sister's return, when there was a change of dynasty, much to our relief.

Oh! how Rachel Thorn hated Ethel, for coming back, yet she feared to show it, and one who did not know the hidden meaning of her deep ways, might have supposed that she doted upon her beautiful cousin—but we knew better, and so did my sister, who amused Ralph and myself beyond expression by the quiet, queenly contempt, with which she received her flatteries, and the cool way in which she not unfrequently unmasked the little actress was inimitable! But why did my sister return to her girlhood's home, and where was her husband ?

CHAPTER II.

MY SISTER ETHEL.

ETHEL PERCY was a belle even before her school days
were well over; alas! too often is this the case in America,
and particularly in the Southern States, where girls mature
so early. With rare perfections both of mind and person,
and being called upon to take charge of the establishment
at Woodburn, where my father entertained a great deal of
company—while yet almost a child, she was, of course,
observed, petted, and admired—nay, might have been
spoiled,—as many have been under similar circumstances
—but some natures are too pure, too firm, to be tainted by
flattery, and resist it, even as adamant resists the corroding
acids, or consuming heat that would tarnish or destroy a
softer gem. My father was proud of her, glad to see her
admired; how could it be otherwise?

Ethel had teachers from the time she knew her alphabet,
and was entirely educated at home, as boarding schools

were held in detestation by my father, and Mrs. Blake, of whom I expressed such a holy horror in the last chapter,—supposed to have white eyes, full of lightning darts, with thunder enthroned upon her brows—being Ethel's last governess, remained at Woodburn after her marriage for our benefit, until one day she informed my father, with a solemn, subdued look, that her scholars (particularly Miss Dunbar and Master Ralph) were entirely beyond her control, and she would be compelled, very reluctantly, to resign her place to some one who could command their respect. The truth is, I have alway had my suspicions that this same middle-aged dame,—being of rather an ambitious temperament—had some lurking ghost of a hope forever haunting one corner of her icy heart, that as gentlemen had been known to marry their housekeepers, or perchance their children's governess, such a thing might occur again, at least it was within the range of possibility, but as time wore on, finding she would be quite as successful in melting an iceberg with her albino eyes, as in making an impression with the same luminaries upon the armor of freezing politeness in which the master of Woodburn incased himself (when she was about)—and having a most cordial dislike to Rachel Thorn, whose spiteful speeches worried her as a sly, vindictive little cat might be supposed to torment a great, surly mastiff;—Mrs. Blake, as other amiable ladies of the same class would doubtless have done under such trying circumstances—threw the blame on her pupils,—and left Woodburn in high disgust, to seek out some more favored abode, inhabited by widowers, with hearts less stony than she believed my father's to be. Poor Mrs. Blake! I did not love her much, and sometimes, may be, worried her a little, but have unceasingly endeavored to atone for all this by hoping she is married!

When Ethel was in her seventeenth year my father took her with him to New Orleans, where (after some persuasion) he consented she should remain with some friends for several weeks, and returned home without her. He regretted this afterwards, but short-sighted mortals cannot rule their destinies, nor the destinies of their children. During that visit it was that my sister met Arthur Linton. Handsome, graceful, and accomplished, she was dazzled by his brilliant, winning ways, though in intellect he was far her inferior. Being a Northerner and a stranger in the city, little was known of young Linton, save that his family was good, his father a man of wealth, and over indulgent to his only son, who was decidedly fast—a genteel correction of dissipated.

Ethel knew not of this,—at least, she turned a deaf ear to those who warned her; saw only the perfections of her lover—for such he soon became—and reputed all reports regarding his dissipated habits, as slanders arising from envy of his fine appearance and fascinating manners, for to my lovely deluded sister he seemed perfection, " an admirable Crighton." and so encouraged by her preference from the first, Arthur Linton followed Ethel to Woodburn.

My father was captivated by the young stranger, who in playing for such a prize played skillfully—and won, leaving for the North in the course of a few weeks as my sister's affianced husband. There was no one there to warn him of Arthur's dissipated habits, for the friends who would have saved Ethel, finding her so incredulous, forbore further interference, and being satisfied as to his family, and position, my father (not on the look-out for faults) was beguiled, as his daughter had been, by ease, grace, amiability—and that, *je ne sais quoi*, so often marking the manners of fast young men, and rendering them attractive. Their marriage was to take place in six months—on her seventeenth birth-day, though at first my father objected to this, on account of Ethel's extreme youth, and wanted the wedding postponed until she was eighteen, but Linton was eloquent, and succeeded in carrying his point.

It was during their engagement that Basil Thorn returned from college—having completed his medical studies in New York, at the age of twenty-five—and fell so violently in love with Ethel. He addressed her during Arthur's absence, though she strove by every means to prevent it, and when at last, she was compelled, in rejecting his hand, to announce her engagement, and approaching marriage with another, his rage knew no bounds, and repeatedly he swore to be revenged upon her, and upon her future husband. He left no effort untried to prevent the marriage, and mixing as Basil Thorn did with dissipated society, he was actually in possession of much information regarding Linton's career, of which my father and sister were ignorant —of course, attributing all he said, and wrote to them upon this subject, to jealousy of a successful rival. His motives were selfish and mean; yet, would to God he had succeeded in breaking off this match, for years of after misery had thus been spared.

One of Basil's letters to my father upon the subject contained something which evidently troubled him much for a time, but which he burned, and we never knew its contents until the truth of what he wrote, alas! had been too bitterly proved.

It was to be—such things seem fated—and spite the warnings of true friends, and Basil Thorn's selfish interference, the beautiful Ethel Percy became Mrs. Linton, and after remaining a week at Woodburn, left us a happy and blooming bride for her husband's northern home. They were to return and spend the winter at Woodburn, which so far consoled us for Ethel's loss that we bore it patiently, if not cheerfully.

A few months after this Basil ended his mad career by committing forgery, as before related, and Rachel came to live at Woodburn.

At first Ethel's letters were full of happiness—she was

charmed with her new home, and friends, and wrote of Arthur as the best, most indulgent of husbands, his father devoted to her, etc., etc.—but six months brought different tidings.

Old Mr. Linton, whose wealth was the result of enormous speculations, had been unfortunate in business, and lost his fortune as suddenly as it was made. Arthur's affluence, being derived from his father's generosity, was thus changed to poverty, and as the old gentleman fell ill and died shortly after his failure, there seemed little hope for their future, as his son had no business capacity. My father immediately remitted funds to Ethel, and continued to do so from time to time, advising them to come South, and promising to assist her husband in his misfortunes.

From these sums (as we afterwards learned) Ethel derived but little benefit, for Linton had been gradually sliding back into his old habits of dissipation—abandoned for some time before and after his marriage—and ere the first anniversary of her wedding-day came round, my sister's letters were so full of wretchedness, that young as we were, both Ralph and myself observing our father's haggard look of misery after reading them, asked him if Ethel was sick?

He put us off by saying she was not well, which answer was far from satisfactory, and with a kind of childish, loving instinct, after talking the matter over, we came to the conclusion that something was amiss with our sweet sister, and that she was unhappy—saying we hated Arthur Linton for taking her away just to make her miserable, and wishing he was dead —which was rather spiteful, to be sure, but quite natural under the circumstances, for we doted on Ethel, and took it for granted, as we were kept in the dark about it, that he must abuse her.

At last a letter came, but not in her hand-writing, which caused my dear father to turn very pale, and immediately after reading it, he requested Rachel Thorn to have his trunk packed, as he should leave the next morning for New York.

This letter, as I afterwards learned, was from an old friend of his, residing in that city, whose painful task it was to communicate that my brother-in-law, after the loss of his fortune, had become excessively dissipated, drinking to intoxication, and constantly frequenting gambling saloons.

In one of these, a few nights previous to the date of his letter, Arthur, while under the influence of brandy, had become involved in a quarrel so desperate that it ended in his killing his antagonist; when to avoid immediate arrest, he was obliged to secrete himself, inducing Ethel by letter to forward his trunk of clothes to a certain place, where he pretended to be called unexpectedly by business.

Vainly and anxiously she awaited his return, until at last another letter came, in which the whole fearful truth was revealed. Arthur represented himself therein as a beggar and a murderer, obliged to fly the country for his life, and entreating that she would return to her father, her husband having forfeited all claim to her love, and would never return to be a disgrace to those who had once loved him.

My sister's condition after the receipt of this letter, as may well be imagined, bordered upon madness; and nothing further being heard from Arthur, Mr. —— wrote, begging my father to come at once and take her home. After his arrival at New York—both for Ethel's sake and to satisfy himself—every possible search and inquiry was made to ascertain the hiding place of her unfortunate husband—but all to no purpose, he had evidently left the country, and all that remained for my father was to soothe his almost heart-broken child, with that tender affection she prized—aye—doubly now—and to bring her back pale and sad to Woodburn, from whence she had so lately gone a happy bride. Thus at the early age of eighteen was my beautiful sister left a deserted wife. My father, of course, reproached himself bitterly for consenting to their marriage—yet completely deceived, as he was, regarding Linton's real character, who could blame him? No wonder that one so noble, true, and good, should be unsuspicious of evil in others, especially when that evil wore so fair a mask, besides being linked with some really good qualities, for Arthur Linton was amiable, generous, and affectionate, and had never been rough or unkind to Ethel personally, though neglect is unkindness, and he avoided her when under the influence of those evil passions which led him on to ruin.

As time wore on Ethel became less sad, and sonetimes I fancied she had a hope that her husband would reform, and return yet to make her happy, until at last—one day, about a year after she arrived at Woodburn—all such hopes were finally dissipated by the receipt of a California paper directed to my father, in which a notice of Arthur Linton's death, "from brain fever," was carefully marked. The young widow grieved piteously at first, but after another year, we could see that she regained her cheerfulness more surely, and naturally, than while pining under the double misery of being the deserted wife of a gambler. Six years had passed since then, to the date of my story, and amid the sweet atmosphere, and lovely surroundings of that beloved home, our darling Ethel had matured into the beautiful woman before whom I knelt caressingly on that fair spring evening, when we were discussing Mr. Clifford's expected arrival at Woodburn.

CHAPTER III.

MR. CLIFFORD.

THE next morning I awoke with that nervous, uneasy feeling, which is apt to possess the minds of young persons, particularly those who are excitable and sensitive in their organization, when something disagreeable is about to happen—something we would feign avoid, but cannot, an inevitable necessity, to which the mind must be made up, as to the pulling of a tooth, and from which we shrink with mental dread, as the body does in anticipation of physical pain. For in spite of our new tutor's pleasant sounding, aristocratic name, with which I pretended to console myself the previous evening, my dreams of Mr. Clifford were none of the sweetest.

The horrid ogreish picture drawn by Ralph, haunted me all night, and once, when with a sudden start and cry, I awoke, to feel my sister's soft hand laid gently on my brow, and hear her firm, sweet voice whispering, "Lie still, Amy, dear; what is the matter?"

I replied, drowsily, "Oh! Sis, I dreamed our new teacher was just as Ralph described, savage as a Bengal tiger, and my start just now was a dodge to avoid the big dictionary, which he seemed hurling at my head."

Ethel laughed, and patting me playfully said, "Go to sleep, little one, and dream of the name which seemed too nice for Ralph's ogre."

Yet still, though I went to sleep again, imagining Mr. Clifford as the patient, dangling, good-natured individual I had pictured in opposition to my brother, from my dreams he still arose, bristling, fierce and inflexible, fastened upon my mind as the "old man of the sea" on Sinbad's body. And when our maid Lucy, with her low voice, whispered, as she drew aside the curtains, " Come, Miss Ethel, Miss Amy, it's eight o'clock, time to get up, mammy says breakfast's most ready," I could scarcely shake off the dreamy conviction that Ralph's Mr. Clifford was storming in the school-room because of my laziness, and waiting there to annihilate me with his green eyes and carbuncle nose. So while Lucy was combing out Ethel's magnificent hair, I sat tardily pulling on my gaiters, looking quite disconsolate and forlorn. When suddenly catching sight of me, my sister laughed aloud, exclaiming:

"Do, for pity's sake, Amy, cheer up; for should you look so dismal when this dreaded Englishman arrives, he will be forced to the conclusion that you are the scape-goat of the family, or that—worse still—you have a step-mother; from which last named calamity the saints preserve us,' she added devoutly. "Your pet, Mrs. Blake, for instance; just fancy now, Amy, if father had been bewitched with that perfect embodiment of all the cardinal virtues, and, clasping us · to his heart some fine morning, whispered into our ears the electrifying intelligence, that the dearest, sweetest, best mamma on earth was already picked out and ready for us! Picture it, think of it, such things have been; and remember, in comparison to such a trial, how trifling is the advent of even a savage teacher; and do you know, I've taken it into my head that he will prove quite a pleasant person after all, and that learning from him will be to you like a draught of champagne, sweet and exhilarating, after being plied with the bitter tonic of Blake's temper for such a time," and she glanced up at me with a beam of sparkling mirth in her eyes, which melting over that matchless face, lighted even its dimple with an expressive glow,

> "Like any fair lake which the breeze is upon,
> When it breaks into dimples, and laughs in the sun—"

continuing, "haven't you dismissed that absurd dream yet, little Sis? Come, let me curl your hair while Lucy is braiding mine, and then look your prettiest, so as to captivate Mr. Clifford at first sight, for I believe he is to arrive before dinner."

"La, Miss Ethel," said Lucy, without stopping for a moment in the pleasant task of which she was so fond, the twisting and plaiting those wonderful tresses, "if you mean the strange teacher-man, he's done come. Master told Archey to take Zebra out to de landing, bright and early dis mornin', as de boat might be up by daylight, but Archey went a coon-hunting wid Massa Ralph last night, and so, nigger-like, he went and over-slep hissef; so who should he meet over dar by de Elgin gate, but a stranger-man, and den Archey say, he took off his hat and, says he, 'Good mornin, massa, is you gwying to Woodburn?' and de gentleman said 'Yes,' for de boat, you see, got up uncommon early, and he borrowed a horse. But now, getting down, what did he do but tell Archey to take de critter back to de riber, saying he would ride Mr. Percy's horse de rest ob de way. Den says Archey, 'I chuckled and laughed to myself,' —you know how Archey chuckles when anything comes over him funny like, Miss Ethel—'for thinks I to myself, dem Yankee men from de North don't know nuffin 'tall 'bout ridin' sich cantankerous creeters as Zebra, and I'll be bound he'll get throwed 'fore he strikes de Woodburn lane. But my stars! Lucy, dis nigger was mistaken once, sure; for no sooner did dat stranger-man put his hand on Zebra's neck—but twixt you and me, I don't believe he's even kin to a Yankee—while he was bowing it up and looking skittish,—then he stood as stock-still as old Bill, when he's tired out ploughing,—and when the new man got up, 'fore de Lord, I believe he thought it was Massa Ralph a mountin' him.' But good gracious, young ladies, dar's de breakfast bell!" and she stuck in the last hair-pin with such a spasmodic jerk that my sister cried,

"Pray don't murder me, Lucy, there's no hurry. Mammy always keeps hot cakes for us, and we are not expiring with anxiety for an introduction to Mr. Clifford; are we, Miss Percy?" and she turned to me with mock dignity.

"Well, any how, Archey tells me he's monstrous fine lookin', and don't in de least dissemble a school-master man," continued the loquacious Lucy, "with that attempt at big words so common among our southern house-servants.

"There now, Amy, with such a description from a person of such undoubted good taste as Archey, you may dismiss all the terrible phantasmagoria of your dreams last night, and go down to meet this elegant newly-imported wonder, in the shape of an English dominie, with unruffled assurance;" and Ethel offered me her arm encouragingly, as Lucy opened the door for us to descend to the breakfast-room.

How lovely my sister looked that morning, in a pure

white muslin wrapper, fastened neatly at the waist by a delicate lilac belt, trimmed daintily round the throat with soft, fine lace, and caught together with a curiously wrought pin of Etruscan gold. No wonder she generally adopted a rare simplicity of dress, when it became her so well.

Mammy, with a suspicion that we would be late, and fearing that her unexceptionable muffins might be baked a trifle too long, had the bell sounded before breakfast was quite ready, to hurry us; so when we entered, my father was just showing Mr. Clifford in through the library door.

"My eldest daughter, Mrs. Linton, Mr. Clifford," he said. "My youngest daughter, Miss Percy. Amy, darling, come and shake hands with your new preceptor;" and then I looked up to meet the large, sad, wonderfully persuasive eyes of my teacher fixed upon me so encourag-ingly, that with a blush and smile of positive delight at finding the ugly monster of a dream—from which I seemed scarcely awakened—as if by magic, transformed into this elegant looking individual; and when with a firm, gentle clasp he pressed my hand between both of his, which were white and finely formed, and indicated gentle birth and breeding, even to the shape and polish of his nails, I felt very happy under the full assurance that Mr. Clifford was my friend as well as my instructor.

Even Ethel, with all her queenly self-possession of

manner, seemed for a moment almost embarrassed, so completely was she astonished at Mr. Clifford's unusually striking appearance, and the ease and polish of his bearing. Such eyes, and such a mouth, would have redeemed any face (even were it otherwise positively ugly), and lighting up, as they did, finely-cut features, a clear, pale complexion, to say nothing of those waving sunny-brown locks, and a soft brown beard, the effect was wonderfully agreeable. In figure he was tall, well proportioned, and muscular. His age I never could have guessed then, for though in the full prime of mature manhood, one might be puzzled to say whether he was thirty-five or past, though afterwards I knew that at the time of his arrival at Woodburn Mr. Clifford was thirty-eight.

And now let me return to the breakfast table: My father's rule was, that meals should be served punctually at certain hours,—never allowing one member of the family to wait for another, and making no exception even in his own favor, so those who came in first always sat down, and those who happened to be a little late, did not come sneaking to the table, in dread of a lecture, as is the case in many "a well regulated household"—less happy in their rigid punctuality than were the family at Woodburn.

So it chanced the morning of Mr. Clifford's arrival, that Ethel had finished pouring out our coffee when Rachel Thorn glided in through the balcony door—her movements were all gliding and stealthy, as a cat—holding in her hand a basket of very large green figs, garnished with roses and white jasmine. They looked very tempting, with the dew yet glistening upon them, and the bearer presented no unattractive picture as she entered, prettily attired in a delicate blue morning dress, round garden hat, and black silk jacket. Rachel's figure was lithe and graceful, her face peculiar, yet rather striking and prepossessing when undisturbed by the worst passions of her nature, and strangers upon seeing her were apt to remark, "What a graceful, pretty girl."

"Ah! Rachel!" exclaimed my father, "you are the only industrious bee about this hive, and have been gathering in your store of sweets, betimes, I see." She had placed the basket before him on the breakfast table. "Many thanks, what a delicious treat, and the first really fine figs we have had this season. Mr. Clifford, let me present you to my niece, Miss Thorn."

I shall never forget the puzzled look of wonder that overspread Rachel's face as she glanced up at Mr. Clifford, who rose at once and bowed with that perfect ease so peculiar to high-bred men who have traveled and seen much of the world.

Just as she was seated, "rattle-te-bang" echoed through the hall. There was a rush, a bark, and then Ralph's merry voice crying:

"Down, Towser, don't you know better, you old rascal,

than to jump with your dirty paws on my new hunting suit? Ho! halloo there, Archey, come and take Lara to the stable, will you?"

Bristol, the waiter, here stepped softly to the hall door, and said, in a rather loud whisper, "Archey isn't here, Massa Ralph, he's dun gone to de river, and please sir they'r eating breakfast." With which, he quietly opened the door wide enough to present a tableau of my gay young brother in his green hunting clothes, with flushed cheeks and tousled hair, just putting down his gun, with a bang, in the corner. His face was partially turned away from the open door, and being unaware of the presence of a stranger, he shouted out:

"Good morning to you all. Father, have you been riding this morning? I missed Zebra out of the stable, and couldn't find that lazy scamp Archey two hours ago, to saddle my horse."

"Come in, come in my son. I have not been out, though Zebra has, (but only a short distance,) owing to your pet Archey's oversleeping himself. He is a lazy dog truly, but we have a surprise for you, Ralph, come in, I want to introduce you to a friend of mine."

By this time he had gained the door, and caught sight of our stranger guest.

"My son, Master Ralph Percy, Mr. Clifford," and they were shaking hands before my brother had time to recover from the dumb, overpowering astonishment which seemed to take possession of him, on hearing the name of our new teacher.

I sent him a triumphant telegraphic glance across the table, and the mischievous curl of Ethel's lip was irresistible, as she said, after a brief pause succeeding this last introduction :

" Mr. Clifford, I hope you can draw, so that Ralph's talent for this art may be cultivated,—as he has remarkable taste for sketching, especially ideal portraits of persons he has never seen."

My brother laughed, of course, as did all those who saw the joke—how could he help it ? But the young gentleman looked uncomfortable, and began to play with his fork in visible trepidation. Mr. Clifford, with a quick perception and keen sense of the ridiculous for which he was remarkable, smiled, with that beautiful expressive smile, which seemed to illuminate his whole face, and bowing to my sister replied :

" I do draw, Mrs. Linton, and shall be most happy to assist your brother in his sketches," for he knew there was a joke and shrewdly suspected (as he told us afterwards) the real meaning of Ethel's jesting sarcasm.

Such was our first breakfast at Woodburn after Mr. Clifford's arrival. Little then we dreamed how strangely he would be identified with us in the progress of coming events. That blessed and perfect wisdom which hides the future from us, is scarcely appreciated,—for, alas, how few happy parties,—how little of jest, or laughter, would there be, were we suffered to gratify the human curiosity,—so presumptuous—which might oftentimes tempt us to sweep aside that mysterious veil, and rashly look beyond it.

CHAPTER IV.

OUR SCHOOL ROOM.

BACK of the house,—detached from it, and so near the hawthorn hedge separating yard and garden, that every breeze, stealing in through the open windows, came loaded with balm,—stood a picturesque little cottage, containing, on one side, our school room, light, commodious and cheerful, and on the other two smaller rooms,—a chamber and study for the teacher. Finished and furnished with oak, curtained with delicate blue chintz—to match the coverings of the furniture—with a dainty little book-case and writing desk in the study, these apartments were a very model of elegant neatness,—and I gladly accepted the pleasant task assigned me by my father of introducing Mr. Clifford to his new domain.

He seemed pleased with all the arrangements, and particularly to find his own apartments thus detached from the main building, "for," he remarked, "here I shall be more to myself, and feel less a trouble to the family, than if obliged to come and go constantly through the house, appearing unexpectedly at unseasonable hours, and perhaps causing the various members of your family, Miss Amy,—who are, doubtless, most amiable under less aggravating circumstances—to wish a certain nameless individual very far off in an opposite direction."

I looked up, smiling, and with the innocent straight-forwardness so common in very young girls, replied, " Well, perhaps if you were cross and ugly, as I fancied you might be, such a thing is possible—but surely, Mr. Clifford, you don't suppose for a moment that any of us could wish you out of the way ?"

" I hope not," he said, evidently much amused at my earnest manner ; "and perhaps there is a tinge of selfishness in my liking this little cottage so much, for, besides disliking to be troublesome, I am very fond of being quiet, when inclined to read or write—and now, Miss Amy, tell me, will you, who are to be my scholars, only yourself and your brother ?"

" No," I answered, "there is another, Pearl Dunbar, who will ride several miles every morning to join our class. She is the adopted daughter of a relation of my father's, whom we always call ' Uncle,' and though, in reality, Pearl is not related to us, she seems like a dear cousin, indeed almost·a sister, so constantly have we been together from our infancy."

"Pearl!" exclaimed Mr. Clifford. "What a very strange, sweet name. Is she remarkably fair—a blonde—to be thus named?"

"Oh, no, quite the reverse," I said; "she was called Pearl when my uncle adopted her, at which time she was four years old, and I know nothing of her previous history. The Dunbars live at Elgin, the beautiful place you passed just before reaching here, on your way from the river. She looks like a Spanish girl; is very talented, handsome, as wild as a deer, a perfect Die Vernon on horseback, and is just a little past sixteen."

I paused, suddenly, for a moment, wondering why Mr. Clifford should look so sad, or rather, so much sadder than usual, while listening to this hasty description of a perfect stranger; and then—fearing he might notice my hesitation—went on:

"And my cousin, Rachel Thorn, to whom you were introduced this morning, intends, I believe, taking lessons in drawing, and German also—if you teach German. So you will have four scholars instead of two; quite enough, I fancy, to try your patience to the utmost. And now, suppose we stroll through the garden, it is so lovely!"

Saying which, without waiting for a reply, I bounded down from the little vine-covered verandah, and through an arched pass-way cut in the hedge, followed by my teacher, who accepted the proposed ramble with evident pleasure; and knowing, as all thoroughly well-bred persons

do, that the chief charm of keeping up conversation pleasantly, especially with a stranger, is by lending an interested
attention to what is said, and never interrupting the speaker,
Mr. Clifford won me completely, by listening, with
apparent satisfaction, to all my girlish chatter about every
thing connected with Woodburn and its surroundings.
Then, to the many questions I asked regarding far-off
countries—having discovered that he was a great traveler—
he replied so fully and so kindly, rather encouraging than
checking my curiosity, that ere our conversation ended, I
came deliberately, to the opinion that Mr. Clifford was the
most fascinating of teachers—if not of men. I had not
known many, to be sure; yet the sincere respect and
admiration of a young heart, as yet unspoiled by the (too
often) contaminating influences of society—is no unworthy
meed of praise.

Our walk through the garden extended all over the
premises, and the great plantation bell was ringing for
twelve o'clock as we sauntered up through that grand old
avenue of live oaks to the front door; my companion
started at the sound, and, turning to me quickly, said,

"Why, that is like a boat-bell! yet, surely, you cannot
hear them thus distinctly so far from the river."

I laughed out—and explained that it was only the plantation bell ringing, to call in the hands from the field to
their dinner.

"Ah, yes; I had forgotten," he replied. "The regulations here are pretty much the same, I believe, as on the places in Cuba."

"In Cuba!" I could not help repeating, "Have you been to Cuba, too, Mr. Clifford?"

"Yes, I lived there once for nearly a year." And then that same unaccountably sad expression which he had worn when I was describing Pearl, again flitted over his face; so I instantly refrained from pursuing the subject; and seeing Ethel at the front door, I ran on to ask her if lunch was ready?

So soon as Mr. Clifford joined us, I left him with my sister, and went into the library, hoping to find my father and Ralph, that they might be consulted about a riding party in the evening, for our new teacher's benefit; that he might be introduced to Pearl, for whom we were to call at Elgin, and then go on to the Cliffs. It was all quickly arranged and discussed as we sat at lunch.

"Ethel must lead the party," said my father, "with Mr. Clifford; as she is a fine rider, and deserves such an escort—if Archy's account of our friend's horsemanship be correct," and he winked at me with a quizzical expression, "for your ability to control Zebra, Mr. Clifford, has convinced this pet darky of Ralph's that you are the very prince of equestrians, as he is rather a fiery animal, and not always very docile with strangers—though I had no hesitation in sending him out for you, as Englishmen generally are fine riders. The cause of Archey's surprised ad-

·miration, however, is, that he thought you were a northerner, and as a general rule they are not brought up in the saddle, as is the case with our southern youth of both sexes."

"Riding is a part also of English education," said Mr. Clifford, pleasantly, "and therefore I deserve little credi for making friends so soon with Zebra; and though grateful for Archey's admiration, I cannot help feeling a shrewd suspicion that mingled therewith was a shade of disappointment at my failing to turn a summerset over the head of your spirited chestnut, Mr. Percy."

At which Ethel and myself were not a little amused, remembering the account of that amiable Ethiopian's "chuckle" at the triumph his fancied Zebra would achieve to Mr. Clifford's discomfiture, related to us that morning by Lucy.

I could see by the expression of Rachel Thorn's face, when my father proposed being her escort, that she would rather have been assigned to Mr. Clifford; for devoted to the society and attention of gentlemen, she never failed, in her sly, insinuating way, to attract the notice of every male visitor at Woodburn, and jealousy of my sister's superior attractions was the master-passion of her life. Yet too wily to let the uncle she had so thoroughly succeeded in blinding as to her real character, have an insight into those sly manœuvres, only a momentary shade of annoyance flitted over her countenance, unobserved by all save me, ere she replied,

"Oh, yes, certainly, with pleasure. You know I don't care always to ride as fast as the rest, so we can jog along as quietly as you wish."

A little shaft of amiability, aimed at our handsome teacher, who was peeling a banana for Ethel, and did not even hear what she said, I think, for Rachel bit her lip upon observing his occupation, as she glanced up at him with her most winning smile, while speaking to my father.

Long afterwards, how well I remembered the lightning glance of concentrated hate and envy she cast on that pre-occupied pair, who were chatting gayly, unconscious of her smiles or frowns. How strangely and vividly such passing scenes, so trifling and uninteresting at the time, seem stereotyped upon the memory, when, from after circumstances, they become as the first links in a chain of events, startling, unexpected, unaccountable.

As we left the lunch-table, Ralph gave me a pinch on the arm, and whispered, "So we are to have one more frolic, Amy, at all events, before the game of Tipps begins; not quite as exciting as a race with Pearl, to be sure; for we must behave our prettiest, to try and make a good impression on Mr. Clifford. I say, what a perfect *stunner* he is —a prince in disguise, no doubt. And now just mark my prediction, if our dear cousin Rachel goes to imbibing German from him, she will tumble head over heels in love !—

not with Goethe and Schiller, but with her teacher, and try, like the sleek, gliding little snake she is, to coil about his heart; and then, if foiled in this, as is most likely, look out for poisoned stings those who stand in her way! I wonder what on earth possessed such a trump of a fellow to come down here, Amy, to be tormented and bedeviled with us—old Blake's leavings!—Jupiter! how the old woman would pitch at him, and roll love-looks instead of thunder-gusts out of her white eyes, should she happen to turn up about this time. It's well she's off, fairly out of the way. You know father offered to let her stay here until another home presented itself: for Rachel Thorn, and our never-to-be-forgotten, or lamented either, Blake, would have fought, and scratched each other's eyes out, over this handsome Englishman, like two tiger-cats fighting over a young elephant."

What a wild, merry rattle-cap he was, and how we laughed together over his absurd conceit: he talked at random, little dreaming who would be the victim of Rachel's poisoned sting.

CHAPTER V.

THE PEARL OF ELGIN.

THE evening was lovely, the moon full, and our plan was to leave Woodburn at six o'clock, and return by moonlight. We were all assembled at the front door, waiting for the horses, except Ethel—who, when she came down stairs, looked so magnificent in her dark blue riding-habit, braided and buttoned with black, a black hat, trimmed with blue velvet, and decorated with a long black plume—that even Mr. Clifford, with all his high-bred self-possession, could not conceal a look of wondering admiration as she joined us. There is no dress so becoming to a handsome, graceful woman, as a riding habit; and even Rachel, although so petite, had looked unusually pretty until my sister appeared, whom she made an effort to embarrass by exclaiming—

" Why, cousin Ethel, how perfectly stunning you do look, and how completely we small people"—glancing at me—"are extinguished, 'when awful beauty puts on all her charms.'"

But Rachel, as usual, was foiled in this attempt to discompose the fair mark at which her flowery shafts were aimed; for, turning to Mr. Clifford, she coolly remarked,

"My cousin's great partiality unfits her for rendering an impartial judgment in my case, so you must excuse her enthusiastic expressions, to which, fortunately, I have become so accustomed, they cease to confuse me—come, let us be going!"

Rachel's attacks upon my sister always reminded me of some foolish child firing off squibs at a stately swan, when, without even ruffling its feathers, the proud bird sails off over the water, as if in disdain of its little enemy; and yet the cutting edge of her repartee was so gracefully covered, that none, save those who knew Ethel's opinion of Rachel and her flatteries, discovered their hidden sarcasm.

Fleetfoot was restive, and I observed Mr. Clifford cast more than one anxious look at the little Arabian, whose rider patted her arched neck quietly and caressingly, while, with a steady hand, she drew the reins, firmly checking the spirited animal, who knew her voice and touch perfectly, and was not in the least vicious.

"You are a confident rider, Mrs. Linton," he remarked, as they rode off in a fast lope.

"Yes," she replied, "confident, but not fearless, for I would not attempt to ride such wild horses as Pearl Dunbar mounts, yet she has never been thrown, though we all tremble for her safety at times, as her daring almost amounts to recklessness."

"What a strong will and high spirit Miss Dunbar must have," he remarked, "I quite long to see her, and yet almost fear the prospect of having such a wild pupil. Is her temper very imperious?"

"Oh, you must not dread teaching Pearl," she answered, "she is impulsive and strong in her prejudices, but warm-hearted, generous, and not the least violent, to us she is very dear, almost like a sister; but come, we are only a mile from Elgin now, let's leave the rest behind, and you shall have an opportunity of judging how prepossessing your new pupil is—at least, in appearance—very soon;" saying which, she gave the reins to Fleetfoot, and they were off at such a swift canter that Ralph and myself only succeeded in catching up with them when turning into the Elgin gate. Pearl was standing with her adopted brother Victor, out before the front door, as we rode up, for they were expecting us, and a little negro-boy stood near by, holding their horses.

Mr. Clifford and Ralph, quickly dismounting, advanced towards them, and, as my brother presented his companion, Pearl threw up the black lace veil that shaded her face, and smiling, with her warm, sunny Southern smile, held out her hand cordially to Mr. Clifford. He took it, and seemed striving to speak in reply to those pleasant, friendly words of greeting; but again that painfully sad expression overshadowed his face, accompanied this time by such a deadly pallor that Ralph looked at me inquiringly, as he exclaimed,

"You are ill, Mr. Clifford—Victor, order a glass of water, while we go into the parlor, please."

But he would not go in; said it was only a sudden faintness which of late had troubled him, and after drinking the water which Victor brought, declared himself quite ready to ride again; and as Rachel and my father came up just as they were mounting, no further allusion was made to this agitation, for there was an intense sadness in the stranger's pale face, which seemed to forbid remark or inquiry.

I was surely correct in describing Pearl as Spanish looking, for she was completely so; from the clear rich brunette of her complexion, the purple blackness of her long thick hair, the starry splendor of her large dark eyes, to the delicate beauty of her hands and feet. Strangers supposed her to be a Spanish Creole; while we, having grown up with her, thought very little about it, save that she was very attractive, and we loved her dearly. Her beauty was such a strange contrast to Ethel's, that it was like gazing at a lovely tableau to see them together.

We knew there was some little romance connected with

my uncle's adoption of the girl, whom he loved as a daughter; but as he was never particularly communicative on the subject, nothing definite regarding the circumstances had reached us, save that when the Dunbars removed from Florida to Elgin, Pearl was with them as an adopted child of my uncle's, who had no daughter of his own, and bestowed upon this lovely little Creole the full wealth of a father's love; she was then only four years old, and had grown up with us a near and dear relation.

Victor Dunbar was not regularly handsome, yet peculiarly striking in his appearance. His temper was haughty, and reserved to coldness with strangers; when provoked he was sometimes unreasonable and violent. Yet those who knew him well could not fail to appreciate his noble, generous nature, and highly cultivated intellect. The love he had ever manifested for Pearl amounted almost to idolatry; and since his return from Germany, where his education had been completed, after an absence of three years, it was whispered that his affection, as a man of twenty-three, for the beautiful girl now in her seventeenth year, was rather less brotherly than when he left her, a little play-fellow of thirteen. Ethel frequently said it made her shudder to see the jealous look he wore when Pearl scampered off on horseback with Ralph; for she was too full of spirit, too eager for enjoyment, to heed his dark moods, or if she heeded, too proud to humor them. Ralph was her favorite companion for racing and frolics of that kind, though she was devoted to Victor as a brother, only thus, we knew, and trembled at the thought of his waking from the delusion that Pearl might be to him more than a sister.

To a lover of nature there could scarcely be a greater treat than to ride through our southern forests, just when the delicate beauty and perfume of spring are melting into the more mature vegetable life and richer fragrance of summer, as was the case on that lovely evening of May 20th, when we rode for five miles through the deep, still woods beyond Elgin, on our way to the cliffs. Amid such scenes the senses of excitable persons become perfectly intoxicated under the exhilirating influences of rapid motion and subtile odors generated by an almost tropical luxuriance of vegetation, which seems draping the earth with a variegated tapestry of vivid green and varied bloom. The magnolia was then in its full glory—so overpoweringly sweet that one blossom possesses too much fragrance for a parlor vase—it scents the outer air to perfection when blended, as at that season, with the bitter aroma of the wild jasmines. Such times, such scenes, such influences, dwell with us, and in after years, perchance, 'neath colder skies, they charm us still strangely, as memory yields, again at our bidding, by a mysterious spell, the light, odor, beauty of those by-gone hours so palpably, that our delight in dwelling upon them is as real, as that of gazing on the pictured charms of some beloved face now lost to us forever. More northern woodlands are neat and picturesque, with their tall trees and soft green pastures—yet they never yield the same varieties of wild beauty, that living panorama of glowing growth and bloom, to be found amid the tangled vine-draped, moss-veiled depths of our far southern forests.

Victor happened that evening to be in one of his most amiable moods, and as Pearl mounted, without waiting for her to scamper off as usual, he courteously proposed being my escort, remarking that it fatigued him to keep up with her head long pace. So that ride is associated with my haughty cousin, of whom I was very fond, and very proud of having him to ride with me, and thus the association is far from disagreeable ; indeed, perhaps, the dewy, dreamy splendor of that moonlit eve would have left less haunting memories had Ralph been my companion. Yet then I was a child, and children are not supposed to dream over whom they may chance to ride or walk with 'mid enchanting scenes, 'neath beaming skies, but children of fifteen will indulge their fancies, and sometimes such memories haunt a life time.

On our return, in passing an old place called "The Glen," which had been uninhabited for years, we were not a little surprised to see lights shining through the windows in various parts of the house, giving unmistakable evidence of its present occupation, which, of course, put all the females of our party on the *qui vive* to know who our new neighbor might be. And after passing we appeared by one consent to check our speed until my father came up,— making him laugh heartily by calling out almost in the same breath, to inquire if he knew who had bought the Glen? He was, however, unable to gratify our curiosity; had heard yesterday, in town, that the place was sold to a new-comer, but could not ascertain his name, so we galloped on caring, less than we thought about the Glen or its occupants.

"Come, Pearl, you and Victor had better go on with us to Woodburn and spend the evening," said Ethel as we neared Elgin.

"Mercy, cousin Ethel!" she cried, "do you want to be the death of Aunt Kate? The dear old soul, is, no doubt, even now in a twitter of anxiety, and beginning to torment herself into the belief that at last Frolic has verified her oracular predictions and pitched me over his head! No, no, I must go home; besides Papa has been absent all day, and would be disappointed not to see me in the evening; Victor, however, can go on if he feels inclined, for I am not the least afraid to ride up alone."

But Victor was not inclined, and while opening the gate for her, I heard him mutter, "Ride up alone! Pearl, how perfectly absurd, just as if I would leave you."

Why did a sick feeling of disappointment and regret steal over me as they left us, and swept swiftly up, through the shadows of that dim avenue? Why will children dream?

Turning back into the road, as we emerged from a dense shade into the broad open moon-light, a dark heavy looking man on a powerful horse dashed past us, going in the direction from which we came; who, though riding very rapidly, jerked up his horse after passing, so suddenly as to bring the animal almost down upon his haunches, and then turning deliberately in his saddle, watched Ethel and Mr. Clifford until an angle in the road hid them from his view, when striking spurs to his horse he rode on at the same head-long gait.

Ralph and myself were behind, having lingered at the gate a moment, so we had full opportunity of observing this peculiar proceeding. "Who on earth was that," I said, "did you ever see him before, Ralph?"

"No, he must be a stranger," replied my brother, "and a very impertinent one too, for staring at sister Ethel as he did."

So we rode on little dreaming then, though we knew afterwards, that the old house which had excited our curiosity by showing signs of habitation, and the dark horseman who turned to watch my sister, were closely connected, for that stranger was master of the Glen.

CHAPTER VI.

DOCTOR FOSTER.

A MONTH had past, and Mr. Clifford was almost as one of the family—for even in so short a time we learned to respect him, as the possessor of a high and honorable nature, to admire his learning and many accomplishments, and to prize him as a faithful teacher and friend.

Who was Mr. Clifford? we all wondered; and why was such a man willing to endure the drudgery of teaching? The refined reserve for which he was so remarkable, forbade questions; and even Rachel Thorn, with all her sly manœuvring—after making a confident boast to more than one of the family, that she was determined to fathom the mystery of his life—had never dared to approach him directly upon the subject, and was obliged to confess herself foiled in every attempt to surprise him into giving some clue which might enlighten her. He seldom joined the family unless invited to do so, and remained, between school hours, so constantly within his own apartments, that at last my father (half-provoked) chided him with being unsocial, and begged, as an especial personal favor, that, unless particularly engaged, he would make it a rule to join our family circle, after tea, in the parlor. He looked gratified, promised to do so, and for several evenings previous to the date of this chapter, we had the gratification of his society until bed-time.

My sister was a fine musician; sang delightfully, accompanying herself with great expression either on the piano or harp. Indeed, I have never heard her singing surpassed by an amateur. Mr. Clifford (who had never heard her until this occasion) stood as one entranced, and when she ceased, his expressions of admiration were so earnest, yet evidently so sincere, that Ethel blushed—though more, it occurred to me, under the eloquent influence of those mild, sad eyes, than from anything he said, for she was accustomed to compliments, and heeded them less than any beautiful woman I ever saw.

Rachel Thorn had marked that look, and the blush it awakened, for her thin lips curled sneeringly, as she remarked:

"Why, Ethel! what a famous Prima Donna you would make, blushing so divinely; for, if the commendation of one person calls up such a becoming color, what might not be expected from the applause of thousands?"

Never before had I seen my sister so justly irritated at Rachel's spiteful remarks. The deep color faded from her cheek so suddenly, that the change was startling, and I almost dreaded her reply. But stinging, cutting, withering as it was, the words were uttered deliberately, and without any evidence of temper in her voice.

"If, by any strange chance, I should ever go upon the stage," she said, "my long and constant association with such a perfect actress as yourself, Rachel, could scarcely fail to prove a great advantage, for, though not particularly proficient in the art of blushing, there are other and more important points to be studied, in which you excel."

There was a look of triumph in Mr. Clifford's eyes, as, while carelessly replacing some sheets of music in the case, he glanced at Ethel, with a meaning smile, which seemed to say : "You have conquered again, and proudly, too."

Rachel fairly shivered with rage, but she knew how far to go, and not daring to provoke my sister further, bit her lips, and was silent ; while, eager to change the subject, I expressed a positive conviction that Mr. Clifford could sing, and begged him to try a duet with Ethel. He consented, and they sang "*Hear me, Norma*" so wonderfully well, his voice being rich and full, and according so finely with her's, that even my father laid down the newspaper, in which he had previously been absorbed, to applaud them.

"Bravo !" he cried ; "why you sing that, absolutely, as if in the habit of practising it together. Fine ! fine ! we must have it over to-morrow evening at Elgin, where, you know, we are all to take tea ; but, by Jove, now I come to think the matter over, no one happens to know it yet, save myself, for I forgot, until this moment, the invitation entrusted to me by good Aunt Kate before dinner. She was on her way here, this morning, when I overtook the carriage, just as that heavy thunder shower came up; so, as the clouds looked very threatening, she requested me to deliver the message, or rather invitation, and turned back. Just think how near I came forgetting it entirely! and, bless me! how righteously indignant the dear old lady would have been, for she was very particular in repeating 'all the family,' 'remember cousin Percy, all, especially Mr. Clifford, for I want him to help entertain our stranger guests,' and who do you think these stranger guests may be? Now, don't all guess at once, for I know you girls are all devoured with curiosity."

"No, we 're not a bit; for it's easy enough to guess one, and the other nobody cares about," I replied, exultingly,' putting on the spectacles my father had just taken off, and looking at him, saucily, across the table. Then, leaning over, I whispered, "It is none other than our new neighbor at the Glen, is'nt it, now, you dear, precious, forgetful old darling?" And again, (more coaxingly,) "Don't tell on me if I've guessed wrong, please."

"But, you're right, you rattle-cap; she wants us to meet Dr. Foster, of the Glen, and our new pastor, Mr. Clare, who is now staying at Elgin on trial,—that is, if he likes the neighborhood, and the neighborhood like him, he is to remain among us.　So, now having relieved my mind from the burden of our most excellent cousin's invitation, taking its acceptance for granted, I shall retire; so good night to you all,'' and my father went off to bed, leaving us to discuss the Elgin tea-party, which we did, wondering—as we had wondered about Mr. Clifford—what the new minister was like, etc., etc., coming to the conclusion that Dr. Foster must be rich, or he could not afford to buy such a property as the Glen; and rather inclining to the belief that Mr. Clare was hum-drum,—such being the style of parsons almost constantly on hand, from time to time, at Elgin; for my uncle seemed to pity, and always befriended, individuals of the cloth, or half-starved artists and school teachers, so unfortunately uninteresting, that less charitable people would not be bored with them.　So, taking it for granted that the present subject—whose merits we would shortly be called upon to judge—must be one of this stereotyped class, I asserted it as my firm conviction, that said Clare was a perfect poke, who would mumble out an everlasting grace over his bread-and-butter, so low that no one could hear it—and then talk very loud, and a great deal—through his nose.　Neither could I resist this tempting opportunity of telling Mr. Clifford what Ralph had said about him before his arrival—hoping I would be as much mistaken as my brother had been—which afforded the subject of said ogreish fancy sketch great amusement, much to the discomfiture of the young artist, who could not be induced to venture an opinion of Mr. Clare.

The next evening, at eight o'clock, we were all assembled in the drawing-room, at Elgin, waiting for the new comers— as Mr. Clare (having been out late to dinner) had not made his appearance. Dr. Foster was, doubtless, too fashionable to come early. So I shall seize the little interval before their arrival, to describe, briefly, the older members of the Elgin household.

Pearl's adopted father, Horatio Dunbar, was an eccentric, humorous, generous Scotchman, some two or three years my father's senior; rather below the medium height, with bright black eyes, whose quizical expressive twinkle at times, when he was telling one of his funny stories, was enough to make the soberest person laugh. Being perfectly bald, he wore a black wig, and one of his favorite jokes was, when there happened to be some very intimate friend with the family, to jerk it off suddenly while they were looking in another direction, and then laugh over their astonishment at seeing a stranger in his place: for the change transformed him so completely that, for a moment, it could not fail to deceive even those on the most familiar terms with him, when they saw it for the first time. He was hospitable almost to a fault; for unreasonable persons frequently abused his generosity; and, as I have said, there was generally one or more itinerant clergymen, teachers, in short, specimens of every species of un-

fortunate individuals who happened to be in the neighborhood, and for the time being without a home, at Elgin.

He had been a widower since Victor's early boyhood, and
Aunt Kate being called on to take charge of the child when
his mother died, ever after remained with my uncle, as he
had never married again. She was a charming exception
to that general rule which, alas, too often most justly stig-
matizes the sisterhood of old maids—(though outwardly
such paragons of methodical piety,—disinterested workers
of charity, and all good works,)—as being, inwardly, moving receptacles of gossip—the very scavengers of society;
feeding upon scandal greedily as vultures upon a dead carcass; digesting their food, and getting up a keener appetite for more by the free use of such tonics as envy, hatred
and malice! Aunt Kate was far from being one of those;
and except for a certain primness in dress and manner,
(those invariable attendants on spinsterism,) no one would
have supposed her to have been an old maid. To a determined disposition, governed by a high code of religious and
moral principles, an almost stern sense of right and wrong,
she added such an unselfish regard for the pleasure and
happiness of others, such a tender sympathy for and with
young persons, in all their joys and sorrows, that Victor
and Pearl loved her as a mother, while all the young people
in our neighborhood regarded a party at Elgin as a perfect
treat—none seeming to view Aunt Kate, (for so she was
generally called,) as venerable maidens are apt to be viewed,

by juveniles, in the light of a severe judge upon all their innocent frolics. They said the reason of her being so good and agreeable was because she was *Scotch*, and I do verily believe that Scotch old maids are better than other old maids; and Aunt Kate was the dearest and best specimen of a Scotch spinster.

But here comes Mr. Clare, at whom we must take a look, for Pearl, though amused at my ideas of his appearance, etc., declares he is quite the reverse—fine-looking, and agreeable. Light hair, fair, with deep, thoughtful grey eyes, a rather slight figure, though tall, and not ungraceful, together with perfect ease of manner and a full, melodious voice in conversation, presented a combination of attractions, which we were totally unprepared to find concentrated in the person of one of the divine fraternity entertained at Elgin. He looked twenty-five, and his whole appearance was altogether prepossessing—so much so that I could not help remarking to Victor, in a whisper, as he entered—

"Why, what a charming looking person! I expected to see a regular stoop-shouldered poke, like our friend Mr. Baldwin, for instance, who is too dyspeptic, you know, to eat butter with his mush."

"Ah, indeed!" he replied, with almost a sneer, as his dark brow lowered, "then you must be astonished at the sight of this lady-killer, for Pearl, and even Aunt Kate, go into ecstacies of admiration over his charms, personal and mental; so he must be something extra, I suppose;

but then, you women generally have a weakness for gentlemen of the cloth.   Heigh-ho! I wish I had studied divinity
at home, instead of going off to Germany!" and he tried
to smile, as I answered quickly:

"Fie, Vic! the idea of your being a preacher!—why,
you're not good enough—not patient enough to teach the
gospel.   But I do really believe good-looking, agreeable
men, are just as jealous of each other's attractions as the
softer sex.   Hark! there's the door-bell—Dr. Foster, no
doubt.   Have you ever seen him?"

"Yes," said Victor; "he is a great, rough bear of a
fellow—vulgar-looking—ugh! I wish father had never
given him the *entre* at Elgin.   But you know that almost
universal hospitality which induces him to take in many,
(by some of whom he is taken in in return,) and if I mistake not, the case in question is to be a striking illustration
of his misplaced confidence.   But it seems this new doctor
is to be our neighborhood physician, and hence my father's
fancy for inviting him here to-night; but judge for yourself;" and as he spoke Dr. Foster entered the parlor.

I have never seen such a queer mixture of gentility and
vulgarity as were presented in the personal appearance of
that man.   His dress was unexceptionable—no flash, no
glitter, which so often marks the *parvenu*.   His hands and
feet were delicate, particularly so for a man of such heavy
appearance, and showed conclusively that his flesh was the
result of indulged appetite, or sedentary habits, perhaps

both, for he looked sensual, especially his mouth, the coarseness of which even a heavy beard failed to conceal. To light-gray eyes, (which, in their cold and furtive expression, were not unlike Rachel Thorn's,) a fair skin and light eye-lashes, he added very dark, almost black, hair, beard and brows—a curious combination, and the *tout ensemble* was far from attractive.

So soon as the momentary silence and restraint, which almost invariably follow the introduction of one person to a number, had worn off, Dr. Foster seated himself by Ethel, and commenced conversation in a free and easy style, which we at once observed was anything but agreeable to my stately sister, who bit her lip, and glanced at me with an almost provoked look, as Mr. Clifford, with whom she had been talking when the doctor came up, walked off, not wishing to interfere with the conversation of a stranger.

I fancied that both observed his look of annoyance—for Mr. Clifford smiled, with a half amused expression—while the new comer moved uneasily in his chair, and then commenced speaking, in rather an abrupt manner, about meeting her out riding with a party shortly after his arrival at the Glen, asked if she was fond of the exercise, etc.? And at last succeeded in fixing her attention for a while by talking of flowers; the fine collection he was making for a conservatory; some rare varieties of cactus, japonicas, etc., he had brought from abroad, for a love of flowers from her earliest childhood had been uppermost in Ethel's appreciation of the beautiful.

Mr. Clifford and Pearl were the best of friends, and his manner towards her ever seemed unaccountably tender—for though after their first few meetings, that agitation to which I have referred as so remarkable, had in some measure worn off, yet the sad look he often bent upon her, told of an inward struggle to subdue some painful recollections awakened by her presence, and even Victor—who was jealous of his adopted sister's partiality for all mankind, save himself and his father, could not object to the gentle considerate care with which Mr. Clifford from the first watched over his high-spirited pupil—nor to the cordial, grateful manner with which she treated him.

They stood talking together within our hearing, while Dr. Foster was with my sister, and I overheard Pearl say, "Oh! doesn't cousin Ethel look too superbly to-night, that pearl-colored silk is so becoming?"

He glanced over at the subject of her remark, and then replied, "Yes, she always looks peerless, and even more so just now than usual; it strikes me, from being in contrast with that new doctor—who I must confess does not impress me favorably—rather than from any peculiar becomingness of dress. What do you think of Dr. Foster, Miss Pearl?"

"Think of him! Why, Mr. Clifford, I perfectly detest the man's looks, and hate to see him chatting to my cousin in that free and easy style; he looks sly and deceitful about the eyes, like Rachel Thorn; don't you think so?"

"Oh! don't draw comparisons, my dear pupil, and try to think as well as you can of Miss Thorn, for she is an orphan, and entitled to much consideration and kindness on that account. Yet, I do agree, with you regarding the sinister appearance of our new neighbor, though appearances are sometimes deceiving; let us hope they may prove so in this case, and that we may be agreeably disappointed in the stranger."

"My dear master," replied Pearl, playfully, "do you expect me to be as considerate and merciful in my judgments of people as you are? Impossible? My likings and dislikings are too strong, yet humbly do I acknowledge myself most culpable in giving such free expression to opinions which might just as well be locked up here"— placing her hand on her heart—"yet, don't think me incorrigible, for, indeed, I am greatly improved since you came; don't laugh now, for they all say so;" and moving up to the table where Victor and myself were looking over some engravings, she appealed to us for a confirmation of this assertion—obtaining which—she commenced again upon the doctor, mimicking his self-assurance so inimitably that even Mr. Clifford was forced to laugh; and then she said, "It's past endurance! he shall not talk one minute longer to cousin Ethel, for I'm going over to make her sing." And from the ready way in which the proposition was acceded to, we had no reason to imagine that my sister was particularly entranced, even by the doctor's floral rhapsodies,—who was officious when Ethel went to the piano, asking for one operatic song after another, in a style that was quite bewildering—nor did he subside in the slightest degree, until Mr. Clifford, by request, came up to sing with her—when the doctor sat sulking near by, and looking, as Pearl said, "unutterable things" the while.

Dr. Foster evidently avoided conversation with Rachel Thorn, and several times during the evening when they happened to be thrown together, he turned away, as if abstracted, and sought another part of the room. I could see she felt cut at his slighting her, and amused myself as we drove home by inquiring her opinion of this odd looking stranger.

"Why, he is a perfect vulgarian," she replied, "and I am astonished at Ethel for allowing him to be so much with her."

"Then, Rachel," said my sister, "I am glad that he did not give you an opportunity of snubbing him, for in our uncle's house to a stranger guest, that would have been rude, so, as it seems, I had more forbearance; it is fortunate for the credit of the family he inflicted himself upon me instead of you."

Rachel tried to laugh, but was evidently annoyed at

being thus suddenly extinguished by her adversary's ready repartee.

Thus ended the evening at Elgin, which we lightly discussed, little dreaming how important a part those two strangers were destined to play in a rapid succession of coming events.

That night I dreamed a vivid, wild dream—in which Ethel seemed standing alone, upon a black and tottering bridge, whose broken arches spanned a fearful abyss, from which there came a sound of angry, rushing water. Pale and helpless, she was forced to cross—and clung despairingly (while advancing, step by step,) to the trembling balustrade. Then I saw her shrink back, horror-stricken; for, up from out that frightful gulf, on to the rotten abutments, over the balustrades, along the slimy stones and boards, hissing, came an army of vipers—and while she clung to the bridge for support, lo! a hideous serpent coiled about her arm; when, suddenly, from the other side of this chasm, bounding recklessly over the slippery bridge, Mr. Clifford appeared. Heedless that it tottered under his weight—heedless that countless vipers were hissing at him—heedless of the gloom above, below, on he sped, swiftly, to where my sister stood petrified with horror, the slimy reptile clinging to her bare, white arm. To seize and tear it off, and then—catching her in his arms—to speed swiftly over that broken, crumbling ruin—seemed the work of a moment; and while they gained a rock on the other side, I woke with a cry, as the whole arch, bristling with serpents,—whose hissing had made me cold and sick with terror through that dreadful dream—tumbled, with an echoing crash, into those yawning deeps of rushing water.

CHAPTER VII.

RACHEL THORN.

RACHEL was very clever—and progressed in her German with a rapidity which appeared to astonish and please Mr. Clifford, whose interest (we afterwards found) she had excited, by informing him (in confidence, for the time,) that it was her intention, by hard study, to fit herself for teaching—being determined, when quite competent, to seek a situation as governess, for she was too proud—now that my father no longer required her services—to remain permanently at Woodburn, and would have left long before, but until now, never had an opportunity of improving herself sufficiently to undertake the task of teaching. All of which Mr. Clifford, of course, believed—it was quite natural he should—thereby increasing the inducement he had to instruct her as thoroughly and perfectly as possible, both in drawing and German.

In the course of these instructions, however, he failed to perceive—for a long time, at least,—what was perfectly evident to all lookers-on, viz. : that Ralph's prediction was verified most completely—for Rachel Thorn, while thus acquiring knowledge, had—lost her heart. Neither did we fail to observe how entirely innocent he was of all design to enthrall the affections of his wily pupil; for— apart from the necessary courtesy and attention to be expected from a teacher—he never gave her the slightest cause to suppose herself, for one moment, the subject of his thoughts—and nothing, save vanity, and the blind love which possessed her, could ever have induced that clever girl to believe possible the impossible task she had undertaken, of trying to win Mr. Clifford—futile and absurd as the delusion which might lure a little child to seek for fairy treasures by traveling to the end of the rainbow !

The growing friendship between Mr. Clifford and my sister, excited in her an uneasy jealousy; and though fully impressed—as I feel assured she was then—that he would never aspire to Ethel's hand—a visible effect of that jealousy was to make Rachel hate the subject of it more than ever for her superior attractions, and by artful manœuvrings, to undermine the exalted opinion he entertained of my sister's character—hoping, that when disenchanted with one whom he must necessarily worship at a distance, she might eventually succeed in winning him by determined devotion.

Thus it was matters stood, when, by going a step too far, she loosened the mask which was destined, ere very long, to fall off, revealing to us the dark duplicity of her nature in all its revolting deformity.

Upon a certain gloomy, drizzling Saturday, in August, I was sitting near the drawing-room window with Ethel, sewing, and Rachel in another part of the room at a table, translating her German lesson for Monday—who kept calling on Mr. Clifford for assistance until we were both provoked at her, and could not help wondering at his endless amount of patience—when a negro boy rode up to the door, with a basket in his hand, which, shortly afterwards, Bristol brought in, and, handing it to my sister, said: "From the Glen, Miss Ethel, and the boy has gone; said there was no answer."

I could not help exclaiming when the cover was removed, "Oh! what superb flowers! did you ever see such cactus? And here is a card, 'For Mrs. Linton, with Dr. Foster's compliments.' Mr. Clifford, Rachel, do come and look at them. I declare now it is really kind in the doctor, isn't it?"

My sister could not help admiring the gift, and yet she looked annoyed, as they rose, attracted by my exclamation, and came across the room to look at the flowers—and while sewing away more rapidly than usual, she said:

"They are certainly very beautiful, yet I scarcely think that my limited acquaintance with the donor warrants his sending me a present—even of flowers"—and then she looked up at Mr. Clifford, to see what impression it had produced upon him, with such an inquiring glance, that he replied, as if to a question:

"I believe it is considered entirely admissible everywhere, and even by the most fastidious people, for a gentleman when he has visited a lady even once, to send her flowers, and quite as admissible for her to receive them; and I believe Dr. Foster has been here, not only as a physician, but as a visitor, on several occasions; indeed, the propriety of such a delicate attention as this, Mrs. Linton, it strikes me, can scarcely be questioned; perhaps," he added, smiling, "if the doctor were a greater favorite, his offering might be more acceptable."

Ethel's color rose as their eyes met, and then the impression first dawned upon me, that had Mr. Clifford been the donor she would not thus have hesitated as to the propriety of accepting this exquisite gift—perhaps he thought so too—at all events his eyes rested on her for a moment, with an expression of lingering, yearning tenderness I had never seen there before, and which appeared to move her strangely—for the color deepened and spread until even neck and brow were suffused with that burning blush.

Rachel did not see it, at which (while scarcely defining the reason why) I was pleased—for, after glancing at the flowers with a queer, provoked expression, she remarked sneeringly, "Dear me! how touchingly lover-like, surely cousin Ethel, the elegant doctor must be smitten with you," and then returned to her German.

No one noticed the remark, for Mr. Clifford and Ethel were evidently thinking of other things, and I was too much absorbed by the new train of thought arising from that eloquent look, to heed her spiteful words.

My sister at last, after struggling—vainly as I thought—to recover her wonted composure, suddenly put aside her work, and saying, pleasantly to Mr. Clifford, that as the flowers were not to blame, and stood there as it were accepted, she would at least put them in water, and left the room to do so. Volunteering to get her some sprigs of geranium and myrtle to mix with those gorgeous cactus and azaleas, I threw on my hat and mantle, and ran into the garden for them.

As I returned, seeing the side door of the conservatory open, I went in there (instead of going round the house) as it was still drizzling with rain, and the conservatory (which communicated with the parlor,) ran back of it a considerable distance towards the garden, and therefore it was the nearest way into the house. Upon entering, I caught sight of a very delicate green vine, (the leaves of which were extremely beautiful,) that hung in festoons over the enormous pyramidical stand on which the plants were arranged, and upon the first few shelves I quickly climbed, to gather some sprigs of it to mix in with Ethel's flowers. While standing up thus, a considerable distance from the floor, just in the act of pulling them, the parlor door leading into the conservatory opened, and I heard

Rachel say, " Come in here a moment, Mr. Clifford, I want to show you such a curious air-plant in bloom; look there, just over your head, to the right."

"That is singularly beautiful," he replied, "and very rare. I wonder where Mrs. Linton got it?" For the green-house was Ethel's own domain.

I kept perfectly still, thinking they would walk round, and be so astonished to see me there, but they were standing still near the air-plant as Rachel said, with a great over-grown sigh:

" Poor, dear Basil brought that to Ethel when he came on from New York, many years ago. Oh! how devoted he was to her, my darling brother, but not more so than she was to him. I suppose you know that they were engaged, Mr. Clifford, that my uncle objected (on account of Basil's poverty) and at last induced Ethel to break off with him to marry Arthur Linton, who was supposed to be a fortune!"

She spoke rapidly, as if afraid of being interrupted before the tale was told, and when Mr. Clifford answered:

"No, Miss Thorn, I was not even aware that you had a brother," she rejoined quickly:

" It broke his heart, drove him to desperation; he left us suddenly to go none knew whither, and from that time has he been lost to me as if dead. Ethel never loved any one but Basil; she never cared for her husband, having married him to please my uncle, and because he was rich.

The last words were spoken as they walked back into the parlor, and Rachel shut the door after her before I had time to climb down from the shelf where I was standing when they came in.

Perfectly stunned and bewildered at what I had heard, knowing it to be utterly false, yet scarcely aware how to act under the circumstances, fearing I might be blamed for listening to a conversation I had overheard so suddenly, and so entirely without design on my part to act the part of a listener. After a moment's reflection I determined to go at once into the parlor and tell Rachel (in Mr. Clifford's presence) that I had overheard her, though most uninten-tionally, and then, face to face, dare her to repeat what she had asserted either in Ethel's or my father's presence. To conceal what I knew would have made me sick and miserable. So getting down from among the plants as fast as possible, I ran round and entered the parlor, but unfortunately for the furtherance of my plan at that time, neither Mr. Clifford nor Rachel were there; but just as I entered, Ethel came in through another door, with her flowers beautifully arranged in a large crystal shell, made for holding bouquets.

I presume my pale cheek and troubled look startled her, for she said, "What is the matter, Amy, have you hurt yourself?"

"No," I replied, "here are some beautiful green leaves to mix in among your cactus, and in getting those vines

out of the green house I overheard Rachel say something
about you to Mr. Clifford, which made me very angry,"
and then I told her the whole, with an earnest assurance
that I had been a most unexpected and unwilling listener.

"What an unprincipled girl she must be," exclaimed my
sister. "Yet as you did not speak at the time, let it pass,
she would only sneer at you as an eaves-dropper; say you
misunderstood her, etc., and as to mentioning the subject
to Mr. Clifford, for the present, at all events, it must not
be thought of. He certainly does not deserve our friendship, if Rachel Thorn's cunning falsehoods can alter his
good opinion of me, and I can scarcely believe it will have
the least effect upon him, but if so, some future dark attempt
to injure me, will reveal Rachel's falseness without any
effort of ours to unmask her, and therefore, Amy, I must
beg you, let this matter remain entirely *entre nous*—unless Mr. Clifford sees fit to speak with either of us upon
the subject, and then of course the truth must and shall be
told, be it ever so much to Rachel's prejudice."

"Oh, Sis!" I said, "it is too bad for her to slander you
thus, and to such a good, true friend as Mr. Clifford; I just
hate her for it, and don't see how you can allow her to
remain at Woodburn after such a daring piece of treachery."

"Now, Amy, that is all nonsense," replied Ethel; "we
knew all along of Rachel's duplicity, and I am not at this
moment more sure of her wish to injure me, than I have
always been. Had I been in the green-house and overheard

what you did, it would certainly have been right for me to speak out then and there to defend myself from her calumnies, but to make her your enemy is a different thing, and she would be sure to deny it, unless Mr. Clifford were present, which is impossible, as nothing would induce me to mention the subject, or have it mentioned to him; if he believes me slandered, it surely is his place to investigate the affair in some way, and then let Rachel know that he is in possession of the truth. Depend upon it, 'twill be far better thus."

Just at that moment there was a sudden rush through the hall, and Rachel entered greatly flushed, and looking as if she was overflowing with important news.

"Oh cousin Ethel, Amy," she cried, "I have got the funniest thing to tell you that ever was in the world." We both stood looking at her in silent wonder. "Just now, I was in the school-room putting away my German books, when uncle sent for Mr. Clifford, who was over in his room. He went of course at once, and I don't think he saw me even, for in going out he left the door of his room wide open, and as I passed through the hall a moment afterwards, seeing what seemed to be a miniature lying open on the writing table, I could not resist the temptation of taking a look at it, and who do you think it was? Pearl—a beautiful miniature of Pearl Dunbar, and set round with pearls too."

"Impossible!" we both exclaimed in a breath.

"Ah! I knew you would not believe it," she replied quickly, and therefore I slipped the picture out of its velvet case and brought it with me—see and judge for yourselves," saying which she drew out from her pocket a small oval-shaped ivory miniature, mounted in gold, and set with large, beautiful pearls, so strikingly like Pearl indeed, that we could scarcely doubt its having been taken for her. Yet so perfectly amazed were we, and also provoked at Rachel's audacity in daring to go into Mr. Clifford's room, and still more, in bringing off the picture, that my sister, while casting a hurried glance at it, said—

"Oh, Rachel! how could you do such a thing? The idea of stealing into a gentleman's room without his knowl-edge, and then to bring the miniature away. Suppose he returns and misses it, what would you do, and what would he think of you?"

"Why, what a fuss you make about nothing," she answered; "in the first place, there's no danger of his getting back before I replace it, as uncle's talks with him are everlasting, and suppose he did, why I should just make a clean breast of it, and say the curiosity inherited from our worthy ancestress, Mrs. Eve, tempted me to peep, and I could not resist; nor a further temptation either, to surprise you with this unexpected discovery. Just to think of Mr. Clifford and Pearl being lovers. Who would have thought it? How sly they have been, and how perfectly furious Victor will be when he finds it out, and I am determined he shall know it. She ought to be ashamed to flirt with two men and be engaged to a third, for I've been told that Cecil Clare is devoted to her."

"Rachel," I said, "you shall not continue to talk in this manner of one who is dear to us as a sister ; though so much like her, that cannot be Pearl's likeness, or if so, she has doubtless only lent it to Mr. Clifford to copy, at his request. At all events, she is incapable of doing anything deceitful or unladylike, and it is certainly neither your business nor ours to meddle in this matter. If right that Victor should know it, she will doubtless tell him herself."

Here Ethel interrupted me, saying—

"Rachel, let me implore you to go at once, replace the miniature, and then candidly tell Mr. Clifford what you did in the impulse of the moment, and ask his forgivness."

"Well, that's a fine joke," she cried. "I shall of course put it back, but as to saying anything about the matter to him, catch me at it." And away she went, leaving Ethel and myself gazing at each other in utter amazement.

"Did you ever see that miniature before, Amy?" asked my sister, looking very white, and speaking in an agitated voice.

"No, nor do I think, spite the likeness, it can be hers, as, had she owned such an one, 'tis more than probable we would have seen it long ago, or at least when it was taken,

4*

and we know she has not been lately sitting for her picture.
Though so wonderfully like, that face looks older to me
than Pearl's. Perhaps Mr. Clifford painted it from memory, and blending her image with that of some dear one
who resembles Pearl—has given the picture this rather
more quiet expression.

"Oh! it must be Pearl, surely," she said, "and the
whole thing is very strange, though Mr. Clifford might
fascinate even a girl so much younger than himself, it is
true, but why has Pearl not confided in us?"

"Don't distrust her, sister; depend on it, Mr. Clifford
is no lover of hers, and it will be, must be cleared up in
time to our perfect satisfaction."

The emphasis laid on "hers" made Ethel look up at me
with a queer, startled expression, as she said hurriedly,
"What if he is? They surely have a perfect right to
love each other! A most outrageous piece of daring that
was in Rachel. I feel mean, actually, for having even
looked at the picture, and now she will certainly make
mischief between Victor and Pearl. I feel wretched about
the whole thing!"

Dear Ethel! I knew (or rather guessed) the cause of
that wretchedness, which she would have then been so unwilling to confess, and was even startled by my emphasiz-
ing a little word, whose meaning awakened an echo in her
inmost heart.

CHAPTER VIII.

MR. CLIFFORD PERPLEXED.

> "And that in seeking to undo
> One riddle, and to find the true,
> I knit a hundred others new."—TENNYSON.

THERE was a queer state of things existing at Woodburn for some time subsequent to the events related in my last chapter. Rachel Thorn's manœuvring was for a while successful, and she, as a matter of course, proportionably exultant; while Ethel looked worried; Mr. Clifford, though kind and gentlemanly as ever, sorely perplexed; and, if looks are an indication of feelings, I must have appeared, as I surely felt, excessively provoked—so much so, it was scarcely possible for me to treat Rachel with even common politeness; and I rarely spoke to her, never, in fact, save when she addressed me directly.

She had taken occasion to inform us—Ethel and myself—that the picture we made such a fuss about was replaced in its case, long before Mr. Clifford returned to his room;

and, as it could not tell tales and she would not, there existed no possible chance of his knowing anything about the
funny little trip it had taken in her pocket. We were perfectly disgusted with her conduct, and made no reply,
though she laughed triumphantly, and was evidently
pleased, as with some very clever performance.

I am perfectly certain, Rachel never for one moment believed Mr. Clifford to be a lover of Pearl's; and even if
she thought the miniature really one of her—which is
doubtful—her idea, no doubt, was, either that he had
painted it, or borrowed it from Pearl for the purpose of
copying; for she was too absurdly in love with Mr. Clifford herself to triumph thus at finding another woman's
picture in his possession, unless quite sure she was no rival, and the secret of her exultation consisted in accidentally discovering another means by which her wily scheme
to separate him from my sister might be forwarded; and
as the days wore away I could see a shade of coldness growing up between them, just a shade, yet it pained me,
knowing he was deceived, and feeling almost sure that she
was also, which state of things annoyed me beyond expression, and I had arrived at a positive determination to try
at least and set matters right, when, by going a step too
far in her most inveterate propensity to make mischief,
Rachel Thorn upset part of her plan and opened a way for
overthrowing it entirely.

About two weeks after Rachel found the miniature in

Mr. Clifford's room, I was sitting at the front door, study-ing one of my lessons, when Archey, shuffling round the corner of the house, pulled off his hat, and said,

"Please, Miss Amy, is you gwin to ride, and shall I saddle Lara or Miss Effie's little filly for you,—dar comes Miss Pearl froo de gate, and she's comin in a hurry, too. Gosh! but a'nt Frolic tryin hissef?"

"No, I am not going out, Archey, this evening, and suppose Miss Pearl is only coming over for a visit—but you can stay and take her horse. It is queer she is all alone, not even little Dick with her to open the gate."

"Lor. bless you, Miss, yander's Dick clippin' it down de lane, but he can't keep up wid his young lady when she's flying like dat no time, de poor little nigger looks, arter ridin' long of her, most always like he had jis got out of a dust pile—"

"Je hollikins! how Frolic is swettin!"

And as Archey took the bridle of the tired animal, Pearl, looking flushed and excited, jumped down, and, rushing up to me, said hurriedly,

"Amy, where is Rachel Thorn? She has told a base falsehood to Victor, just for the purpose of trying to make mischief between us, and I must see her at once, in your presence and Cousin Ethel's, for she shall take it back."

I followed her into the parlor, knowing perfectly what was coming, highly delighted at the prospect of having such a mystery cleared up, and not displeased, I must confess, at the chance of seeing Rachel placed by her vile scheming in a rather uncomfortable corner.

Soon after Ethel came in, who looked surprised at Pearl's visible agitation, and asked her, "What was the matter?"

"Wait until that little viper comes," was her reply, "and then you shall know."

I saw in a moment, from my sister's expression, that she knew herself mistaken with regard to the miniature, for her face cleared and wore a relieved look.

Just then Rachel entered, looking unusually pale and troubled, as when sent for in such a hurry by Pearl, she no doubt guessed the object of her visit, who, so soon as she appeared, exclaimed,

"Rachel Thorn, how dared you tell Victor Dunbar that you knew a gentleman to whom I had given my picture? It was false, and you knew it—and I demand, as a right, to hear why such a story was forged, or what possible foundation you have for it?"

"The best foundation in the world," replied Rachel, doggedly—though her look was anything but confident, and her voice trembled; "I saw your miniature on Mr. Clifford's table, and brought it in here for cousin Ethel and Amy to look at—ask them if I am not telling the truth."

"You certainly had in your possession, and showed to us," said my sister, "a beautiful miniature, which you represented as belonging to Mr. Clifford—and which was most wonderfully like Pearl; yet, it does not follow, as a matter of course, that this picture was taken for her, and from her manner of denying the fact, I am quite sure it was not."

"The idea of my giving such a likeness of myself to Mr. Clifford at all, is perfectly ridiculous, of course," Pearl exclaimed; "but had such an one been in existence, you would all have seen it, and papa would not have suffered me to give it away. Yet, even granting, Rachel, that you believed the miniature to be mine, what could possibly induce the insinuation made to Victor, that Mr. Clifford was my lover? You must have known, you did know, this to be false; and I cannot forgive such a piece of mischief-making on your part."

"I never dreamed," replied Rachel, "of making mischief, by informing your adopted brother that Mr. Clifford was in possession of your miniature, Pearl; brothers are not generally in the habit of blazing out at their sisters for having love affairs—perhaps, however, as Victor, in reality, does not bear that relationship towards you, I may have mistaken your position to each other."

The high-spirited girl cast upon her impertinent tormentor a look of such withering scorn and contempt, (as eyes like hers alone can flash) while replying:

"As my brother, or my lover, either, Miss Thorn, Victor might well have been provoked at me for presenting my miniature to a gentleman without his knowledge or consent;

and your insolent curiosity regarding the relationship in which we stand to each other, shall never bo gratified by me. Amy, will you be kind enough to see if Mr. Clifford is at home—as it is my wish to havo this amiable young lady informed (in the presence of witnesses) whether he has now, or ever has had, a likeness of me."

I left the room at once, to comply with Pearl's request, and have no further knowledge of what transpired between them, until after I returned with Mr. Clifford—who was not a little astonished at being sent for so particularly and unexpectedly by Pearl.

Rachel looked as white as a ghost when we entered; indeed, she could scarcely help feeling both angry and mortified at having her perfidious conduct thus exposed.

So soon as we entered, Pearl, walking up to Mr. Clifford, with flushed checks and flashing eyes, asked boldly:

"Have you a likeness of me, Mr. Clifford? Rachel Thorn told Victor that you had, and as my denial of the fact seems insufficient to convince her—for she asserts having seen the picture, and had it in her possession—I determined to bring her face to faco with you, and let others, beside myself, hear the truth."

"Don't be so agitated, my dear pupil," responded her teacher; "you astonish me beyond measure, by asking such a question, as I cannot imagine how or where Miss Thorn could ever have seen a miniature of mine which does certainly resemble you exceedingly, but which was painted, I fancy, before you were born, as it has been in my possession for more than sixteen years. It is the likeness of a very dear friend long lost to me, and to whom your remarkable likeness caused the violent agitation I evinced upon the occasion of our first meeting. I have no likeness of you, Pearl; nor would I ever care to have a better one than this chances to be. And now, Miss Thorn, may I inquire where you happened to obtain this said miniature ?" turning to Rachel with grave politeness.

" Yes," she replied, (by this time worked up by anger to a high pitch of bold effrontery) "I saw it on your table, while passing through the school-house hall—could not resist taking a peep, just to see who it was—and then, amazed at beholding, as I thought, a very handsome likeness of Pearl Dunbar, I ventured to bring it off for a moment or two, that cousin Ethel and Amy might have the benefit of my discovery. They both looked at it, and believed, with me, it must have been intended for Pearl. And now, as this most solemn and important conclave is, I presume, at an end for the present, with the full satisfaction of all parties, I shall beg leave to retire."

Saying which, she swept out of the room.

So soon as we had recovered (in a momentary silence) our astonishment at Rachel's insolent insinuation, that Ethel and myself were mixed up with her examination of, and comments upon, Mr. C.'s miniature—if not with its actual removal from his table—my sister, in an agitated voice, said :

" Oh ! Mr. Clifford, you will not, you cannot, for one moment, believe that either Amy or myself encouraged Rachel in the shameless effrontery she evinced, first in daring to enter your room and bringing off the picture, and then, in braving the whole matter out, as if not in the least ashamed of it. She took the miniature out of her pocket, and held it up before us in such a way as to insure our having a full and perfect view of it—and so much we could not avoid ; but we both chided her severely for touching it, and neither of us even took the picture in our hands to examine, though, of course, it was impossible not to observe the very singular resemblance it bears to Pearl, and I believed it to be a likeness of her, though Amy did not, and said she thought the face looked older than Pearl's, though so exceedingly like her."

He did not interrupt Ethel while speaking, but stood gazing in her anxious face, on which such an eager wish to prove herself innocent of all blame in this matter, was so clearly written—with that same earnest, eloquent look I had marked when she was questioning him regarding the propriety of receiving Dr. Foster's flowers—then, when quite done speaking, her eyes fell, while she stood before him as if waiting a reply, Mr. Clifford said—

" Mrs. Linton, I am just as sure that neither Amy nor

yourself countenanced Miss Thorn in looking at that picture, as I am that she wished to serve some purpose (unknown to us) by showing it to you; and since this little affair serves to reveal in some measure the character of your cousin, I feel equally certain that she had a motive, also, in taking me into the conservatory some time since, (under pretence of showing me a curious flower,) simply that said flower might lead to a certain subject; and regarding a friend of mine, from whose history she volunteered to relate some episodes so naturally and feelingly, as for a time to deceive me,—I say it with shame,—and to alter the high opinion I had formed of her integrity and truth. That friend, Mrs. Linton, was yourself. The subject of Miss Thorn's communication we can discuss, if you wish it, at some future time. So far as I am concerned, they need no further denial; and my humiliation is deep indeed at the thought of having doubted one I knew so well, from false representation; though while imploring your forgiveness, I can only say, if it will, even in the slightest degree, excuse my weak credulity, that your cousin's earnest, innocent manner of speaking might deceive even a more suspicious person than myself."

He paused, held out his hand to Ethel, which she took; and, seeing them friends again, I could not repress an exclamation of delight.

'There, sister! I knew it; Mr. Clifford was deceived

by Rachel's artful representations. Now all this might
have been avoided, had you allowed me to speak at once
about it."

Mr. Clifford looked surprised, and evidently wondered
how I came to know anything about his conversation with
Rachel in the conservatory, so, as the time had come
for a general explanation of mysteries, a full account of
the way in which I happened to overhear it, was forthwith given, when, quite contrary to my expectation,
upon hearing how positively Ethel had objected to my
making any denial of Rachel's story regarding Basil and
herself to him, Mr. Clifford looked particularly well satisfied.

What queer creatures men are, to be sure! I fancied
he must of course feel exceedingly grateful to me, for having entertained a wish to set him right at once, by denying
the artful falsehood with which Rachel had beguiled him,
and also a wee bit hurt at Ethel for being content to run
the risk of losing his friendship, when, lo! to my amazement, from some cause or other, his admiration for my sister appeared, if possible, greater than ever, while, if he felt
any gratitude for my friendly intentions, it must have been
too deep for words. I will try at all events to think so;
but one thing is quite certain, Mr. C. and my sister, after
their reconciliation, were so completely absorbed with each
other, and so entirely forgetful of Pearl and myself, we

came speedily and wisely to the conclusion, that our com-.
pany was not then and there particularly desirable, and
when our eyes had telegraphed this much to each other, we
silently withdrew. I don't believe they even missed us.
What ungrateful people !

CHAPTER IX.

THE PARSONAGE AND CECIL CLARE.

"Strong as a man, and pure as a child, is the sum
of the doctrine,
Which the Divine One taught, and suffered, and
died on the cross for.—LONGFELLOW.

"Miss Rachel has a headache, sir, and wont be down," said Bristol, when my father inquired why her seat was vacant at dinner.

"Poor thing!" he said, "I am afraid she studies too hard. Mr. Clifford, those long German lessons are rather perplexing; don't you think such close application injurious to health?"

Glancing up at Ethel and myself with an expression half amused and half worried, my teacher replied, "I fancy Miss Thorn's indisposition is not the result of over-fatigue in that way, Mr. Percy, as she commits with great readiness, and is not obliged to labor over her lessons."

"Ah, well! I am glad to hear it. Ethel, you had better see if your cousin is ill, after dinner; perhaps she would like some tea."

My kind, thoughtful father, he knew nothing, as yet, of
the darker phases of Rachel's character, and was ever thus
mindful of her comfort as of ours.   I feared Rachel's perfidy, and wanted him undeceived; but Ethel, pitying the
girl's lonely condition in life, and knowing her entire de-
pendence upon us, declared she never would unmask her
to my father until justice to some one of us should render
further concealment impossible.

Rachel's indisposition lasted several days, as she had
tact enough to keep out of sight, for a while after making
such a disagreeable impression on the man whom she was
striving even by such extreme and desperate efforts to
win.

Foolish Rachel! she little knew the truth and purity of
that noble nature.

On the following Monday Dr. Foster called, bringing a
superb bouquet to my sister, who was more stately than
usual, I fancy,—as later in the day I heard my father tell
her, he had taken the doctor off for a walk, because of her
exceeding formality; and that he pitied "the poor fellow,
who it seemed kept a conservatory for her especial benefit,"
and then his look was so comical that even Ethel laughed,
though at the same time she said:

"Please, dear father, don't even joke me about the attentions of that horrid man, for, without being exactly
able to define the reason, he is excessively disagreeable to
me.   I only tolerate them because he is at present our

family physician, and sincerely wish he would move away."

He was evidently astonished at my sister's earnestness, and kissing her fondly on the forehead, said:

"Well, well! I won't jest about him again, my daughter, but try and be as civil as you can, for though not prepossessing as a beau, he certainly is a first-rate physician, and therefore—unless he is impertinent—I trust you will all refrain from treating him with marked impoliteness, as the loss of his medical skill on the plantation would be a severe one to me."

And seeing my father was in earnest, we all promised to be as civil as possible.

Mr. Clare liked the neighborhood, and the neighborhood liked Mr. Clare, so he remained, and with his mother had been for some time settled at a lovely parsonage adjoining our little church, and situated midway between Elgin and the Glen. They were universally esteemed, and had been very generally entertained by our hospitable community. Mr. Clare's persuasive eloquence had gained him an influence over the congregation, never so fully possessed by any of his predecessors, while the genial charm of his social qualities secured a popularity separate and apart from his holy calling, seldom enjoyed by ministers, and never by those who make the religion of Christ incompatible with all pleasures and amusements, be they ever so innocent; representing the gentle Nazarene as a severe judge, instead of a merciful Savior, thus too frecquently closing the door of salvation upon the young and light-hearted, who unwilling to renounce all enjoyment, fear to enter in, and are not unfrequently led into a sinful excess of worldly follies, which the cheerful, healthful influence of true religion might have prevented.

For He, who as a wedding guest, converted water into wine,—who even "set at meat with publicans and sinners,"—came not to have his love on earth as a cold, dark shadow, 'neath which the young and happy might dread to dwell, but as a "burning and a shining light" to those, he teaches, "to pray, and not to faint,"—nor "to wear a sad countenance, as the hypocrites do"—but to keep them from the evils by making it easy and pleasant to continue in that right path, "which leadeth unto life eternal." Of this pure and perfect class—among those whose mission it is to proclaim the gospel of Christ—was Cecil Clare,—hence was he beloved not only as a minister, but as a man, and his mother well deserved the blessing of such a son. I need scarcely award her a higher meed of praise. On the Friday following the events just related, we were to take tea at the parsonage, all save Rachel, who (still pleading indisposition) would not join us, which was a relief, especially to Ethel and Mr. Clifford, who both seemed to feel in her presence as if under the influence of an "evil eye." As the weather was fine, we left, as usual, on horseback, calling at Elgin for Pearl and Victor, the old folks preceding us in a carriage,—for dear Aunt Kate would scarcely have considered herself in greater danger poised upon an elevated tight-rope, than on horseback, and was continually in the habit of predicting that some of us (most probably Pearl) would come to an untimely end sooner or later by this mad practice of "racing through the country." Good, kind aunty! how we laughed at her fears, and how pleasantly she took it. Alas! we little dreamed how soon and how very nearly her predictions were to be verified. As we rode up towards Elgin, Pearl and Victor met us in the avenue. He looked out of humor, and she a shade more thoughtful than usual,—indeed, we had not failed to remark of late that Pearl was less wild in her mirth than formerly,—not quite so fond of riding races with Ralph, and rather fonder of going to church since Mr. Clare's arrival, yet still she was not changed, only softened—to which no one objected save Victor, who had been jealous of the minister's influence over Pearl from the first. For a short time, however, this jealousy was diverted into another channel, by Rachel Thorn's malicious gossip with regard to the miniature, at which time believing himself to have been deceived,—the storm, pent up so long, burst forth and vented itself in a torrent of reproaches against the being dearer to him than all the world besides, for which, so soon as the matter was explained, he became, of course, very penitent, feeling heartily ashamed of his unreasonable and unjust anger, as very high-tempered people are so apt to be when brought to hear reason.

The pleasant mood succeeding this outbreak, however, was of short duration, and I afterwards learned that his ill-humor on the evening in question resulted from meeting Pearl and Cecil Clare strolling through the Elgin garden together the day previous; and hence the reserve and gloom of his manner when they met us, for he had no wish to go, and only consented because his father and Aunt Kate particularly requested him to do so.

Victor's dislike for the minister resulted entirely from the fact that Pearl liked to hear him preach, and took pleasure in his society; and he often spoke in a sarcastic tone of her being " wonderfully devout since this charming lady-killer had made his appearance—all of which Pearl bore most amiably, replying somewhat to the effect that she only wished he would find a charm either in the minister or his sermons, which might induce him to like church-going a little better.

Poor Pearl! she did not define her own feelings then, and we did not know until afterwards that Victor, faulty as he was, had some cause for what we then regarded as absurd and unreasonable jealousy.

" Come, Pearl," said Ralph, " let's be off and distance the crowd." She hesitated, glanced up shyly at her companion, and said, " Victor, won't you join us for once in a gallop ?"

"No, I won't," he replied, in a surly tone, " racing is not much to my taste; and besides, I am not, perhaps, quite as anxious to reach the parsonage as you are."

The speech was rude, unkind, uncalled for, and all feeling for Pearl, we pretended not to hear it; but I saw her great dark eyes fill up with tears, as bending towards him, she said in a trembling voice,

"I do not deserve such unkindness from you, Victor," and then she dashed on with my brother.

I was provoked at my cousin's rudeness to Pearl, and yet, no way displeased as they rode off, leaving Victor with me. I cared more for him than she did—at least in such manner my foolish heart argued—and why should he not stay with me?

He called me "little coz," regarded me as a perfect child, though scarcely a year younger than Pearl—and still I nursed the hope that perhaps one of these days, finding Pearl only cared for him as a brother, when I should cease to be so like a child, he might—but no matter, it is very foolish and idle in children to dream.

After our arrival at the parsonage, so bright, so cheerful, such a beautiful picture of a minister's home, and where so cordial and warm a welcome awaited us, the cloud arising from Victor's ill-temper soon dispersed— for he was far too well bred to show the darker phase of his nature before those whose hospitality he had accepted, even though unwillingly; so the evening wore pleasantly away, Pearl being her own bright self again after a little whispered chat with Victor, in which I am sure he begged her pardon for his recent harshness.

Mr. Clare and his mother were so earnest in striving to please, and yet so totally free from all fussiness in their style of entertaining, that it was a real treat to visit them.

Once during the evening, when fortunately for the preservation of Victor's equanimity of temper, he happened to be looking in another direction, I saw Pearl blush and tremble when our host, bending over to present a dainty bunch of sweet violets, touched her hand—of course accidentally, such things are always accidental—whispering, at the same time, something too low for me to hear; yet I found myself wondering what he could have said.

To be sure, it was, or ought to have been nothing to me. What right had I to think or care about it? Perhaps Mr. Clare was saying something to her about joining the church—however, she would not be apt to blush at that—and so, without exactly knowing why, this soliloquy ended in my feeling very happy to see our own pastor so taken up with Pearl, and also that she liked him well enough to change color at the *empressement* of his manner in presenting a bunch of violets.

CHAPTER X.

OUR RIDE HOME, AND WHAT CAME OF IT.

THERE was a partial moon when we left at ten o'clock, and feeling particularly amiable and generous under the influence of certain conclusions arrived at after witnessing the little tableau referred to between Mr. Clare and Pearl, I said to my escort, just as we were mounting,

"Come now, Cousin Vic, be good-natured, and ride back as fast as Pearl wishes, for that speech of yours wounded her; besides, I have something to say to Ralph, so he must go with me."

He acquiesced with evident delight, so much so that it cooled, in a slight degree, the ardor of my generosity as they rode off together, taking the lead of our party, Archey being, as usual, sent on a-head to open the gates.

Thus we rode along pleasantly enough until when about a half mile beyond the parsonage, where there was a very sudden and abrupt descent in the road, rising as suddenly on the other side, forming a gully which resembled the bed of a stream long gone dry.   Just as Victor and Pearl descended, (as Archey rode upon the opposite bank,) the figure of a man, wan and wild looking, with long matted hair and tattered clothes, rushed swiftly through the centre of this gully—which on either side of the road was filled with tangled vines and shrubs—starting out of the thicket on one side and disappearing on the other, with a cry not unlike the war-whoop of a savage, just in front of their horses' heads.

It was certainly enough to frighten the gentlest animal, and neither of these was particularly quiet.   Frolic gave a sudden plunge, so sudden that even Pearl, helpless to avert the consequences, being entirely off her guard at the time, fell over his head into the road.   It was a fearful sight, for Victor's horse reared madly and then dashed on, apparently over the very spot where Pearl had fallen; but a strong hand and stronger bit averted that, for the frightened animal was checked about a yard distant from where she was lying, while Frolic bounded over the prostrate form of his mistress, ran furiously, and was already off far beyond Archey, who had jumped down, and stood with his eyes rolling, crying out,

"W-o-o-h.   Oh Lord she's kilt!"

Victor bounded down from his horse so suddenly, our first impression was he had been thrown also, but in a moment he was staggering up the little hill with Pearl in his arms, scarcely less pale than the insensible girl he was supporting.

I never shall forget the frenzied exclamations of agony which appeared wrung from him while gazing down upon his apparently lifeless burden, for the blood was pouring from a cut in her head, and the deep swoon into which she had fallen was startlingly like the stillness of death.

"Oh, God! she is dead! My darling, my beautiful Pearl," he cried, "she will never, never speak to me again, and I—oh—I have been so harsh and cruel to her of late."

And sitting down by the roadside on an old log, holding her to his heart, that strong, stern man burst into a passion of tears.

We had all dismounted and gathered round Victor, as he sat down—Mr. Clifford alone having presence of mind enough to dispatch Archey after the carriages, in which Aunt Kate and my uncle had preceded us some fifteen minutes, charging the negro not to alarm them by looking so ashy and rolling his eyes, but simply to say,

"Miss Pearl was a little hurt, and would be obliged to return in the carriage."

I felt sure that Aunt Kate's first look at Archey's face would convince her to expect the worst; but there was no help for it. Indeed, both Ethel and myself were so perfectly unnerved, and overcome with grief, believing Pearl to be either dead or in a dying state, that we were entirely unfit to act or suggest, and therefore Mr. Clifford ordered everything.

" Mr. Dunbar," he said to Victor, " we must take her to the parsonage as soon as possible, without waiting for the carriage, (which may overtake us before we reach there,) but not a moment should be lost in removing her to a place where restoratives may be obtained, and also a physician.   Ralph, my dear boy, ride over at once for Dr. Foster, and now, Mr. Dunbar, by placing Pearl gently upon this thick saddle blanket, we can carry her up to the parsonage much more easily and with less pain than in any other way."

Saying which, he fastened the horses to a tree, and, aided by Victor, (who obeyed him without a word of opposition) placed the senseless girl upon the blanket between them, and lifting it up firmly and gently, walked on quickly towards the house, followed by Ethel and myself.

A sorrowful group ! and oh ! how different from the merry party who had set out from there less than half an hour before.   Victor was at first bent upon taking Pearl home directly the carriage arrived, and appealed earnestly to Ethel to know if she did not think it best.   We all coincided in the opinion that such a step would be madness, and prove almost certainly fatal to her whose life now seemed trembling upon a breath.   Then he said, with heart-rending earnestness, to Mr. Clifford :

"Tell me, really, do you think she is dying or dead?"

"No, my dear friend, she is not dead, and I trust in God's mercy, not dying; though her pulse beats very feebly, and I fear she is badly injured; but prompt and energetic measures may, nay, I trust will, restore her. On, steady now, we will soon be there, and I believe, sincerely, it is far better to carry her thus, and less apt to increase pain than the jolting of a carriage."

The light from Mr. Clare's study was now quite visible, and we were inside the gate before even a distant roll of the carriage could be distinguished.

Pearl was on a soft white bed, with Mrs. Clare's gentle face bending over her, watching the effect of cold water and other restoratives, while she strove to staunch the blood still flowing from the wound in her temple, when poor Aunt Kate and Uncle Dunbar arrived, for, seeing our horses tied, they knew, of course, that we had returned to the house.

"Poor, dear child," said the good old lady; "my forebodings and predictions are verified; she will die, or be a cripple for life. Oh! God have mercy upon our darling."

And she knelt down by the bed-side, weeping and kissing the little white hand which lay cold and helpless within her own; while my uncle, with a grief too deep for utterance, stood near her pillow, looking years older than when he left home, as the great tears coursed silently down his furrowed cheeks.

It is very, very touching to see old men weep.

So completely engrossed had we all been with Pearl, that no word was spoken in regard to the strange looking being, whose sudden appearance and startling cry had been the cause of so much mischief; and after coming to the conclusion that it must have been some poor drunkard who had wandered out from town, I scarcely gave the matter a thought again (until, going out to give some necessary directions about the carriage, etc., and also see if my brother and the doctor were coming,) Archey, with a kind of solemn importance, beckoning me to the end of the gallery, whispered :

"Miss Amy, does you know who dat wild lookin' creeter was, what give Frolic such a great skeer? Kase I does."

"No, Archey, but I fancy it must have been some drunkard from town or the neighborhood," I replied.

"No, Miss, it an't nudder—fore de Lord, Miss Amy, sure as I is a livin' nigger, dat was the poor crazy creeter what Dr. Foster keeps fastened up in de room wid iron bars cross de winders; all de niggers round here been keepin' tellin' me 'bout him, steddy, for eber so long ; but dey's all so fond of tellin' skeery lies, I never b'leaved um till dis here blessed night, when I seen him wid my own eyes, and no mistake 'bout it."

I was astonished, though rather incredulous, at what the negro said, and told him :

"If Dr. Foster kept a crazy man fastened up in a room with prison windows, it could scarcely happen to be out roaming at large through the country."

"My stars, Miss Amy," said the boy, "dat's no great wonder; for dat big ugly nigger, Gabe, de Dr. sets to take keer of him, is awful 'feered of de crazy man, so sometimes he knocks Gabe down when he comes wid his vittles, and den runs so fast, he's clean out in de woods fore de nigger git's time to holler—and den maybe de Dr. don't lick him. Golly! but ain't I glad dis is master's darkey, sted of b'longing to sich a savage man as dat new Dr.; for if Archey was set to take keer of a crazy creeter, he'd run off—fore de Lord, he would—but, good night, Miss, I must be a gwying, and yonder comes Massa Ralph and Dr. Foster. He's a monstrous wicked man, but dat's none of my business, and I do hope he'll cure Miss Pearl, for she's sich a nice, pretty, kind young lady."

And pulling off his hat with a bow, Archey shuffled round the corner of the house, just as my brother and Dr. Foster came up the steps.

So completely puzzled and bewildered was I by what the black boy said, it overcame, for a few moments, the intense fear—which had overpowered us all—that Pearl would die. It is an unaccountable anomaly, when the heart and mind are thus diverted awhile from an absorbing sorrow (be it ever so intense) by something startling and unexpected—and my brain was so full of Archey's queer story, that when they walked hurriedly up to me, I could not speak until startled out of my abstraction by Ralph's frantic manner, as he said:

"How is she, Amy? Why don't you speak? Is there no hope? Is she dead?"

Almost shrieking the last word, he seized my hand so fiercely, that in actual pain I cried out:

"No, no, she is not dead; her pulse beats somewhat stronger. Mercy, Ralph! don't break my fingers. Come in, doctor, we have been most anxiously watching for your arrival."

Cecil Clare was standing in the hall as we entered, looking very pale, and oh! so wretched! There was no outburst of grief or wild anxiety from him as there had been from my brother and Victor; but sorrow, thus controlled, is suffering, and leaves far deeper traces upon the countenance than when relieved by tears or exclamations of grief—and that pent-up agony left an expression on the minister's countenance which surely told that Christ's spirit had hushed the passionate storm within, even as he did the raging of the winds and waves, with one deep, holy, eloquent whisper:

"Peace, be still."

CHAPTER XI.

A TIME OF TRIAL.

How full of anxious misery to us all were the moments during which we awaited Dr. Foster's decision regarding our darling Pearl! After staunching the wound in her temple, pronouncing it deep, but not dangerous, he said,

"There is some severe injury to the back, or one of the hips, and the right arm is broken, hence this long swoon, from which Miss Dunbar is now recovering, was the result of extreme pain; but unless there is some internal injury, of which I am not yet aware, there is no reason why time and careful nursing should not restore her to health, though if the hip is seriously injured she may be slightly lame for life : indeed, even with the most favorable results she must be lame for a long time."

It was a great unutterable relief, even with that fearful possibility of lameness, and a fervent ejaculation of gratitude to God escaped involuntarily from her adopted parents, which found echo in the hearts of all those anxious watchers, and then remembering the utter wretchedness expressed on the white face of that watcher outside her chamber door, I whispered to his mother, that perhaps as Mr. Clare would be anxiously awaiting the doctor's decision, she had better go to him, and my proposition was gratefully accepted, for, while resigning her place to me, she whispered,

"Ah, yes! I must go to him—poor Cecil!"

Slowly the sufferer revived, and at last, after a sudden shudder, evidently convulsing her whole frame, the long black lashes were lifted from her palid cheek, and we saw again those beautiful eyes looking upon us with an expression of wonder and alarm, which but a short time before appeared closed forever in the sleep of death.

The fair, mutilated arm must be set at once, and then followed another deep, long swoon from renewed agony. The hip *was* injured, though to what extent could not as yet be fully ascertained; but in moving her it evidently caused great suffering, and, together with the wound in her temple and fractured arm, brought on a fever and delirium, for which the doctor was in a measure prepared, and which continued in such an aggravated form as to render it impossible to remove her from the parsonage for many weeks; indeed, so extremely ill did she become at one time that we despaired almost entirely of her life.

Aunt Kate and Ethel were with her constantly; indeed

the former, whose love for that beautiful girl was the absorbing passion of her life, never left Pearl, even with my sister, until the fever abated, when, being quite ill from constant watching and anxiety, she was taken almost by force to Elgin for a day or two of rest, by her brother, whose sufferings were scarcely less than her own, and both looked years older from the effects of this bitter time of trial.

The lessons at Woodburn still went on; but our school-room, so cheerful before, was dreary enough now, for we missed the bright presence of one whose coming had ever brought as it were a flood of beaming joy into our midst; and Ralph, poor boy, grew so pale and listless that we scarcely knew him as the gay, frolicsome lad he had been.

Rachel was sulky over her lessons, when, as time wore on, she found Mr. Clifford unalterable in his freezing coldness towards her. He told me that once, in a hurried and agitated manner, she had attempted to excuse her conduct regarding the miniature, and also that, so far as Ethel's conduct to her brother was concerned, she blamed her uncle more than any one else, as he was the cause of her marrying Arthur Linton. To all which her teacher listened in silence, and then begged that in future she would not revive the subject, as he had no objection to her seeing the miniature, and to her brother's or Mrs. Linton's secrets he had no right to listen; yet feeling sure whatever either

Mr. Percy or his daughter had thought proper to do in such a case, must be right and honorable, and that upon this one point nothing could ever change his opinion, so it was best to drop the subject. And so Rachel grew sullen and silent; but the fire of her nature, treacherous as that of a volcano, was not quenched, only smothered.

Still, Cecil Clare continued to preach—Sunday after Sunday rising up with that white, still face, whose very calmness told a tale of fearful inward struggle; and once, when the prayers of the congregation were requested for Pearl, (when the fever was at its height,) his voice grew so low and tremulous, we knew that it swept over a well of unshed tears, like the sad wailing winds of autumn, when through some lone valley it comes, with a sobbing sound, drearily sweeping over deep, still waters.

Dr. Foster continued sending flowers to my sister, who received them ever with the same stately indifference. She could not refuse to do so now, while the doctor was in daily attendance upon Pearl, and sometimes they were sent to the invalid, as he was smart enough to know that this would please Ethel more than receiving them herself; and as Pearl grew better, she took great delight in the fragrant bouquets and baskets of exotics which were constantly placed within her reach.

Victor was gloomy and desponding during these weeks of trial, as he rarely saw Pearl save for a few moments at a time, and never alone. Her being so long at the parsonage, thus increasing each day her debt of gratitude to the Clares, was a great source of trouble to him, and once or twice during the occasions of his brief visits he happened to meet Cecil Clare coming out of Pearl's chamber, which added to his annoyances, though under ordinary circumstances it should not have done so, for the minister is considered as privileged to enter upon such occasions as the physician; but Victor was jealous of Cecil Clare; and to make matters worse, good Mrs. Clare, as a kind of apology to him for her son's visits, regarding Victor as Pearl's brother, told him that while the delirium of fever was at its height, she had called for Mr. Clare, and would not be satisfied until he stood beside her.

Poor lady—she meant so kindly—little knowing the deep wound her words inflicted, for Pearl had never called Victor during her illness—but on the contrary, rather dreaded his coming—though, of course, we never told him this, and fearing she might during the delirium express something of the kind in his presence, Ethel always begged him not to stay long with, or talk much to the suffering girl, as the doctor forbade all excitement as highly injurious.

She told me afterwards what was held as a sacred secret at the time—that once, just as the young minister had left the room, Pearl beckoning to her said :

"Don't tell Victor that I care for Cecil Clare, or I believe he will kill him."

My sister was frightened at the wild, earnestness of her words, which, though uttered in the aberration of fever, were evidently prompted by some all-powerful feeling which had haunted her when free from hallucination; and Ethel expressed herself as fervently thankful that Mr. Clare had left the room ere she spoke thus; and, of course, while Pearl continued wandering, she could not dismiss a nervous dread that either in his presence or Victor's she would utter the same words, or some of a similar bearing.

Rachel Thorn rode over occasionally to see the invalid, and whenever she chanced to meet Dr. Foster showed an evident desire to attract his attention, and was always sure when they met, to address her conversation mostly to him, though the desire he had evinced to avoid her upon their first meeting continued, and this very fact while it, no doubt, annoyed and puzzled the wilful girl, I feel sure, rendered her all the more desirous to cultivate his acquaintance.

One afternoon it so happened that while I was preparing some lemonade for Pearl, and Ethel combing her hair and bathing her temples with ice water, Rachel sat near the bed with a light fan keeping off flies, when Dr. Foster entered.

She was sitting where he usually stood when feeling Pearl's pulse, and I observed, with some surprise, that after the usual formal salutation to us all, he walked round to the opposite side of the bed, (as it appeared to me,) in order to avoid coming near Rachel. It was just when Pearl's fever was at its height; and after feeling her pulse and watching the flushed cheeks and wild eyes for a few moments, he asked me to send for certain things required towards the preparation of a soothing medicine, when before I could put the lemonade I was stirring out of my hand, Rachel saying:

"Let me bring them."

Went quickly out of the room, and after returning with the desired articles, she stood near the doctor, and much to his annoyance, continued watching him while he prepared the medicine, asking questions and making remarks, which we observed were responded to in a most disobliging manner.

At last having finished, he pushed away his chair from the table as if provoked, and strode off to a little dressing-room adjoining the chamber, where he was in the habit of washing his hands—rolling up his sleeves partially as he went.

"Oh doctor, you have no soap," exclaimed Rachel, and picking up the soap-dish (which by some accident had been left on the bureau) she ran after him just as he dipped his hands in the water. I did not hear him speak, but from some cause (then unknown), as my cousin put the dish down on the marble washstand, the noise of which I heard, (though as the dressing-room door was only half way open, I could not see either of them,) for she appeared to drop it down suddenly out of her hand, and crying out :

"Oh merciful God!" in a trembling, excited tone of voice, rushed back as white as a ghost.

"What on earth is the matter, Rachel," I said, going quickly up to her; and Ethel asked hurriedly :

"Are you ill ? "

"No," she said, "only I grew suddenly dizzy, and felt like falling, from a rush of blood to my head; it will soon pass off."

And putting her hand to her forehead, she sat quite still for several minutes. In the meantime Dr. Foster came back, looking quite cool, and remarked carelessly :

"Are you in pain, Miss Thorn ? "

To which she replied :

"No, only dizzy."

He sat down very quietly by the table, and commenced writing out a prescription. He was some time writing, and I saw him after scribbling over half a sheet of note paper (as if dissatisfied with it) throw the paper aside, and commence on another piece, which, completing in much less time, he folded up, and handed to Ethel—while as she glanced over it, he caught hold of the discarded scrap, and rather crumpling than folding, stuffed it into his pocket.

Rachel sat with her head still buried in her hands, while the doctor gave several directions to Ethel regarding Pearl's medicine, etc.; and just before leaving, with apparent civility, which we thought queer, because so very unusual, he walked over to where she was sitting, and remarked :

"I would prescribe a few grains of ammonia for that dizziness, Miss Thorn, and have some here if you will accept it."

Saying this he took a small lump out of his pocket, and rolling it up in the identical scrap of note paper on which he had written, and then crumpled as if worthless, he handed it to my cousin, who, scarcely glancing up, thanked him, and slipped the parcel into the pocket of her dress.

I felt puzzled and worried at the whole scene, wondering what on earth could have happened to make Rachel scream out so (for her dizziness was evidently all feigned,) and also why Dr. Foster should become so suddenly polite towards one he had particularly avoided on former occasions ?

After he left, Rachel complained of feeling sick, and urged me to return home with her at once (as we had come over together that afternoon in the carriage) so it left me no opportunity to talk the matter over with Ethel just then, though we exchanged more than one look of wonder.

My cousin remained profoundly and gloomily silent during the ride—and immediately upon our arrival at home, went to her room, telling me she was sick ; did not want anything but quiet ; not to let the servants disturb her ; and after shutting the door, I heard her turn the key, as if to insure solitude. My last thoughts before going to sleep that night were of Dr. Foster and Rachel— wondering what he did, or said, to make her scream! and feeling as if I would give a great deal to see that paper in which he had wrapped the ammonia.

CHAPTER XII.

PEARL'S SECRET.

"My mind is troubled like a fountain stirred,
*And I myself see not the bottom of it.—*Shaks.

WHEN Pearl was convalescent, and quite in her right mind, one morning as Ethel and myself were sitting with her, while we chatted away pleasantly, and among other things were discussing the queer scene between Rachel and Dr. Foster, the invalid fell quietly to sleep, after which we continued our conversation in whispers, for fear of disturbing her, and an hour or more elapsed before she woke. When fixing her eyes with a troubled expression on my sister, Pearl said anxiously—

"Cousin Ethel come here; I feel very sad and want to consult you about something that is haunting me and making me miserable night and day. You can understand and sympathise more fully with me in this matter than aunt Kate, and therefore it is best even before speaking to her, that I should ask your advice."

My sister immediately took her seat close by Pearl on the bedside, while I rose and was about to leave the room, thinking she might wish to be entirely alone with Ethel, when she said quickly—

"Don't go away, Amy. I trust you as fully as cousin Ethel, though she perhaps can advise me better, and want both of you to hear what I am about to say."

I drew near silently, taking her thin, white hand in mine with a gentle pressure, as she proceeded.

"Just after Mr. Clifford's arrival, most unexpectedly Victor made me a declaration of love, in his wild vehement manner, saying his happiness—nay, his very life depended upon my becoming his wife. This pained me exceedingly. I told Victor we were, and always had been, too much like brother and sister to think of any nearer connection, and begged him to give up all thought of such a thing. Furthermore urging that as his father and aunt Kate had always regarded our relationship as brother and sister with so much pleasure and satisfaction, I did not think either of them would approve of his becoming my lover; but here he interrupted me with the assurance that he had spoken to both of them on the subject, and far from disapproving, they were higly gratified—especially papa, who said nothing could happen that would afford him such happiness as a marriage between us, for he loved me dearly, even as an own child, and though Victor and myself had been reared togther, yet as we were no relation to each other, of course there could be no plea of that kind urged against our union, and so far as my parentage was concerned, he did not care whether I was born a princess or a peasant, for he knew me to be worthy of all love, and good fortune, and prayed God that Victor might be so blessed as to win my love."

" It is scarcely necessary to tell you how perfectly astonished and overcome I was by all this, as nothing of the kind had ever been hinted before, and Amy would be almost as well prepared to regard Ralph as a lover as I was to look on Victor in that light.   Yet I loved him dearly, and if papa wished it, did not every feeling of gratitude and affection within me urge a ready accession to his wishes, who had been such a dear kind father to me?   Then, when I hesitated Victor whispered so pleadingly, so earnestly,

" ' You will learn to love me darling, you are so young, such a child yet, that you scarcely know the meaning of love; but promise only that you will try, and I am content.'

" Then he drew me up to him and winding his arms about me, kissed my forehead, lips and eyes so fiercely, that it almost frightened me, and as he continued,

" ' Tell me shall it not be so; will you not promise to be Victor's own little wife—provided he can succeed in making you love him well enough ?'

" I answered 'yes,' for what else could I say, cousin Ethel, when papa, Aunt Kate and Victor all wished it ?"

And throwing her arms round my sister's neck, Pearl burst into tears.

" I see and understand it all, my dear child," said Ethel caressingly, "and cannot wonder, under the circumstances, that you should promise to try and love Victor, as he wishes; but why be so distressed? Do you find it impossible to love him, except as a brother? If so, surely he is good and noble enough to release you."

" Oh! cousin Ethel," replied the weeping girl, " you don't know how passionate he is. I dread to tell him, for when angry Victor is unreasonable, and will be very angry with me. You remember of my telling you of the stormy scene between us, when he so absurdly believed Rachel Thorn's malicious story about Mr. Clifford's having my picture; and before and since that he has been fierce or sullen by turns, because — because. Oh! my dear cousin, it is hard to speak of this matter, even before you and Amy. But he is jealous of Mr. Clare, and thinks I care more for him than for any one else."

And here the sick girl began to sob so passionately, that we were afraid of her lapsing again into fever. Poor Pearl! how innocently, yet how completely, did she betray her secret in this outburst of emotion. My sister at last succeeded in calming her, and then said—

" It will not do for you to fret, and give way to such depression in this matter, my darling Pearl; cheer up, and pray for guidance to that all-wise and merciful Friend of whose wisdom and goodness Cecil Clare has taught us so many true and beautiful lessons; trust to him for strength to act as your own pure and truthful nature dictates. Remember, you only promised Victor to try and love him well enough to be his wife, and finding that impossible, would it not be wicked in you to stand up before God and man and perjure yourself by vowing to love and cherish forever as a husband one who is, and you feel can only be, loved by you as a brother! Surely Victor will see and acknowledge all this, my child; he cannot covet an unwilling bride. So when you are strong enough to speak more calmly upon the subject than at present, tell him how you feel without reserve, and I feel confident that though disappointed and unhappy, he cannot be unreasonable and angry.

"But papa and aunt Kate, they know of the understanding between us, and it has made them so happy, what will they think of me, cousin Ethel?"

"Only that you are a sincere, conscientious girl. Can you believe for one moment that either of them would wish you to marry a man whom you find it impossible to love, save as a brother?

"No, oh, no! I am sure they love me, and are not stern or passionate as Victor. Yet, their hearts being set upon it, may they not be made unhappy by my apparent waywardness, for he is so worthy of my love—ay, of one far brighter and more talented than I am—for Victor is so smart, so cultivated, so agreeable."

To all of which my fluttering heart said " amen," as in

mute despair I sat with a sick, dreary feeling, the blood seeming to curdle cold about my heart while listening to Pearl's recital of his great love for her, and the unhappiness caused thereby, and wondering why things in this life are ordered so strangely.

"They will not think you wayward," responded my sister, "and your best plan is to speak upon the subject, when strong enough, to them, even before speaking with Victor, as their opinion and advice will, I am sure, be calculated to strengthen you in pursuing the right course towards him."

Pearl grew quite calm after this conversation, and promised to act as Ethel advised. Foolish child that I was to feel thus forlorn at hearing this verbal confirmation of a fact which had been evident to me so long, viz.: that Victor loved Pearl, and wanted to make her his wife. Yet as a kind of antidote to this feeling, now arose the certainty that his love for her was hopeless, and I clutched it eagerly as one wounded by a nettle will seize the soothing weed which often grows near by, and is known to cure its sting.

CHAPTER XIII.

THE MANIAC.

ONE fair Saturday evening in August, a few days after the scene related in my last chapter, I had been spending the day with Pearl, who was far more composed since her conversation with Ethel, and was gaining strength much more rapidly than before, though still entirely helpless. Aunt Kate and Mrs. Clare were sitting with her on the evening referred to, so I proposed, just at sundown, to my sister, that we should take a walk, as she looked pale and drooping for want of fresh air and exercise. Ethel assented, and early twilight found us wandering leisurely along a road skirted by dense woods, in the direction of the Glen—for Dr. Foster having made his daily visit to Pearl, we were not afraid of encountering him. I chatted away, as we walked along, about Archey's improbable story of the wild man who had frightened Frolic—of which we had frequently spoken together before, and which my sister persisted in ridiculing as perfectly absurd, maintaining always that this crazy-looking individual was no other than a low man in the neighborhood much given to intoxication.

On the present occasion, I asked her how she accounted for so many of the servants telling the same story to Archey, and why it should be connected with Dr. Foster's cruelty to Gabe, said to be the keeper of this unfortunate lunatic? She laughed at the idea of my crediting such nonsense, and·said,

"Some drunken guest at the Glen knocking down one of the servants, would be quite sufficient for all of Archey's romances—and ten times more."

As she ceased speaking, startled by a sudden rustling in the undergrowth near us, and feeling rather nervous from our conversation, I cried out—

"Oh, sis, what's that? Do let us turn back, for just suppose we were to meet the crazy man!"

"I presume it is a cow or sheep," she replied, "or perhaps nothing larger than a *rabbit*. Amy, don't be so silly. I wish Master Archey would hold his foolish tongue, and almost wish some one would give him a good shaking on the strength of his absurd stories."

At that moment I gave (involuntarily) a piercing scream, and grasped my sister's arm, pulling her towards me so suddenly and violently, it caused us both to totter—

for there before us, out in the open road, where he had leaped with a cat-like bound from the tangled thicket— stood the same wild stranger whose sudden rush through the old bayou had caused Pearl's horse to throw her six weeks before.

Gaunt and sallow, with long, light locks matted together, hanging about his neck and over his eyes, a great mass of yellow beard covering entirely the lower part of his face— with soiled and tattered clothes dangling loosely about his attenuated form—his hands scratched and bleeding from rude contact with thorns and briers—this frantic-looking being, from whom even my brave sister shrank back amazed and terrified, as he stood before us, burst into a fit of wild and fiendish laughter.

We both comprehended instantly and fully our fearful situation in being wholly and helplessly within the power of a maniac. After a moment or two—though I strove to drag her away—Ethel, partially recovering her presence of mind, and knowing how useless, nay, perhaps, fatal, would be any effort to escape by running from a creature who could leap and bound with the activity and suddenness of a panther, said, in a gentle, soothing voice, though tremulous with fear :

"What makes you laugh so ? Is there any one trying to catch you, from whom you are glad to get away ?"

"Yes !" he shouted; "I'm glad to get away from him, and I'll hide forever in the deep, dark woods rather than go back there "—pointing towards the Glen—" I'd rather sleep with the snakes and toads, or in the thickets with bears and wild-cats, than go back to that cell. I hate him! and I'll kill him yet. I would like to bite and tear his flesh, as the ugly beast he hunts me with tears *mine.* My brother! who says he is my brother? how do you dare to say that devil is my brother?" and he advanced as if to seize Ethel, who, retreating very cautiously a step or two, replied:

"I did not say so. It must have been some one else—for we don't think he is any relation to you," for she knew that the only way to appease lunatics is by agreeing to whatever they may choose to say; "but if he treats you badly, why don't you go home?"

"Home," he said—and from a shrill, frantic pitch his voice suddenly subsided into an almost plaintive whisper in the utterance of that single word—"home! ah, yes, I had a home once, and a wife too, who was very fair. She must have looked like you, but I don't remember; it has been so long since he took me away from her, and I have grown so old since then; but, ah! I forgot, he told me she was dead when I wanted to go back home, and kept me locked up—but he lied, I know he did, because he always does, and I'll kill him yet—ha, ha, ha!" and as that fearful laugh rang out again, appearing to hear some sound in the distance, he looked back, and almost shrieked,—

"They are coming with chains to bind me, and the

hound to tear my flesh, the two devils—one is white and the other black, and I can't kill both together—hide me. Oh, where shall I go?" and again the wretched maniac would have seized hold of us—this time in terror, as if we could protect him, observing which, strengthened with fresh courage, Ethel, turning quickly, said:

"Come on, follow me—I know where you can hide in safety, but be quick."

And almost in a run, we set off towards the parsonage, the lunatic following us, until suddenly diverging from the road, Ethel led him by a path through the woods, a short distance, to where stood an immense hollow oak, and pointing to the cavity, said hurriedly,

"There, go in quick, they won't find you now, if you keep quite still for a long time, 'till they have gone by."

Stealthily he crept into the tree, coiling up among the dry leaves and moss, as if accustomed to such lodgings; seeing which, my sister whispered,

"Now don't move till I come back to tell you they have gone by;" and then pulling me off, after gaining the road, we ran until inside the parsonage gate, nearly a mile distant from where we left the poor hunted wanderer.

Then, when the danger was past, Ethel's strength gave way, and falling down on the grass she sobbed out convulsively,

"Oh, Amy, was it not too frightful? Poor Archey, I fancy his story must be pretty nearly correct, after all.

But who can this miserable being be? If actually in Dr. Foster's care, his brother or some near relation, I presume; but if so, the treatment he receives must be harsh, else why this dread and hatred of his keepers? I cannot understand it, yet all of his raving confirmed the story you heard about the negro Gabe, for he said there were "two devils, and one of them was black." Oh! mercy, how cold and sick I turned at the sight of that wretched, frantic looking stranger, and nothing but my perfect trust in the goodness of God, to whom 1 prayed earnestly for help or direction, ever enabled me to act as I did."

Few women would have acted with such perfect self-possession under similar circumstances," I replied; "but here comes Mr. Clifford, who promised to ride home with me this evening—do, dear sis, let us tell him of our startling adventure, and ask if he has ever heard anything calculated to throw light upon this mystery."

As we walked up to the house—for Mr. Clifford dismounted and led his horse—I gave a full recital of our adventure with the lunatic, and also what Archey had said to me the evening Pearl was thrown, and we were astonished in no slight degree to find that Mr. Clifford had heard all about Dr. Foster's crazy brother, the room with prison windows, etc., pretty much the same, indeed, as had been related to me by the negro; but he was greatly shocked at the fearful danger from which we had just escaped, and avowed an intention to speak to my father and Uncle Dunbar on the subject at once, and regarding the propriety of insisting that Dr. Foster's vigilance in guarding his brother must be such, in future, as to prevent his escaping thus, to the discomfort and danger of all in the neighborhood.

Before reaching the parsonage, we heard the deep baying of a blood-hound borne from the direction where Ethel had secreted the stranger, and then loud shouts, accompanied by a frantic yell, such as he uttered when with us in the road, upon fancying he heard the voice of his pursuers. Ethel turned very pale as she said to Mr. Clifford,

"It makes me perfectly sick to think of the dreadful treatment that wretched being may be subjected to, and I do think the matter should be investigated, and his sufferings relieved, if possible; for surely Dr. Foster might be compelled to send his brother to an asylum. Might he not ?"

"I scarcely know," he replied, "yet rather fancy that the doctor has a right, as his brother, to retain the lunatic under his authority; particularly if there still remains a hope of restoring him to reason. It is scarcely possible that he would support such a burden, unless influenced by affection; and yet these stories of cruelty, together with the miserable appearance of this crazy man, would indicate quite the contrary. It is certainly a very odd affair, calculated to excite wonder and sympathy."

That night another fearful dream arose from the haunting memories of our startling adventure, in which Ethel and myself were together, wandering through a dismal swamp, where a perfect curtain of grey moss swept down from gigantic cypress trees, through which the winds moaned dolefully, causing the moss to sway back and forth with a dreary, sighing sound, among the dark, gaunt branches; for it was winter, and the oozy soil under the cypress trees was covered with dead and mouldy leaves. I thought we were alone—lost in the forest amid that spectral gloom, and frighted at every shadow cast by a faint and shimmering moonlight across our path. At last we came to the borders of a great, black, slimy-looking lake, where the road came to an end, cutting off all possibility of continuing our journey in that direction, while to retrace our steps through the swamp was almost as hopeless, for we knew not whither to turn towards home. So at last, overcome by fear and weariness, we sat down weary and desponding, on a great damp log and wept in each other's arms. Soon there came a splashing sound, like the dipping of oars in the water, and then we strained our eyes over the dismal lake, hoping for some friend in a boat, who would take us to Woodburn, and yet fearing that it might be the lunatic again. Presently a slight canoe came winding to shore, through the green slime, in which

with horror we beheld Dr. Foster's crazy brother. Our
terror was overpowering and voiceless, for neither spoke,
as we cowered down behind that great, dark, wet log, upon
a mould of rotten leaves and moss, to hide from him, but
all in vain; for pulling up the canoe, he bounded out and
came leaping towards us, with peals of frantic laughter, as
he cried,—

"Ah, yes, I have found you at last—come on—for I
will row you over this deep black lake to perdition, for betraying me as you did by sending those devils to the hollow oak, where she pretended to hide me—ha! ha! come
along."

Saying which, he appeared to seize and drag us fiercely
towards the boat, into which, shoving us before him rudely,
he jumped, and catching up the oars, rowed away so
swiftly, that the swamp, with its tall cypress trees, soon
faded away in the distance—while before, around us,
stretched that great waste of slimy water, enveloped in a
cloud of murky fog. Suddenly, I thought the maniac
jumped up, flung away his oars, and seizing us both as he
shrieked,—

"Come down into hell with me"—plunged madly into
those inky deeps, dragging us after him; and I struggled,
suffocating with the sullen water and the thick, clinging
slime.

Then, quickly as we had gone down, were we snatched
from that frightful grave, and by daylight breaking

through the fog, found ourselves in a great wide boat, rowed towards a pleasant shore by Mr. Clifford;—when I awoke with the morning sunlight streaming into my face through the parted curtain, as Lucy drew back and whispered,—

"Young ladies, time to get up, it's most eight o'clock."

CHAPTER XIV.

SOME LEAVES FROM PEARL'S DIARY.

SEPTEMBER found Pearl still at the parsonage, much better—well enough to be moved to the parlor sofa for a change—yet still very feeble, quite unable to walk, or even put her foot to the floor, for the injury to her hip was severe—and a slight lameness seemed almost inevitable—though we yet hoped that time and care might overcome it, as she was still so very young. And here I can scarcely continue this story so satisfactorily, as by inserting some leaves from Pearl's diary, which came into my possession years afterwards, and which, of course, I have her full permission to publish.

September 10th.—I must leave the parsonage; must go home to-morrow—would that I had gone long ago; for Rachel Thorn was here this morning, and whispered to me at parting—"Pearl, if I were you, I would go home, yes, even if it killed me—rather than remain longer in the house of a man who every one says is in love with you. Indeed, they hint that his love is not unrequited—and then Victor is so awfully jealous, you ought not to stay another hour." Oh! how I hated her for that cruel speech, and how fiercely I threw off the hand and arm she slily tried to wind round my neck while speaking. May God forgive me for being so angry—but I told her she was a wicked, deceitful wretch—that no one had ever thought, much less said, such a thing save herself, and she only did so to torment me. It was wrong—but I am quick, and her speech was so brim-full of spite, though masked by pretended friendship and kindness. And then the provoking way in which she said : " Don't get in a passion, Pearl, you'll make yourself worse ; I only meant it as a little sisterly advice, to be taken or rejected, as you please—so, good evening," and off she glided like an adder, leaving, as usual, a sting behind her ! Yet, why did her words make me so angry ? Were they entirely untrue ? If so, why not have treated them with cool indifference ? No, they were not untrue—far from it. Cecil Clare does care for me—he has shown it in a hundred ways—and am I indifferent to him ? Oh, no, my poor weak heart cannot deny that he is the only man whose coldness or indifference would serve to make me utterly wretched. And feeling so, ought I to remain here so long ? Is it kind, or just to Victor (after promising that I would try to love him well enough to be his wife) for me to remain, from day to day, under the influence of one who is drawing my heart off further every hour from its allegiance? And innocently, too; for Mr. Clare regards Victor as my brother, and does not dream of an understanding between us. Victor is "jealous," as Rachel Thorn said, and I have not yet had the strength or resolution to speak candidly, as cousin Ethel advised. I wonder if she suspects the real reason that now renders it impossible for me to love him as he wishes? Yet, remaining here, has been no fault of mine—for papa and Aunt Kate both vetoed my going home last week, though I almost insisted upon it; but now, after what Rachel said this morning, I cannot, must not remain. Papa will not refuse to take me back to Elgin if I pine to go—but do I pine for home? Alas! no, and spite my sufferings, the weeks spent here have been the happiest of my life. Yet I will say it is best to go; the change may help to strengthen me, and if Aunt Kate is obstinate in refusing her consent, I shall not scruple to tell her what Rachel Thorn says.

September 11th.—Just as I finished writing yesterday, Cecil Clare came in to bring me a bunch of violets; we were quite alone—so I told him, that feeling very much better, I intended asking papa to take me home the next day. "My stay here has been already too long, and caused dear Mrs. Clare and yourself a vast deal of trouble," I said, trying to smile, as I looked up and our eyes met.

"Trouble," he exclaimed; "how can you make use of

such an expression, when the joy I have in seeing you is so great, and my mother loves you;—do you want to leave us then, or what has caused this sudden determination? For Dr. Foster said yesterday, you must not be moved for a week."

I was confused, and remained silent, while toying idly with the dewy violets he had given me; for how could I tell him what Rachel said, and what other excuse was there to plead for disobeying the Doctor's orders?

"Why are you silent," he said at last, "Miss Dunbar? Has anything happened to offend you?"

The name sounded cold and formal, for he had always called me Miss Pearl of late.

"No, Mr. Clare," I answered, "nothing but the greatest kindness and attention have I received in this house—what could offend me? Both you and your mother have been all devotion to me, and it would be the basest ingratitude were I to leave even a shade of mystery or uncertainty over the cause of my rather sudden departure. I was told this morning by a friend—and the word was uttered with sarcastic bitterness—that my prolonged stay here either was, or would be, a subject for disagreeable remarks," and the hot blood tingled up to my cheeks while speaking.

"Friend!" he repeated; "yes, you may well utter that word in mockery, for I happen to know who your visitor was this morning, just before I came in—and can well imagine her capable of such malice; but do not heed it, I beg of you, for, even were I living here alone, the constant presence of your aunt and cousin would prevent remark—and with my mother—oh! you cannot, will not be driven away by such an abominable piece of spite."

He spoke so earnestly, and appeared evidently so wounded at my determination to leave, that at last I consented to remain until the end of the week. There would be some gratification, too, in showing Rachel Thorn that her opinion was disdained and disregarded.

September 12*th.*—Aunt Kate gave me a package to-day, brought up from New Orleans by Michael McAlpine. He is a son of the good old Scotch people who had charge of me before I was adopted by papa. How wonderful it is to think of my being rescued from the waves by a fisherman, upon a lonely shore, almost dead, and tied to the broken spar of a shipwrecked vessel! I can scarcely realize it. How merciful and good is the God who preserved me from a watery grave, to be blessed with such true, kind friends, and such a lovely, happy home.

Dame McAlpine is dead, and her last request to her husband was, that Michael might take a package to me containing the handkerchief which was round my neck and the clothes I had on when old McAlpine carried me home drenched and insensible to his humble cottage.

Thus runs a part of his letter to papa:

"My dear old dame had stowed the things away so carefully she forgot all about them until after you had removed to Elgin, and then we ventured to keep them as a memento of the bonnie bairn we loved so dearly for two years—thinking it could be of no use, having no name upon it, and only some queer worked figures. The clothes she had on were torn, but my poor wife put them all carefully by in a trunk with the handkerchief, and I promised her to send them to ye, good sir, for our bonnie bairn, as perhaps they may by some chance yet one day lead to a discovery of her parents—though God bless her winsome face—I doubt me not she is an orphan. Michael is a good lad, and if you can find employment for him it will be a blessed day for us—as the fishing business is rather falling off of late, I can barely support him, poor laddie, and scantily enough too—so he wants to help himself, bless his brave heart! and I think, perhaps, you may befriend him—for which the Lord will bless you and the bonnie bairn, (who must be a bonnie lassie now)—how my old heart would warm with a sight of her fair face, and I never would have given her up, except that I knew ye would rear her tenderly, and make her a fine lady, as she ought to be, for she's a born lady if ever there was one."

Poor old man! how I should like to see him, and the good dame, who was a mother to me for two years. Alas ! I can never thank her now for all that kindness. But papa has often sent them money in my name, and I know he will always continue to befriend the poor lonely old fisherman who rescued me from drowning. Michael is to stay at Elgin, aunty says, to help work in the garden, and also in taking care of the horses. I am so glad, and I shall take such pleasure in being kind to the motherless lad who used to call me his little sissey. This handkerchief is a dainty, pretty thing, a very marvel of fine needlework, and though the good old fisherman and his dame could find nothing but queer figures upon it, I can see very plainly that the design in one corner is a crest—while those delicate vines wrought into letters round the other, form themselves into "Olivia." I wonder if that was my mother's name, and if she was lost in trying to save my life? And these pretty little baby clothes! how odd to think I could ever have worn such tiny things. There is no name on them. Oh! how I wish they had been marked—and yet why? I am perfectly happy as Pearl Dunbar, and could not be more so were I to find my own parents—though, of course, I should love them, oh yes, so dearly. There is a natural instinct, causing the hearts of those who have never known their own parents to yearn for them sometimes as I do, but never sadly, or repining —how could I with such friends and such a home?

September 13*th.*—Mr. Clifford has just left, after paying me quite a long visit. What a noble, true, good man he is! I do wonder how he ever came to be a teacher? Not that there is anything beneath the dignity or standing of a gentleman in teaching—but then it is so tiresome, and he looks too grand for such weary work. How much cousin Ethel likes him, and they are so suited for each other! He loves her, I am sure, every look and action tells it—and how could it be otherwise when she is so fascinating and they are so much together? I wonder if cousin Ethel knew all about Mr. Clifford, if she would not marry him? One thing is certain, she never blushes in any other presence but his. How perfectly absurd it is in Rachel Thorn to show her love for Mr. Clifford in the way she does! every one sees it, and also that it is scorned by him. Oh! the cold gleam of hatred in that girl's eye at times when she looks at her rival frightens me,—she looks capable of anything and everything desperate, and Dr. Foster too—their eyes are wonderfully alike—is as jealous of Mr. Clifford as Rachel is of Ethel. He is a good physician, and I thank him for curing me, but papa pays him liberally—so that I am at liberty (without being ungrateful) to dislike the man, and I do most cordially— for he looks wicked, and I cannot help believing the stories about his harshness to that poor lunatic brother—for when papa spoke to Foster about the propriety of keeping a stricter guard over him—after that evening cousin Ethel and Amy had such a fright in the woods—he represented his brother as such a " furious maniac, that even with the greatest severity and the strictest watching he would manage to escape sometimes."

"Then," said papa, "you should send him to an asylum."

Upon which the Doctor pretended that he had such great control over him (even in his wildest moods) there might yet be some chance through that influence of eventually restoring him to reason, urging this as a plea for keeping the poor unfortunate being under his immediate care. But I cannot believe his motives good, nor help fancying he has some hidden mean reason for this apparent act of fraternal devotion; he is a selfish, cold man, and would never assume such a burden unless there were very cogent reasons urging him on. Mr. Clifford thinks pretty much as I do regarding Dr. Foster. Oh! he must be selfish and vulgar to have made such an unfavorable impression on this just and noble Englishman, who is so careful and unprejudiced in his judgments of people. How tender and kind is the interest he takes in me, because of my likeness to a dear, lost friend—partly—though I am sure Mr. Clifford likes me for my own sake too. I wonder if the original of that lovely miniature, which they flatter me by saying I resemble so much, was his lady-love? Perhaps so—for I doubt not his history is full of interest and romance—he looks as if it were, and I am sure his love for Ethel Linton, with Rachel's jealousy and Dr. Foster's, to say nothing of the crazy man, is enough material for a novel, and if I were as clever with my pen as Amy, I'd set about writing one forthwith, founded on all these striking events.

Then there is poor, dear Victor, too, with his mad

jealousy of Cecil Clare. Mercy! I wonder why people can't live without falling in love? The last time he was here, Victor said, as he pressed my hand almost fiercely at parting, "Pearl, when you return to Elgin, that matter between us must be decided positively; I cannot live thus; and your ultimate decision shall influence me, whether to remain here, or go abroad for years—perhaps forever." I grew cold and faint, and would, nay, ought to have spoken candidly then, as Cousin Ethel bade me, but lacked the courage, and could only murmur, half inaudibly, as he left me, "Yes, we will talk about it when I come home."

Ah! how perfectly silly it was in me, allowing such an opportunity of expressing my real feelings to pass in this way. Yet I am feeble, and the least excitement makes my heart beat so fast. In spite of what Cousin Ethel says, I fear papa and Aunt Kate may be hurt with me for driving Victor from home, as he will be sure to go abroad after hearing my decision; and yet how can I help it? They have always been so kind, let me not doubt their forbearance on this trying occasion.

Elgin, Sept. 20th.—My diary has remained unopened for a week, and no wonder, for I can scarcely command myself even now sufficiently to relate the stirring events which occurred the day after my last notes were written, and the one previous to that on which I left the parsonage. The evening was so lovely, that Mrs. Clare had my sofa rolled up close to the library window, opening on to a little verandah overlooking the garden, and as I had a pleasant book to read, Aunt Kate and my kind hostess left me there for awhile alone, while they went off for a drive. Cecil Clare was absent in town, and not expected home until dark. How I enjoyed the sweet sunny breeze that crept in to me through the window, loaded with the bitter aroma of the Madeira vine with which the verandah is covered! How sweet it was, after such a long confinement and so much suffering, to be so near the outer world of beauty and fragrance once more. I read but little, for my heart was out in the garden, with the merry little birds among the autumn roses, and then off to Elgin with poor Frolic, wondering if I should ever ride him again? And then I fancied myself mounted once more on my little favorite, galloping through the grand magnolia grove between here and Woodburn, as once I did with Cecil Clare, just before that fearful accident which has lamed me perhaps for life. The warm air, the song of birds, the hum of bees among the vines, were soothing, and lulled me so pleasantly, that from waking dreams I passed gradually into a soft and peaceful slumber, which lasted I know not exactly how long, though it was yet quite light, when, startled by a slight noise, and that mesmeric influence produced by the light of waking eyes on the mind of a sleeper, I awoke, beneath the gaze of Cecil Clare, who stood there, bending upon me a look I had never seen so fully expressed in his face before. A look of deep, unutterable tenderness, long hidden, and thus suddenly breaking forth, mingled as it was with the full and perfect purity of holiness within, illuminated his countenance as sublimely as the halo of glory emanating from the heads of pictured saints and apostles.

" How long have you been here, Mr. Clare?" I faltered out, striving to hide my agitation as best I might. "Your mother did not expect you until dark, and this may possibly account for the unusual circumstance of my being here alone, and asleep in your sanctum sanctorum, where I was tempted to come at Mrs. Clare's suggestion, because this window, opening down to the verandah, affords such a beautiful view of the garden. Aunt Kate has taken your mother off for a drive, and I fancy they will be back before long; so now that you have my apology for being an intruder here, please push my sofa back into the parlor again, will you?"

My manner was full of confusion, though I strove in vain to hide it,—for still those deep, clear eyes were shining on me, earnestly and full of love.

" No," he said, "I cannot help you back into the parlor, nor allow you to leave this spot, Pearl, until you hear what I have to say, what must be said before you leave this house, for you are strong enough to answer me now. I love you dearly, devotedly, Pearl, and, child as you are, would have you promise to be my wife. Tell me, could you be content to dwell with me in this quiet little home?"

He caught my hand, and, sinking down on his knees beside the sofa, pressed it to his lips, ere I could sufficiently command myself to falter out,—

"Oh, Mr. Clare, stop, I implore you! Don't say anything more on this subject now; for I have no right to listen—nay, must not, being almost pledged to Victor Dunbar, who has loved me from childhood, and whom I have promised to try and love in return."

The words were scarcely past my lips, and he still clung to my hand as if bound by a spell not to be broken, when there was a sudden rush from the parlor, for we were just opposite the door, accompanied by a frantic exclamation of anger, which caused Cecil Clare to start up— only for a moment, and then stagger, falling heavily backwards on to the verandah floor, beneath a fierce blow dealt upon his head by Victor, who stood by me, white, and trembling with rage.

"Lie there, you sneaking, hypocritical parson!" he cried: "I'll teach you to rob me of the treasure I coveted so madly! And you, Pearl—perfidious, ungrateful girl— whom I have loved so dearly ever since your childhood, how could you so basely deceive me into believing that you had the wish, the will, and would at least try to return my affection, while thus encouraging this strange preacher, and suffering all my hopes to be crushed so suddenly, without one word of warning, by finding you thus almost in his arms!"

These words rained out in such a perfect torrent of fury that I scarcely drew my breath while he was uttering them; and then, ere there was time to reply, he had gone, as suddenly as he came, and I saw him in a moment afterwards, through the long parlor window opposite, riding at a frantic pace down the avenue.

What could I do? To move from the sofa was impossible, for I was unable to stand; and there lay Cecil Clare, the man I loved—though strengthened to check his avowal of affection from a sense of duty—prostrate and insensible, on the verandah, against the iron trellis work of which he had fallen, cutting his head, and from this wound the blood was pouring, while I sat gazing upon him, cold, sick, and for a few moments, bereft of voice, as well as the power of moving. At last, by a great effort throwing off this dumb dread, I called loudly to the servants for help, but they were not within hearing, as no answer came. Then, when almost exhausted from calling, a desperate resolution possessed me to slide down from the sofa, and try at least with my handkerchief to staunch the blood trickling down that white still face; but just as I turned, in making an effort to move from the sofa, there was a ring at the front door bell, when mustering all my failing strength, I called for help so loudly that Mr. Clifford was at my side almost before the bell had ceased ringing. At one glance he comprehended the whole, and Cecil Clare was lifted up, carried by that powerful man into the parlor and rested in a great easy chair, before I could utter one word of explanation; indeed, my senses were so completely stunned by what had happened, and terror overcame me so entirely, it was not until after Mr. Clifford succeeded in restoring Cecil Clare to consciousness that the cold, wretched feeling which had possessed me gave way, and then, falling back on my pillow, I burst into a passion of tears—always such a blessed relief to high-strung natures, and but for this I must certainly, after such terrible excitement, have relapsed into fever.

When sufficiently calm, I informed Mr. Clifford, as briefly as possible, of all that had happened, for the circumstances required that he should receive my fullest confidence. Part, at least, he had surmised from Victor's distracted manner, as they had passed each other on the road, for though he had called out to know "if anything was the matter," Victor made no reply, and dashed on.

Cecil Clare had been stunned into insensibility, and soon recovered, having received no real injury save the cut on his head, which was not very deep, so that the blood was quickly staunched, and save an excessive paleness, there remained no evidence of Victor's violence in his appearance when Mrs. Clare and my aunt returned, for the cut was easily concealed by the great waving masses of his fair hair ; so we agreed not to speak of the event which might be kept secret between us, and was calculated to cause great pain to the friends of both parties; therefore, ere the ladies returned from riding, Mr. Clifford had left for Elgin, where he hoped to see Victor before there had been time for him to speak to his father upon the subject, which he would be sure to do when that fierce fit of passion wore off, leaving him to reflect clearly upon the madness and wickedness of his conduct. I wrote a hurried note to him by Mr. C., stating exactly what had passed between Mr. Clare and myself, showing him how hasty and unjust he had been towards me, as I had no thought of encouraging the love of any other man, while bound by a promise to him, from which I had intended to absolve myself immediately upon returning to Elgin, having found it impossible to love him otherwise than as a brother, and, had I ever wavered in this intention, his conduct upon the present occasion certainly confirmed me in it, and that henceforth he must not think of me, save as a sister deeply distressed and mortified at his sinful and unreasonable fury."

My prayers were more fervent than usual that night. I had much to be thankful for, as Cecil Clare might have been killed by that dreadful blow,—and the declaration of his love had taught me how dark a shadow would have fallen upon my existence, had Victor's violence resulted fatally; and then I prayed for him too, my poor dear adopted brother, whose love for me was so overpowering, it caused him to forget God, Heaven, everything but his own wild passion.

CHAPTER XV

PEARL'S DIARY CONTINUED.

Though jealousy be near akin to love,
Yet nurse them not together—for if so,
Be thy love blessed—yea, even thrice blessed
Tainted by jealousy, it will corrode.
If unrequited—jealousy doth spoil
The purity and perfectness of love ;
With its fierce passions, 'til they change
To dark deformities.

September 21*st*.—The next morning early, an answer came to the hurried note I had sent over by Mr. Clifford to Victor, which ran thus :

" Pearl, my sister—for now, alas ! I know you can never be more to me. My dear sister, will you, can you ever forgive the madness and wickedness of my conduct last evening ? Your note, of course, exonerates you from all blame, and renders my behavior even more culpable than it would have been had I felt assured that Cecil Clare was your accepted lover, (which the circumstances warranted me in believing for a moment), yet even had that been a certainty, there is not the slightest excuse for the sinful fury which might have left the brand of Cain upon my brow.   Forgive the folly inducing me to believe it possible you might in time learn to love me, for it was evident from your manner of granting the promise, that it was given entirely for my sake, and because you thought from what I said that my father and Aunt Kate wished it.   Let me then absolve you from that unwilling pledge, and if you love Cecil Clare—as I believe you do, Pearl—let not a thought of me interfere with your happiness, despite the foolish abuse I heaped upon him last evening.   I know he is good and true, and far more worthy of you than I am, or ever can be; and yet I craved the blessing of your love God only knows how much, and its possession might perhaps have made me a better and a humbler man, though as good Aunt Kate says, his almighty wisdom knows what is best for us.   I would have told my father all, but Mr. Clifford, good, noble Mr. Clifford, advised me to spare him the pain of knowing the part I acted in that shameful scene of yesterday, as fortunately, the injury sustained by Mr. Clare is not serious enough to render its exposure necessary, and therefore I only told *our* Father that you found it impossible to love me, except as a brother, freeing you from all blame in the matter, and assuring him that you had acted most honorably—so do not fear on your return to Elgin to speak freely with him on the subject Pearl, for believe me you are as dear to that noble heart as I am, and were he to blame either of us, I am sure it would be me, knowing as he does, my passionate nature.

7*

Show this letter if you wish to Cecil Clare, and beg his forgiveness. Pray for me, Pearl, for I am very, very wretched. Being unable to risk my fortitude so far as to see you again, and yet miserable at the thought of leaving home for an indefinite time without bidding you a last farewell, I shall go this afternoon, as my kind father has given his consent, and furnished ample means for me to travel abroad, so long as it may suit me to remain. There is a fearful struggle going on between the love I have cherished for you since childhood, which has possessed and encouraged the better part of my nature, and the madness of my jealousy, which springing from the worse and stronger part, threatens to conquer, destroy, blot out all that is good and pure within me. When I can pray, it shall be for your happiness, and you shall hear from me again when I can write more calmly as

" Your devoted brother,

" VICTOR."

I wept over this letter, and longed to see the writer once more, yet dreading another outbreak, forbore to urge his coming over to say " good-bye," and determined upon postponing my return home, fixed for that day, until the following, when he would certainly have left. Poor aunty Kate was in great distress when informed that all was over between Victor and myself, and went off to pack his trunk with a sadder heart, I fancy, than she had borne since the night they were summoned to my side after that dreadful fall. Yet Ethel was right. Neither my dear papa nor aunt Kate blame me for not marrying Victor, though such a union would have made them very happy. They know nothing yet of Cecil's love. I gave him Victor's message, but did not show the letter, as it refers to my love for him as almost a certainty, and I could not allude to that subject, save so far as to remark (as I did) that Victor was going abroad, and we were in future to be as brother and sister only.

Just then our conversation was interrupted, but his face lit up with joy, when I uttered these words, and the forgiveness his rival craved was most freely granted. Hopeful lovers can afford to be generous on such occasions—but Cecil Clare is good and pure enough to be equally so even to a successful rival.

September 25th.—It is so strange at Elgin without Victor, and yet though we miss him so, I am glad for his sake that he has gone—as the quiet monotony of a country home life would have been insupportable in his present unhappy and excited state. Poor Amy is altered since he left, and has lost half her sprightliness. Yesterday, when Bang—Victor's favorite dog—came and rested his head on her lap, as she bent over him I saw the big tears dropping sadly from her pale cheeks upon that faithful creature's shaggy head, who, missing his master, goes whining about the house and yard as if seeking the absent one. Amy is not such a perfect child after all, being in her sixteenth year, and wonderfully matured. Perhaps when Victor returns to find her grown up a bright and beautiful woman, as she promises to be, he may fall in love with her. She is certainly well suited for him, being so clever and appreciating, and I do hope it may be ordered thus.

Archey was here this morning with a note for me from cousin Ethel. The boy was possessed, as usual, to chatter about Dr. Foster and his crazy brother, and also of a matter which astonished me not a little, viz. :—a sudden and unaccountable intimacy between Dr. Foster and Rachel Thorn. They are, to be sure, enough alike in disposition to be congenial spirits ; yet, his constant effort to avoid her at first, makes this recent friendship appear most singular. I only wish he would fall in love with Rachel, and persuade her to accept a home at the Glen—she is to me like a dark shadow in the midst of so much brightness and beauty at Woodburn.

The Glen is a fine old place, and I rather fancy she is mercenary enough to be tempted thereby into marrying its master, even in spite of her ridiculous love for Mr. Clifford, knowing as she must, that it is hopeless. But the Doctor's aspirations, unfortunately, aim at rather a higher prize than Rachel Thorn.

Eugh ! it makes me sick to think of that great, pompous, vulgar lump of humanity in the shape of a doctor (stuffed into broadcloth) having the assurance to love Ethel

Linton!   But I must not forget Archey's funny communication.

"Miss Pearl," he said, shuffling up to me, hat in hand, "just as sure as we is livin', dar is sumpin or anudder gwying on twixt dat dar strange doctor and de young white 'oman massa 'lows to live at Woodburn—sum of de niggers calls her 'Miss Rachel,' but I speaks of her all de time as 'Miss Torn,' for she's nun of my mistress, and I was never no ways sociable wid her.   Well, long about a week or two past, I's seed dem two walkin' togedder in de lane back of our house, wid dar heads close enough togedder to be hatchin' mischief, and whenebber dey sees me or anybody cumin' she bows and goes back to de house, as if dey had met on accident, den he walks off to de quarter and gits on his horse to go home ; and dey's been a doin' so ebber since the doctor's been tendin' on uncle Abe.   Lord Miss, how dis nigger chuckles when he see dat little sly white 'oman bow and walk off as if she jist happened to be dar, and did'nt care 'bout stoppin' to talk wid de doctor ; and well I might chuckle, for I's watched um two or tree times while I was squattin' down behind de corn-shucks piled up in de barn lot, and dey thought deyselves all alone—and if you b'leve me, I was dar watchin' um de fust day she went out dar and overtook him as he went down from seeing massa at de house.   Den she whispered sumpin in his ear which he did'nt seem to like, for he turned as white as your hand, miss, and then when she whispered again, looking up right quick at her, he said, 'because you 'oman's have sich damned long tongues '—begging your pardon, Miss,—' but if your's is too long, I'll cut it out for you.' Gosh! but dis nigger hugged de corn-shucks close den, for he looked as savage as a meat axe."

I reproved the boy, telling him he had no right to listen to the conversation of white people; and that Miss Ethel would be provoked at him for it.

"I don't be given to it, mam," he replied; "but blast me if I kin help watchin' dem two, for dey both looks so monstus wicked like. Dat's all I heered um say, and I'll try not to listin no more if you wishes it, Miss," and Archey bowed himself out.

It was a queer conversation, and I shall certainly talk the matter over with cousin Ethel. The doctor thinks a month more of care will put me on my feet again, with the assistance of a crutch. I hope so, as that will be in time for the Christmas tree. Poor Victor! 'it is so sad to think he will not be one of our party. Michael McAlpine proves a good lad, and takes such an interest in the flowers, that Aunt Kate has given him almost entire charge of them. He brings a fresh bouquet to my room every morning, and I find great pleasure in asking him questions about the two years I lived in his father's cottage, for he is several years my senior, and often had charge of me when I was to him as a sister. It is hard to realize that I should have lived in a fisherman's cottage, as a daughter to those poor, good people! · And yet, I must be the child of gentlefolks, else that dainty handkerchief would not have been about my neck, and the clothes I wore would not have been so fine. How I delight in looking at that delicate work, the crest, and the name, too—my mother's name it must be—so gracefully embroidered—wondering if the future will ever reveal my real name?

Mr. Clifford comes over every evening after school to hear my French and German lessons. It is a real pleasure to learn from such a master—so delicate in his feeling, so considerate, so full of manly kindness! I do wonder if uncle Percy can see cousin Ethel and Mr. Clifford so much together without thinking that they may happen to fall in love with each other? Poor, dear, beautiful Ethel!—if they could only have met before her first miserable marriage! Yet, when I suggested this to Cecil Clare, the other day, he looked very grave, and said:

"Don't suppose, because events are contrary to what our feeble judgment may deem best, that it is so, or that we could better the order of things by arranging them to suit ourselves—for, by cultivating such thoughts, we put our little mite of earthly wisdom up in opposition to that Almighty one who never has erred and never can err. Had your cousin met Mr. Clifford in her early youth, they might not have been congenial in disposition and temper, at they now appear to be, for she has doubtless been softened and strengthened by early trials; and, though we know nothing of his history, there is a sad, firm, calm look about Mr. Clifford, which indicates that he has borne some heavy weight of sorrow patiently, and met reverse of fortune bravely as a man; resignedly as a Christian. Perhaps they both needed this to make them what they now are, and (if destined for each other) it is far better they never met until now; for God orders all things well. Suppose you, or I, or any other human being, had the government and direction of everything even on this little globe of ours (to say nothing of the boundless universe) for one day, how would it end? In misery, confusion, and ruin. Let us not then even presume, in the weakness of human folly, to doubt the wisdom of God."

It is a blessed thing to possess the confiding faith of a true Christian, there are few so pure and good and wise in their Christianity as Cecil Clare.

October 21st.—Victor has been absent a month, and though Cecil Clare has been a constant visitor at Elgin since his departure, not one word in reference to that fearful scene, which occurred between them at the parsonage, ever escaped his lips until last night, when he asked me if I were quite sure that all understanding between Victor and myself of a tender nature was at an end? and upon being answered very positively in the affirmative, he said a great deal, which might look very foolish written, being doubtless but a repetition of love-making—though perhaps somewhat different in style from that fair antediluvian morning, or evening, when Adam whispered soft nothings to his lovely companion amid the bowers of Eden, down to the present time—yet the voice of his wooing filled my heart with a joy unknown before, a joy too perfect to pall, and now that I am pledged to Cecil Clare, with the consent and blessing of all who love me, my heart overflows with gratitude to that Almighty Friend, whose protecting care rescued the shipwrecked child, and again saved the girl's life when in almost as fearful danger, to bring her thus to an earthly haven of peace and happiness.

CHAPTER XVI.

RACHEL THORN'S BANISHMENT.

How hard it is to realize the changes sometimes occur-
ing in a few short months !

From the last date of Pearl's diary up to January 1st,
events so unexpected (and some of them very startling)
transpired, crowding each other with a rapidity perfectly
bewildering. After Victor's departure, Elgin was never
the same place to me ; Pearl's lameness necessarily made a
difference too ; the house was far more quiet than formerly.
Our rides were less frequent, and never so pleasant either
to Ralph or myself, for we missed those two bright absent
ones—Victor far away, and Pearl so lame that the question of her ever being able to ride again was a doubtful
one. My brother grew pale and sentimental after Pearl's
engagement, read Byron assiduously, sang forlorn love
ditties, and for several months looked the picture of a youth
laboring under a weight of disappointed affection. We

knew his malady to be only temporary in its nature, and therefore both Ethel and myself teased him without mercy, until at last in a fit of desperation he eschewed sentimentality in toto, and thereafter we missed his copy of Byron from the centre-table, wherein sundry and divers passages (of great significance in his case) had been fiercely marked, while in places of sentimental airs we heard him whistling the gayest tunes from comic operas. Poor Ralph! he was for a while very fretful and discontented, and evidently suffered more from this first disappointment than we supposed his light and joyous disposition capable of suffering from such a cause.

My temperament is too elastic, too full of vigorous vitality, to yield readily to depression, and my regret at Victor's absence was from the first brightened by a hope of his returning (perhaps sooner than was anticipated) when on moon-lit eves to come in riding and walking together, he will think more of me, and less of another, than in the by-gone times when I was petted as "little coz." For time was passing, and I would not always be a child.

Before the end of autumn Dr. Foster was generally looked upon as a discarded lover of Ethel, and the truth is he had addressed her more than once, dwelling upon his great wealth as an inducement for her acceding to his proposals, and "a home anywhere she pleased."

"The idea of a home anywhere, even were it an earthly paradise, with such a man," she exclaimed when telling me about it, "and then the 'crazy creeter,' as Archey is pleased to call that poor unfortunate lunatic! Amy, what a time I would have with the fat vulgar doctor, the black giant Gabe, that ferocious blood-hound Wolf, and the crazy man! mercy! what a charming little family circle." And then she laughed so gayly. Oh! my darling sister, how sadly that merry ringing laugh echoed in my memory at no very distant period. Ethel had answered Dr. Foster's first proposition (which was in writing) promptly and positively, by returning his letter with a simple expression of wonder at its contents, and when he renewed the subject shortly afterwards in person, she could not help treating it as a joke, and possessed by a spirit of mischief, at times beyond control, said to him :—

"Why, Dr. Foster, it appears to me the circumstance of your brother's most unfortunate condition, and your great devotion to him, would prevent all possibility of your marrying, as it must necessarily divert your attention somewhat from him, and the presence of a crazy person in your establishment might be rather an objection to most ladies, I fancy;" and then she smiled so wickedly, that any one less vain and conceited than the doctor would have fathomed at once the irony of her mood; but catching at this expressed objection as if he thought it the only one which could possibly exist, he went on to assure her that such reasons for rejecting his suit were entirely ground-less, as he had only been prompted by motives of the greatest fraternal affection to keep his brother so long with him, ever hoping by kindness and care to restore the broken constitution and shattered mind of the sufferer, which now being hopeless, it was his determination in any event to place his brother in an asylum. Then, with a fierce impetuosity, both astonishing and amusing to my sister, he began, in the most Bombastes Furioso style imaginable, to pour forth the rhapsodies of love, imploring her to give him a hope at least of future success, until at last, though almost unable to gain a hearing, she begged him to drop the subject forever, as her decision was and would remain unalterable, and she must consider any future attempt to renew it offensive in the extreme, when, flying from the extreme of love to that of rage, he left the house in a violent passion, and refused to enter it afterwards, even when sent for as a physician.

Ethel joked my father about the loss of his favorite medcal adviser, saying, she "believed he would rather accept Foster as a *son* than lose him as a physician."

Our dear, unselfish father!—he could well endure such jokes,—whose every thought was for our happiness.

Rachel looked black as a thunder-cloud at our sallies of fun about the doctor, and one day, when she had swept out of the room as if highly offended at me for mimicking his pompous manner, Ethel exclaimed,—

"Amy, don't you wish he would marry Rachel, she would suit him exactly?" I gave her credit for the suggestion, and avowed a determination to tell our fair cousin since she had come to admire our neighbor so much of late, it would not be a bad idea to set her cap for him.

"Oh, how angry it will make her!" I said; "for she's dead in love with Mr. Clifford, though for some mysterious reason unknown to us, Foster evidently possesses a wonderful influence over her. What a nice time poor Gabe and the crazy man would have, with such an amiable trio as Rachel, the doctor, and Wolf!—He is just the person to suit Rachel, and about the only one who could keep her in order."

I carried my threat of bantering her on this subject into execution the very first opportunity. I know she was angry enough to strike me, and in thinking it over since, feel well assured that the pent-up fury of that moment urged her on to commit the crowning act of perfidy which caused my father, after she was unmasked, to banish her from Woodburn. We were alone at the time, and her only reply was,—

"Hold your tongue, you saucy little jade; I would rather be without beaux forever than glory in breaking hearts as your lovely sister does!"

I was provoked at her spite, and said as she glided out of the room,—

"There is no danger of *your* acquiring the right of glorification over that kind of butchery!"

When next we met, there was rather a more malignant

expression than usual lurking in her cold eyes, but otherwise I observed no sign of displeasure, and avoided further allusion to our late conversation.

A few days afterwards, as Mr. Clifford, Ethel, and myself were sitting in the library, arguing about the pronunciation of certain words, for which he was searching in Webster, Rachel, entering, as I thought, in rather a flurried manner, said quickly to my sister,—

"Ethel, while you were riding this morning, a note came for you from Pearl, and as you were absent I told the boy he need not wait, and threw it into your portfolio, which was lying open on the table—but let me run and get it."

So, without waiting an instant for Ethel's reply, she sped off, and was down again before we had time to express more than an exclamation of wonder at her sudden fit of obliging amiability. As she entered, my sister, seeing the portfolio instead of the note in Rachel's hand, remarked,—

"You need not have troubled yourself to bring down that great book—where's the note?" at the same time holding out her hand to take the portfolio, which however the crafty bearer managed to slam adroitly, as if by accident, against the back of a chair, causing it to fall, and scattering the entire contents before us on the carpet.

"Dear me!" cried the artful creature, "what have I done? But, mercy on me, Ethel! where *did* you get such a perfect likeness of Basil?"

And catching up a miniature of her brother, which had fallen from my sister's portfolio, she began kissing it, as if in an ecstasy of delight.

Mr. Clifford and myself forthwith proceeded to gather up the scattered papers, both confused, and scarcely knowing what to think, when simultaneously we caught sight of an open letter, apparently long kept, and all on one page, written in a large, bold hand so distinct that neither of us could avoid seeing the beginning and ending—

"My darling Ethel—and your devoted Basil."

For the eyes will take in such words, when clearly written, without any intention of reading a letter thus suddenly spread out to view. I crumpled it quickly, snatching up the portfolio and cramming in the papers *en masse* with a rapidity I could scarcely account for, being bewildered beyond expression—after Ethel's positive denial of anything like an engagement with Basil Thorn, to find his miniature and a *bona fide* love letter from him in her possession.

Mr. Clifford looked as I had never seen him look before, and turning away from me after the papers were collected, left the room. Then I cast an inquiring look at Ethel, for all this occurred so quickly, that Rachel was still kissing the picture when Mr. C. went out. My sister's lovely face was so perfectly rigid with intense excitement that it frightened me, and I sprang forward to hold her, as she deliberately advanced towards Rachel, when snatching the picture from her hand, she said,

"How do you dare to ask where I got this likeness of your brother? Base, deceitful girl, you put it there to forward some vile purpose unknown to me, and which I do not care to fathom; one thing I know, and that is you have played out your last act of perfidy at Woodburn, for my father shall hear of this.

As she spoke, the whole truth flashed upon me, Rachel had forged the letter and placed it there with the miniature to convince Mr. Clifford that her assertion regarding the engagement of my sister and Basil was correct. I hated myself for not seeing through it on the instant, and felt condemned that I had doubted Ethel even for a moment."

"Stop," I said, as she turned to leave the room, "you did not see this letter which fell out with the miniature," and drawing out the crumpled manuscript, I placed it in my sister's hand.

"A vile forgery!" she exclaimed, "for I never received a line from Basil in my life, save the letters he wrote warning me not to marry poor Arthur, and they were all destroyed. Rachel Thorn, why have you been guilty of so wicked an act? I should think one case of forgery in your family a sufficient disgrace, without your following it up in such a shameful manner."

Rachel seemed gasping a moment for breath, and then replied with hardened effrontery,—

"Ethel Linton, it is very well for you to strive and hide your perfidy to Basil by hurling accusations at me. I did not write that letter, and I swear Basil wrote it and sent it to you with the likeness; but you don't want Mr. Clifford to know this, for you love him, Ethel, as well as you are capable of loving, and when aware, as he must be now, of your engagement to, and base treatment of Basil, he will scorn you as you deserve to be scorned. Do your worst. You can turn me away from Woodburn, but rest assured you shall suffer for it yet."

And she ran out, slamming the door in a fury, while we stood gazing at each other, stupified by such monstrous and daring falsehoods.

Long afterwards, Mr. Clifford told me that Rachel had followed him into the garden, when as they met suddenly at a turn in the walk, she exclaimed,—

"Well! do you believe me now, or is Ethel Linton still the angel of perfection you thought her, when I told you of her engagement to my brother, and that she broke it off to marry Arthur Linton, because he was rich? Her heart was more Basil's then than it is yours now, though you think she loves you, Mr. Clifford."

The last was hissed out spitefully, and as she waited a reply, he said, coldly and calmly,—

"Miss Thorn, you have no more right to make that latter assertion than I have for supposing that Mrs. Linton regards me otherwise than as a friend. I have no claim upon your cousin's confidence, but if any explanation of this matter should in future be called forth from her, be assured, whatever she tells me respecting your brother and herself will be accepted and respected as the truth, in spite of all you have said or may say to the contrary."

And with these few decisive words he left her.

My father was both shocked and grieved at Ethel's account of Rachel's conduct, and thought we should have given him an earlier insight into her character, determining forthwith that she should leave Woodburn at once and forever. It is useless to dwell upon the stormy interview which followed the announcement to Rachel of this determination, which was made to her by my father in person, for the bland softness of her manner towards him was lost, swept away by a perfect whirlwind of passion.

She was almost angry enough to refuse further pecuniary assistance from the uncle, who had for so long a time been as a father to her, but love of self triumphed even over her spite, and she ended by assuring him that the handsome allowance he made her should only be accepted until such time as she could "obtain a situation as governess."

"A most capital idea, Rachel," he exclaimed, "I admire your spirit."

What an amused, quizzical expression he wore when telling us about it.

We could scarcely appreciate what a perfect incubus that girl was upon our happiness, until she was fairly gone. Ethel's explanation to Mr. Clifford, I presume, was a perfectly satisfactory one to all parties, for when I happened to go into the parlor, the evening after Rachel's departure, they were sitting very close together, my sister's cheeks wore a deeper tinge than usual, and there was a look in Mr. Clifford's eyes expressing, as plainly as words, that all doubt of her was banished from his heart, as finally as the dark shadow that cast it there had been from our happy home.

CHAPTER XVII.

WHAT ARCHEY SAW IN THE WOODS.

"O, most infamous!
The Count of Lara is a damn'd villain!"—LONGFELLOW.

RACHEL left during the first week in December, and a few evenings afterwards, when Ralph and myself had just returned from a ride, as Archey was leading off the horses, he paused a moment, then hitched them to the rack, and coming back to where we stood, before the front door, took off his hat with a shuffling bow, as if about to ask for something.

"Why, you unreasonable scamp!" exclaimed my brother; "you surely don't want any more tobacco, when father gave you so much day before yesterday."

"Lord help you, *no*, Massa Ralph! I don't want no more bacca—don't spect to get more now, no how, fore Christmas. I was only gwying to tell you, bein as how dat young white oman's done gone, and my speakin out can't do no sort of harm to her now, dat I beleves—"

"Who in thunder are you talking about? you black rascal! Can't you call people by their names?"

"Gosh! Massa Ralph, you blazes out at dis nigger so, it skeers all de sense out of his head, and all I was jist gwying to tell is got mixed up togedder, like de mess in de big pot down at de black folks' kitchen, when it biles up so hard you can't tell pork from beans! Do, for de Lord's sake, don't holler so, Massa Ralph," and Archey began to chuckle. "I 's talkin about de young white oman some of de niggers calls Miss Rachel, and I calls Miss Torn—for she's none of *my* miss. What was it I was tellin about her jist now? Let me steddy over it a minit, please, sir."

"Talk fast, then," replied my brother; "and mind, Archey, don't tell me any of your infernal lies. What have you to say about my cousin Rachel?"

"Well, only dis much, sir—and I aint no ways given to lyin," said the boy; "I has a very strong notion, from certin tings dat come under my inspection, dat Dr. Foster and Miss Torn, sir, is gwyin to get spliced—yah! yah! yah!—kase, de odder evenin, when I rode over to Elgin to open de gate for her, he jined her on de way home, and rode most up to de Woodburn lane; and once, when dey sent me on for to open de gate,—long fore we got to it,—I spected somting 'r anudder was gwying on dat I might as well know; so, knowin de gate was open,—for dar ain't none dar to open, for its broke clean off, and ain't nebber been fixed,—at a turn in de road, I dodged into de woods like, drapped down off old Billy, who 's so dratted lazy he wont nebber move, no matter whar you put him,—

and squatting down behind a log near de road, jist waited
for dem two to come along to see what dey was about; and
presently dey come in sight, ridin powerful slow; and as
dey passed, I seed him hand her a little black ting shut up
like a box, and a letter—fore de Lord I did, Massa Ralph;
and he called her "Rachel," he did; for I heerd him say to
her wid my own years,—

"Rachel, if your damned plotting gets me into trouble, I
shet you up—you know whar."

"It was a rough way, sir, of speakin to a gal he's got
notions on; but he's a savage kind o' man any way: and
I would'nt a had him ketch me behind dat dar log for all
master's plantation, darn me if I would; but dis nigger's
too sly for dat sure; and I was astraddle ob old Bill in no
time, and cuttin froo de woods, got to de gate fore dey did.
So, bein's how de lady's your cousin, I felt like it was a
kind ob duty to speak about dis matter; for dat dar doctor's an awful man, and den de crazy creeter, you know,
Massa Ralph!"

"Hold your tongue, you tattling fool!" said my brother,
"or I'll give you a licking. What business have you to
watch white people, and listen to their conversations? I
only wish Dr. Foster had caught you there!"

"De Lord have mercy! dont't say dat, my dear young
massa, for sure as he had, your poor nigger would'nt have
a whole bone in every bit of his black hide dis here minit;
but I never tinks, I don't, of listenin to good white folks;

but dem two looks so darned wicked, wid dar heads togedder, I could'nt help keepin my eye on em dis long time, and I'm monstrus glad to find dey's got notion of marryin each odder, instead of finishing somebody else. And now, Massa Ralph, I know you aint gwyin to lick a darkey for nothin 't all; and I aint dun no harm, but, fore de Lord, I meant to do good.—W-ho-o, Gypsey—dat dar skittish little mar's about to break her bridle, sir. I shall try to deform about listen, as you don't disprove of it, Massa Ralph!" and Archey shuffled off, leaving us in a roar of laughter at his ridiculous attempt to talk "dictionary," as the black people say, when trying to use big words.

After we went into the house, the whole affair was related to Ethel and Mr. Clifford, who were as much puzzled as ourselves to account for Dr. Foster's intimacy with Rachel; and then the black box and letter, could they have any connection with the miniature and letter she had placed in Ethel's portfolio?

If so, how had Basil's likeness come into the doctor's possession? It was in vain to speculate upon a subject so perfectly enveloped in mystery, but we were now rather disposed to believe with Archey, that there must be some understanding of a tender nature between them, as he had called her "Rachel." And surely the negro never could have invented this singular story.

Twice had we heard from Victor since his arrival on the continent through letters to his father and Aunt Kate, but to Pearl he had not yet written, and his mood appeared gloomy enough.

One morning, just before Christmas, while we were at breakfast, Archey came in from town with quite a package of letters, and those with foreign post-marks were not, as usual, all for Mr. Clifford—there was one from Rome for "Miss Percy," and my heart gave a great leap of joy when (as it was handed to me) I recognized the marked and very peculiar handwriting of my cousin Victor. The style was more hopeful than his former letters. He still called me his "dear little coz," evidently striving to shake off depression while giving an account of his travels for my amusement—chiding himself for having neglected me so long—begging me to write and tell him everything.

" Don't forget to mention poor Bang—how he will whine after me !—and Wizard should be ridden constantly, or he will become unmanageable and lose all his fine gaits, and as father may not think of this, please ask Ralph to see about it, and be sure to pet poor Bang for the sake of your loving cousin Vick."

It was thus the letter ended—only in a P. S. he sent love to Pearl, and said he would write to her soon. At all events this interest about his dog and horse was a healthy sign, and showed that his mind was making an effort against morbid melancholy.

Ah ! what a comfort that letter was to me. How often I read it; and before sleeping that night how (even more

than usually) earnest were my prayers for the dear wanderer.

Poor dreaming child! far better for me had he never
written; but I was now sixteen, and Victor the beau ideal
of my fresh young heart. Hope told a pleasant, flattering
tale, and I listened, as many a deluded girl has done, and
as, alas! they will continue to do, looking forward through
that magical glamour which a first love weaves over the
future, trysting fondly in the accomplishment of what we
hope for, driving away desponding thoughts, ever pursuing
the bright phantoms that lure us on, until, at last, they
leave us despairing in a waste of disappointment—as a
beautiful mirage of the desert, (seeming to offer bright
cities, cool fountains and bowers of rest to the weary wanderer who pursues them) disappears at last, and leaves him
mourning over a delusion which promised that which reality
teaches him can never bo obtained.

CHAPTER XVIII.

THE CHRISTMAS TREE.

At last our great delight, the Pearl of Elgin, was so far recovered as to walk once more, though only as yet by the aid of crutches—which it was most probable she would be obliged to use during the winter. She was slighter and paler, so much paler that even the olive tint had partly faded with the rose from her complexion, entitling her more to the beautiful name she bore.

On Christmas eve there was a large party assembled at Elgin, for our annual celebration of the Christmas-tree, held alternately there and at Woodburn.—In the early part of the evening we danced, played games, acted charades or tableaux,—after which the family and company, followed by the house servants, were ushered by the host or hostess into a room, where stood the tree loaded with presents, a tempting and beautiful sight, when some one was appointed to cut down and distribute the gifts.

Long years' have gone by since those happy meetings—some, whose eyes were brightest and whose voices gayest, giving light and life to the passing hours, were called away from earth, ere yet the beam had vanished, that made lip, and cheek and eye so fair, ere yet their hearts had felt the chilling pall of disappointment or regret,—perhaps t'was better thus. Some whose heads were then white with the glory of approaching age, have since laid down in peace, crowned with years, loved and venerated, well satisfied to obey their Master's bidding—and who when he called found them watching.

Some are scattered, dwelling far away from their fair, warm, southern homes, and changed in every thing save the changeless love for those cherished scenes and those beloved ones who, though severed from us or lost forever, are still as dear as when we met their smiling eyes, lit up by the great glowing Christmas fires at Woodburn and Elgin, in that far off vanished time.

Pearl's partial recovery and Victor's more cheerful letter, made us all feel particularly gay and happy on that especial evening, and the guests were prepared for, and set upon a delightful frolic.

Pearl wore a soft full dress of India muslin, with ornaments of rose-colored coral on her neck and arms; her purple black hair, rolled in a massive twist, was coiled up gracefully low down on the back of her finely shaped head, and entirely devoid of decoration, save one perfect star-shaped pink japonica fastened at the left side.

Ethel was radiantly beautiful in a rich robe of black velvet, with pearl ornaments, and a white japonica amid the masses of her shining hair.

Being still considered as rather a "little girl," my dress was not of the slightest consequence, yet the thought did flash upon me, while glancing in the mirror, that my new blue silk was particularly becoming—neither was I un-mindful that the figure reflected there, looked much more womanly in its proportions than on the preceding Christ-mas, and my head would give a proud little toss at the thought that when Victor returned he might find a grown young lady, in place of his little coz. The tree was more beautiful than any we had ever dressed before, and one universal exclamation of delight and admiration burst forth when it was first disclosed to that expectant company, the wonder of the evening—with its magical crop of presents !

All the rooms were beautifully decorated with holly and misletoes, vases of rare exotics were gracefully disposed upon the table and mantels, and the whole scene illumi-nated by a soft, rosy glow from many wax candles, together with the more ruddy sparkling cheerful light of a huge fire of hickory logs, which crackled and roared and flashed in the great open fire-place.

There was a fearful storm raging without, which caused

the warmth, light, mirth, and beauty within those brightly
curtained rooms to seem even more attractive, and tended
in every way to intensify the enjoyment of our Christmas
party.

Mr. Clifford had been appointed to cut down and distribute the presents, which he did most gracefully, having
some pleasant and appropriate word for each recipient, and
our gayety was at its height,—when, in handing to Pearl one
of many pretty trifles, she accidentally dropped her handkerchief, which lifting quickly he playfully spread out on
her lap, over the crimson satin mouchoir case he had just
given her—worked by Ethel—on one side of which
" Pearl " was beautifully embroidered with white silk floss.
The embroidery of the handkerchief being fully and clearly
revealed on the dark satin, when Mr. Clifford's eye fell
upon it, he exclaimed, in a voice whose intense excitement
was painful in the extreme, attracting the attention of all
present,—

" Oh! God of mercy! Pearl Dunbar, where did you
get that handkerchief? "

His manner so startled the feeble girl, that for a moment
she appeared on the point of fainting—for it was the handkerchief Michael McAlpine had brought, and which she
believed had belonged to her mother.   At last she gasped
out—

" It was on my neck when, when—but, Mr. Clifford,
papa can tell you all about it; for, indeed, I do feel so sick

and weak," and leaning back in her chair, poor Pearl looked so very pale it frightened us.

Meanwhile Mr. Clifford picked up the dainty little thing which had caused so much excitement, and without one word of explanation or apology, rushed out of the room, followed by uncle Dunbar, whose kind black eyes lost their twinkle of mirth, and looked sadly troubled, for he always had a dread that something would "turn up" unexpectedly, calculated to clear away the mystery of Pearl's life, and that he might, perhaps, lose her, after so many years of tender care and love—Mr. Clifford's agitation inducing him now, of course, to believe, as we all did, that he must know something with regard to her parents.

When my uncle found Mr. Clifford, he was standing under the hall lamp, examining minutely the delicate work on this mysterious handkerchief.

"Mr. Dunbar," he said, " you will excuse my extreme agitation and sudden departure from the company when informed that this is my crest, and the name embroidered here, ' Olivia,' was that of my wife ; and this is either the handkerchief (or an exact copy of it) I presented her after the birth of our little daughter, which she did not long survive—and that child was lost at sea some fifteen years ago. And now tell me, in heaven's name, when, where and how did it come into your daughter's possession ?"

"This is strange, passing strange, Mr. Clifford," replied my uncle, " for this handkerchief was round the neck of a beautiful child, about two years old, who was rescued from the waves after a furious storm, one morning some fifteen years since, off the coast of Florida, by the master of a small fishing smack. The child was tied to a bit of broken mast, and had evidently been dashed about for some time, as she was quite insensible and almost drowned when saved by the fisherman. The wrecked ship went down just as the little fishing vessel was putting out to sea for the rescue of those on board. All the passengers were supposed to be lost, and with the exception of some three or four of the crew, who escaped in a life-boat, that fair child was the only remnant left from all that freight of human life. Diligent search was made, but no clue to the little girl's parents could ever be obtained, and at last, supposing them to be certainly lost, the old fisherman, McAlpine, adopted that beautiful shipwrecked infant, and for two years it was cherished by him and his wife, in an humble cottage, as their own; when a curious chance brought her under my care, and by me she was regularly adopted as a daughter. The fanciful name given to her by that rough, warm-hearted old sailor, because he had picked her up out of the sea so pure and so fair, was never changed—for still we call her Pearl."

Mr. Clifford, who had listened with rapt and breathless attention to this narrative—when the narrator paused—grasped his hand convulsively, and gasped out in a broken whisper :

"I see. Oh ! yes—it is all very clear to me now—there remains not the shadow of a doubt upon the fact, that your adopted daughter is—oh ! merciful God, how almost impossible it seems—my own long lost child !   No wonder she is so like Olivia !" and he sank down in a chair, breathless—overpowered.

Some half an hour after they had left us, Uncle Dunbar returned and whispered something to Pearl, who immediately rose and left the room with him, prepared for something startling, but (as she told me afterwards) totally unaware, until folded in Mr. Clifford's arms, (when the story was quickly told) that in him was found her long lost father.

She did not return to join the company again, for the meeting of a father and daughter, dead to each other during almost the whole of her young life, was too sacred for other eyes than those whose love had been to her in place of that lost parent—and no one save them—not even Cecil Clare—saw Pearl again that night.   Aunt Kate (who was sent for by my uncle soon after he led Pearl away) returned with her cap, if possible, in rather a more remote position on the back of her head than usual, and her dear, good, honest eyes quite red from weeping.   She described it as such "a touching scene," yet trying to look cheerful, and to answer in her pleasant, blunt, Scotch fashion, to the best of her ability, the endless questions put in rapid succession by that wonder-stricken assemblage of

guests.   Cecil Clare was visibly agitated, and left with his
mother almost immediately after hearing this most singularly romantic story, the particulars of which must of
course remain unknown until Mr. Clifford should be sufficiently composed to relate them.   Indeed, after Aunt Kate
finished distributing the presents our Christmas party
broke up, not sadly, but wonderingly—and all, very
naturally, on the *qui vive* to hear a story, the late episode
of which was so "uncommonly novel like," as Aunt Kate
said.   Dear old lady! what a perfect twitter she was in,
and how her nervous fingers did twitch and work; now
arranging her spectacles, and now giving that nondescript
cap of hers a spasmodic jerk, until at last she ended by
bringing it on a line perpendicular with her eyebrows,
producing an effect more original and ludicrous than becoming—for Aunt Kate was not handsome, and her rather
quaint, peculiar style of adornment rather served to
heighten the effect of her large features and angular figure;
but then she was so thoroughly good, and sensible, and
true, that those who loved her scarcely marked her plain
physique, and I could not help thinking what a fine subject there would be for some great painter when my beautiful sister, while restoring that queer specimen of a head
dress to its proper place upon the cranium of this living
example of spinster perfection, (with an amused expression
that would flash out of those expressive eyes as she peeped

at me over the old lady's head) kissed her so gently, so kindly, saying :

"Good night; don't fret about losing Pearl, aunty, for I know Mr. Clifford will never take her away from you."

And so we left, and so ended that Christmas eve which had furnished us such large material to speculate upon until the whole truth should be revealed.

The storm had abated, and as we drove through the gate a gentleman dashed by us on horseback. It was Mr. Clifford; for the startling revelation of that evening had left him too much absorbed and too deeply agitated even to think of handing Ethel into the carriage; and not until we, who were the last to remain, had left, could he tear himself away from that newly found treasure, the beautiful Pearl, he had so mysteriously discovered under the shadow of our Christmas-tree.

Pearl's guardian angel might have dropped a tear of joy and love—if angels are allowed to weep—while bearing up to God that night the holy incense of her prayer; for it was met by another as earnest and as pure. The spirits of father and daughter mingled their thanksgivings tenderly together before the throne of grace.

CHAPTER XIX.

MR. CLIFFORD'S STORY.

"There's a Divinity that shapes our ends,
Rough hew them as we may."—SHAKSPEARE.

THE next day we heard the following remarkable story, which I shall endeavor to render as nearly as possible in the words of the narrator.

Lenox Clifford was the son of an English clergyman, and remotely connected with a noble family. His uncle having been a man of large fortune, now inherited by an only son, delicate and dissipated, the uncertain life of this profligate cousin only stood between him and an almost princely inheritance. His father, with sound sense and far-seeing judgment, being unable to endow his children with fortune, spent a large portion of their moderate means in securing for them fine educational advantages, for he believed—and a wise belief it is—that a store of mental wealth must eventually secure, at all events, a more satisfactory position than heaps of treasure can command for shallow brains or uncultivated minds. His only sister was married, and with their widowed mother, now resided in ———shire; for Lenox Clifford had been called home suddenly from college to see his father die. After that, his education was completed in Germany and France, for the purpose of acquiring both languages perfectly; and it was at Paris he met with the singular adventure which became the opening chapter to his afterwards most romantic history. How mysterious and beyond control are oftentimes the coming of events, whose *denouement* gives rise to those real life stories, whose strangeness is so deeply colored with romance!

One night in returning to his lodgings, as Mr. Clifford passed by a fashionable opera-house, from which the audience had lately dispersed, he was attracted by a sudden gleam of light flashing from something upon the pavement before him, which, on closer inspection, proved to be a bracelet, elegant and costly in design, for it shone a perfect blaze of jewels as he raised it under the street-lamp; a serpent in form, and of such cunning workmanship that it writhed between his fingers, for the delicate gold scales set with opals were all separate, causing it to twist about and quiver like a living thing, while on the flat head shone a large diamond, whose pure white light was in fine contrast with those wonderful changeable scales and the fiery flash of its ruby eyes. Underneath the head, and just over the fine spring clasp, now broken—which had evidently caused its loss—in a quaint style of green enamel, were the letters O. L. What should he do with it? At present, nothing; for to seek the owner of a lost trinket at that hour, through the mazes of such a gigantic city as Paris, would be worse than folly; so depositing the fairy thing safely in the inner breast pocket of his coat, Lenox Clifford went his way, wondering—as most young men in similar circumstances would—whether the arm was fair to look upon, from which that rich bracelet had fallen—or if he should meet its owner, and where and when? The next day was spent in fruitless endeavors to find her, and sorely perplexed at night, he went to the same opera-house, still hoping, by diligent inquiry among those he knew, to obtain some clue to the fair unknown; but all in vain. After leaving the opera, he went into an eating-saloon, and while taking his supper, overheard detached portions of a conversation which startled him into close attention, accompanied by a resolve to thwart a most villanous scheme, then, and there, revealed to his astonished ears. The speakers were only divided from him by a cloth partition, or screen, and were either ignorant of his proximity or carelessly free from the fear of being overheard.

"A priest," exclaimed the first speaker, "I hate the very name, Orliff, my sudden fit of sanctity was only put on as a plea to accomplish my plan of getting to Paris; I have always been determined to break away from the cursed quiet of a monastic life, and now, when the fire of a fierce uncontrollable passion is consuming me, the temptation becomes stronger than ever. You have promised to serve me, and now is the time, for my determination is unalterable. Olivia Lacy shall be mine; fair means have I tried in vain, and now"—here the other speaker evidently expostulated with him in an undertone, so that "exposure," "detection," "penalty," were the only words Lenox Clifford could hear distinctly, and then the first speaker replied angrily,

"Your cursed cowardice shall not snatch this prize from me, there are others to help me through if you back out, and cowardice it is, Orliff, for your conscience, we know, is not large enough to be troublesome," and he laughed, a reckless coarse laugh, "my secret is very safe with you, however, whether you help me through this little affair or not, no fear of your betraying me, no, no, we both know too much of each other's private history to try that game, don't we, old fellow? But you won't back out now,—to-morrow is Friday, and in the evening she goes alone about twilight from the con—well then, to madam"—

"Hush, Henrique," said the other, "you may be over-heard."

"Well, home to her aunt's, then," he resumed, in a lower tone—but this way is by far too much frequented for me to attempt forcing her off there by violence—no, we must use stratagem, and I have a plan all arranged, which is almost sure to succeed. To-morrow afternoon, before the time she generally leaves, a handsome carriage, which I have hired and which you are to drive, must be sent to the convent in haste, with a message from Dr. Le Branch (the name was almost whispered, yet loud enough for him to catch the sound) to Miss Lacy, begging her to come at once to her aunt, who is extremely ill;" your pretty little nephew can act as footman, Orliff, and deliver the message well, as whatever you tell him he believes is right, and on this occasion he must not have a suspicion that he is acting a part. The girl's impulsive nature will induce her to go at once, and then you must drive in the right direction until nearly there, when turning suddenly into the Rue ———, stop for a moment—I will jump in and stifle her cries so quickly and effectually that you can drive on out of the city without fear of detection."

An involuntary cough from Lenox Clifford just at this moment betraying his close proximity, the rest of their conversation was carried on in whispers, from which he could only glean an occasional word, yet were these sufficiently significant to reveal all the horrors of that infamous plot.

"On board the steamer." "Can say she is mad"— "pass for my wife"—"Florence, 'till I am tired of her."

It was enough—and the young Englishman vowed inwardly, not only to thwart their vile plot and save the innocent girl, of whom he knew nothing, save that her name was "Olivia Lacy," but also to bring Henrique and his more cautious companion, Orliff, to justice, and therefore when they rose to depart, he did so likewise, determined to have a look at these men whom it might become necessary for him to identify hereafter.

Orliff was tall, sallow, vulgar and hard-looking to a degree of fierceness; yet there was a look about his eyes indicating cunning caution, while Henrique was coarse, thick set, with that bold, sensual expression, so often acquired by young men of gentle birth, who, defying the authority of parents and the laws of God, give way with daring recklessness to their worst passions. Little did those scheming villians dream as Lenox passed them, that their dark plot was in the keeping of this young stranger who had the strength and will to thwart it.

Olivia Lacy! the name had a strange connection in his mind with something—what was it? And Lenox Clifford sat dreaming over this adventure in the solitude of his chamber too much excited to sleep for hours after his return.

At last the letters enameled on that dainty bracelet found at the door of the opera-house, and for whose owner he had sought so diligently, flashed before him—for in the absorbing interest of this late adventure, it was for the moment well nigh forgotten. The initials made no particular impression upon him, until thus, as it were recalled by the sweet name so freely spoken, by the sensual lips of Henrique. And then he drew out the glittering trinket to find those delicate letters corresponding with that name. It was a curious coincidence, and yet the same initials might suit a number of names. So he began with that unaccountable perversity by which the human heart and mind delights in perplexing itself, to enumerate all the female names he could imagine, begining with O. L.—Ophelia Lyman, Orphia Laton, Octavia LeRoy—together with every other probable and improbable name that could be thought of, and at last settling down to a firm conviction that the initials on that identical bracelet, belonged to no other than Olivia Lacy, and therefore he must strive to find her out on the morrow, (even were she immured within the walls of a convent, or guarded by some fierce old uncle or aunt, always more formidable than parents,) return the trinket as a pretext for seeking her, and then should his conviction prove correct, reveal the plot of Henrique and Orliff; or if this failed, the street must be watched where Henrique was to jump into the carrriage, and the intended victim rescued, even were it at the risk of his life; and with that determination young Clifford slept, to dream of ruffian priests, glittering serpents and Olivia Lacy.

CHAPTER XX.

THE RESCUE.

"What news is this that makes thy cheek turn pale,
And thy hand tremble?"—LONGFELLOW.

UNFORTUNATELY Mr. Clifford had failed to hear the name of the convent or school where Miss Lacy was, as the cautious Orliff had interrupted Henrique, so as to render what he said regarding it entirely indefinite, but youth is sanguine and the great difficulty of not knowing, or even having an idea in what direction to turn, while thinking over his plans for her rescue at night, never occurred to Lenox, and indeed, until fairly started upon his adventures in search of this fair unknown, he failed to realize the uncertainty of such an undertaking, for seeking after a person to be found somewhere in Paris, is well nigh as perplexing, though less dangerous, than threading the mazes of the Cretan labyrinth. Whither should he turn? The *Sacré Cœur* was in high repute, and if at a convent at all, perhaps she might be there; at all events he would inquire. So forthwith to the *Sacré Cœur* he went first, and calling for the Mother Superior, was speedily ushered into the presence, or rather partial presence—for an iron grating rose between them—of a tall white nun, so cold and stately in voice, manner, and appearance, that she cast a chill upon him, such as one might imagine to come from sailing under the dismal shadow of an iceberg.

"Miss Lacy," she replied, in answer to his inquiry as to whether there was such a young lady under her care; "yes, there is a girl of that name among our scholars—but are you a relation of hers, for it is only a plea of near relationship which induces us to allow one of your sex to see a young lady under our care."

"I am a stranger to the lady," he replied; "in fact, have never seen her; but having found a bracelet, which I am induced to believe belongs to her, I am anxious to see Miss Lucy for the purpose of restoring it; and then, by an odd chance, I happen to be in possession of certain information of great importance to her."

The tall, white nun hesitated a moment, and then said,

"I can receive the bracelet—though she seldom goes out, never wears trinkets, and therefore it is almost impossible the bracelet you refer to can be hers, though perhaps I may be mistaken, and will ask her, communicating the information you have at the same time, as our scholars are allowed no secrets from us; will this not answer—Miss Lacy is engaged with her lessons."

"No, I would rather see her, or, if that is impossible,

can you not direct me to some friend or relative in the city; the bracelet I might send, but the communication is of vital importance, and must be explained in person, either to the lady or some one deeply interested in her welfare."

"'I am, of course, interested in her," said the holy mother, in a piqued, cold tone of voice, " yet, if you insist upon it, the girl may have an interview with you in my presence," and she swept haughtily away.

Restless and impatient, young Clifford waited her return, for time·was wearing away, and she might not, after all, be the Miss Lacy referred to by Henrique; he had a difficult, nay, almost impossible task before him, and but a short time in which to accomplish it. What was she like? And straightway he began drawing ideal pictures of Olivia Lacy, making her a·perfect angel of beauty—though was it not quite as likely that she possessed only good looks, nay, indeed, might be positively ugly?

" No !" his reason and heart both responded, this is scarcely possible; for such desperate risks are not apt to be run by hardened villains like Henrique for homely women; and indeed even good men are not often apt to resort to extreme measures, be they ever so lawful, in order to gain possession of the plainer specimens of the feminine gender. He walked up and down the room for nearly half an hour, unable, in his present excited and impatient state, to sit still; and believing that revenge for his unwillingness to trust her had incited the frigid looking nun to keep him waiting thus, caused his reflections concerning her to be none of the most amiable; and though we know Mr. Clifford was good, he rather admitted, when recounting this narrative, that, while striding up and down that dismal room, he did not bless the stately white devotee, and could he by one wish have utterly annihilated her, I am afraid that holy presence would have appeared to him no more.

But at last she came, followed, not by the vision of beauty Lenox had conjured up, but by a little, sallow, white-haired girl about fifteen, with red rings round her eyes, and drawing back shyly, as if alarmed at the prospect of seeing a stranger. This yellow complexion turned almost green in its paleness, as advancing close to the grating the young stranger saluted her politely, though in truth well nigh dumb with astonishment and disappointment. Drawing out the bracelet, however, he presented it to her, saying,—

"Miss Lacy, I found this near the door of the opera house, and presuming from the initials it might be yours, came here to inquire."

A look of wonder and admiration lit up the cold eyes of the tall, impassive nun even, as they fell upon the matchless splendor of that jeweled serpent, and the sickly-looking, red-eyed girl, starting back, as if frightened by the writhing snaky motion of those opalescent scales, exclaimed, in a little, squeaking voice,—

"Oh, mercy! that's not mine! I never owned a jewel in my life—never an ornament save this," touching the cross and rosary about her neck, "and a bracelet made of the hair of all my sisters and brothers, and father and mother, and Uncle John, and Aunt Maria, which fell off my arm the last time we went walking with Sister Cecilia; so I thought maybe that it might be that you had found," and putting her handkerchief up to her face, the sallow young lady began to sniffle, and rub her eyes, giving vent to sundry and divers sentimental little sobs, at the sight of a valuable bracelet in place of the variegated, hairy ornament she had described.

"It is rather queer that there should be two Olivia Lacys," said Mr. Clifford, who, though provoked beyond measure, could scarcely help laughing at the absurdity of the scene.

"Mon Dieu!" squeaked out the little woman; "my name is not Olivia; who said it was?—my name's Anna Maria Lacy!"

"I thought you told me Miss *Olivia* Lacy was one of your pupils!" exclaimed Lenox, almost in a tone of fury, turning upon the holy mother a look full enough of fire to melt this monastic iceberg, if anything could; and a spark of his anger was reflected by an answering flash from hers, as she answered,—

"Young man, you asked for Miss Lacy, without giving her first name, hence this foolish mistake was your own fault, not mine. Anna Maria, you may return to your lessons. Sir, I presume our interview is at an end," and she bowed slightly, as if giving him a signal to withdraw.

True, he remembered now—in the excitement and anxiety of the moment, he had failed to give the whole name, for his mind was full of *one* Miss Lacy, and he never thought, until aggravated by loss of time, that there might be another.

"I beg your pardon," he stammered out, quite ashamed of his late wrath; "I remember, now, it is all my own fault truly, and I regret having troubled you." Saying which he hastily withdrew, and soon found himself sorely perplexed again, wandering about the streets of Paris. Several other convents were visited, and then some of the first boarding schools, but no Miss Lacy could he find, and at last, weary and dispirited, with the day far spent, he was on the point of abandoning the search, and determined to go alone with the first policeman who would credit his story, and watch the street indicated by Henrique as that where Orliff should stop the carriage, when suddenly remembering the name of Dr. Le Branch, as the friend and physician who it was to be pretended had sent for Miss Lacy, he determined to try and find that person, learn from him where to find her, or, if too late for a warning, prevail upon this gentleman to go with him, and attempt at least the rescue of the deluded girl: for Lenox Clifford felt a strong conviction that Henrique's plot was artfully contrived, and would scarcely fail to succeed. After various unavailing efforts, he was at last directed to the office of a physician of that name, and where, though almost constantly engaged he might be found; but it was then afternoon, and he trembled at the thought that, even did he find Dr. Le Branch, it might be, alas! too late to save Olivia Lacy: yet still he would make this last effort, and, if again defeated, go alone to the Rue ———.

This time he was successful, however, in finding the gentleman he sought—for no sooner did he say (after introducing himself):

"You are, I believe, a friend of Miss Olivia Lacy," than the fine benevolent countenance of Doctor Le Branch lit up pleasantly, as he replied:

"Yes, I have the happiness of being numbered among her friends, having been for many years a particular friend of her grandfather and her aunt, Madam Armond."

"For God's sake come with me then, at once, and quickly too," said the young Englishman hastily, "if you would save her from a fearful danger, worse than death, and catching hold of the astonished stranger, he hurried him into the street, saying:

"We must not loiter a moment, and you shall hear my story as we go along."

So completely was he absorbed in relating Henrique's plot to gain possession of Miss Lacy, that the bracelet he had found and the coincidence of the letters upon it, corresponding with her initials, was for the time forgotten, and without going into particulars regarding his adventures of the morning, Mr. Clifford simply stating that all his endeavors to find the young lady had proved fruitless, expressed an overpowering fear, (as they hurried onward,) that those two villains had already succeeded in accomplishing their dark scheme, and ere then perhaps Olivia Lacy might be in their power beyond the reach of assistance.

The excitement of both became so intense while dwelling upon such a possibility, that after stopping for a moment to secure the company of a policeman, (a necessary and wise precaution,) their rapid walk merged into a run upon nearing the locality indicated by Henrique, where Orliff might expect to find him. At last, weary and almost breathless with fear and fatigue, they neared the corner of the Rue—where they saw a boy (perhaps twelve years of age) looking with eager curiosity at a carriage some considerable distance up the street, and driving furiously in an opposite direction. Lenox Clifford comprehended the whole in a moment, and felt quite sure this same lad was the " pretty little nephew " Henrique had appointed to act as footman to Orliff.

" We are too late," exclaimed the doctor, " poor, dear child ! but be quick," he said, turning to the policeman, " we must pursue them ; bring the lightest carriage and the swiftest horses you can find, and he poured some gold into the man's hand, while Lenox going up to the boy, asked him :

"Why he was watching that carriage so earnestly, and who was in it?"

"Mister Henrique," replied the child, (looking up in innocent wonder,) "he's gone off to be married with, Oh! such a beautiful young lady. I thought she was going to her aunt's until just now, when Mr. Henrique jumped into the carriage, and then Uncle Orliff, who is driving (for he's a great friend of Mr. Henrique), winked at me, and laughed, and said :

"'They are going to run off together, you can jump down now, and don't tell anybody,' and I would'nt only may be you're her brother, and I've heard mamma say it was wicked in young girls to run off from home to be married, but don't tell on me and I will tell you something"—putting his lips up to Mr. Clifford's ear,—

"When Mr. Henrique got in and slammed the carriage door the young lady screamed, (just as I was jumping down,) and I said :

"Poor thing! uncle, what makes her do that? and he said, 'She's screaming for joy, she's so glad to see him,' and then he cracked his whip, and the horses dashed away so fast, you see they are nearly out of sight. Please don't tell Uncle Orliff I told you anything about it, or he will be very angry ; and he's kind to me, and gives me nice clothes and good things, but I wish he had'nt been mixed

up with this matter, for spite of what he said, I don't believe the lady wanted to go, or she would'nt have screamed
like that."

"No she did not—you are a bright boy, take this,"
(giving the child a coin,) "and be warned by me to keep
out of your uncle's way, and Mr. Henrique's too, for they
are both wicked men, and will teach you no good."

The boy hung his head, and went off looking pale and
frightened, just as the light chaise they had sent for came
dashing up—when the three set off in full pursuit of
Henrique's carriage, which was now entirely out of sight,
and must be more than two miles in advance of them. On,
on they sped for two hours, following the fresh tracks,
yet fearing, at every cross road, that the fugitives had
turned off, and thus were escaping, though wherever they
inquired the same answer met them :—

" A carriage closely shut and driven very fast had gone
by about three-quarters of an hour before ; " and so they
dashed on out beyond the city limits—where the road
turned off from the river Seine in a southwesterly direction,
when suddenly the policeman (who was driving) drew up
where three country roads branched off from the highway,
and they paused a moment, perplexed to know which to
choose, (for two showed signs of being recently traveled,)
deciding at last in favor of the one which appeared most
unfrequented, and evidently led towards a lonely broken
district. Another hour's hard riding brought them in

sight of a forlorn looking house, that might once have been a way-side inn, but now sadly dilapidated, weather-stained, and apparently uninhabited; it presented no very inviting appearance as they drew up to it, determined if possible to find some one on the premises, who might give information regarding the objects of their pursuit—and besides the jaded horses must have rest before continuing their journey.

As they approached near enough to obtain a closer view of the surroundings, though windows and doors were closely shut, the keen eye of the policeman detected, by the uncertain light—for dusk had overtaken them—a close carriage standing underneath a broken shed near by, while the flicker of what might be a solitary candle shone through the black slats of an upper window shutter.

"We have caught our game, I fancy," he whispered, jumping down and motioning us to alight, by a broken, zig-zag path that led up to the door, over a slight decliv-ity, and then he pointed out the carriage, which evidently could not belong to such a dismal looking establishment; but there were no horses near it.

"Be quiet and cautious," he continued, "for such wily birds are swift of wing, and may escape us even yet; for I am satisfied they are here, feeling secure against pursuit in such a dark nest."

Catching the reins round an old post, he signified that the doctor and Mr. Clifford should go up stealthily to the front, while he crept round to the back door of the house, from which it was most likely the two men would strive to escape, when advised of our presence. Knowing the desperate characters they were to deal with, all three of them were of course armed, as Lenox Clifford, having undertaken an uncertain adventure in the morning, concealed a small dirk and pistol about his person, and the doctor, to whom he left no time for arming himself, in their sudden departure, had been provided with a pistol by the policeman.

So stealthy was their approach, that no alarm could have been taken by those inside, at all events until they had gained their respective positions at the back and front doors, and even the gentle knock Mr. Clifford gave was not calculated to excite alarm; it was repeated rather louder before a dark elfish looking face was protruded through a window, which at last was cautiously opened, to the right of the door, and its owner, apparently a girl of some fifteen years of age, said, in a surly, half sleepy tone of voice,

"Who be ye, and what do ye want here !"

"Travelers," was the reply, "we are weary, and want some supper."

"Well, it's not here ye'll get the likes of that," said the girl bluntly, for there's nobody here but me and granny, and she's gone to bed, and we don't keep a tavern no way, so you'd just as well go on," and the dark, blowsy head was partly withdrawn, when the doctor arrested her attention and hand at the same time (for she was about closing the shutter,) by holding out a gold coin, of which her eager eye caught sight in the twilight, as he said,

"We will pay you well for even a glass of water, and water for our horses, if you will let us come in for awhile, —if granny's asleep, she won't mind, and we'll be very quiet, come now, open the door."

And he held up the tempting bait again, which her cupidity could not resist; and making a motion for them to be very quiet, she closed the window cautiously, and in a moment was heard withdrawing the bolt and unlocking the door.

So soon as they stood face to face with this gypsy-like lassie, the coin was slipped adroitly into her hand, as the doctor and Lenox Clifford edged their way into the passage, for she held the door, as she had the window, only half open, and was evidently half frightened at what she had done, after they were fairly inside; observing which, and seeing they were quite alone with the girl, as the passage doors leading into other rooms, and also the back door, were close shut, Mr. Clifford whispered,

"You have other visitors. Where are they?"

The large, lazy looking eyes dilated in evident terror, as she replied, hurriedly,

"No, we a'nt; there's no soul around, except me and granny."

"Does your granny keep a fine carriage, then?" he continued, half inclined to laugh at the absurdity of such an idea, "for we saw one under the shed, and hark ye, girl, we know there are three people here now, though you are taught to deny it—two men and a young lady, who was taken from home against her will, and whom we are here to protect; show us where she is, and you shall be liberally rewarded, and protected against your granny's anger and that of the men by us; refuse, and we will not only find her we seek in spite of you, but afterwards you shall go to prison."

The last word either startled, or the hope of gain tempted her into obedience, for laying her finger on her lip, she led them into a great, dreary looking room, where there was no light save a few flickering embers on the hearth.

"Hush," she whispered, "for granny's asleep in there (pointing to another door), and he's there, too (the one that drove), drinking brandy. Oh, I know they'll beat me for letting you in," and the dark girl began to tremble as we approached the door.

"Go outside, then, and hide in the shed behind the carriage, until we tell you it's safe to come back, only first tell us where the lady is and the other man."

"Way up in the third story, you'll see a light through the crack of the door, and the stairs lead up from that room there," (pointing in the same direction.) She left them hastily, and they heard her shut the front door softly on going out. Peeping in through the empty keyhole into the next room, they saw a man before the fire, near a table whereon was a bottle and tumbler, from which he had doubtless been quaffing potent draughts, now having their effect, for he was asleep in his chair; and no sooner did young Clifford's eyes rest on him than he recognized the tall, dangling figure and sallow visage of Orliff.

"Go, open the back door, and beckon in De Lon," said the doctor, "for this chap must be left in his keeping, and the old woman kept from howling, until we seek Olivia and deal with Henrique. Mon Dieu! it makes me sick to think we may be too late to save her from infamy."

In another moment De Lon (the policeman) was with us, and then softly unclosing the door, his strong hand fell on Orliff's shoulder, and the words, "you are my prisoner," were hissed in his ear before he awoke. Startled and astonished, and jumping up with an oath, demanded by what authority we were there? But his potations had been strong enough to unsettle his equilibrium if not his mind, for, staggering backwards, he was soon forced into the chair again beneath De Lon's powerful grasp, who said hurriedly:

"We are three to one; it is useless to resist." For Orliff was evidently striving, in a half-drunken, fumbling style, to feel for some hidden weapon.

"It's just as I said," he drawled out, (hiccoughing between his words) " damn Henrique's folly ; let me go," and he made a spring forward. But the strong hold was only relaxed long enough to get out hand-cuffs, while, with our assistance, he was secured before the old hag, designated as " granny," and who was snoring on a narrow cot in a far corner of the room, awoke and gave a shrill screech which must have sounded throughout the house, and fearing that Henrique, alarmed thereby, might make his escape, young Clifford and the doctor bounded up the dark, tottering stairway, leaving De Lon to guard Orliff and silence the old woman. The stairs were narrow, and in some places so dilapidated as to be almost unsafe ; but by striking a match or two they gained the third story speedily, and when on the last step, heard a voice, as if in agony of despair, cry out :

"Help ! Oh God !"

Then there followed a struggle, and ere they gained the door (through which a light was visible) a sharp, angry cry, as if wrung from a man by severe pain, rang out, as Henrique, who no doubt by this time heard their footsteps, (yet hoping to escape) burst through the door and strove to rush past them, but was caught and held between those two strong men as if in a vice, while the light, streaming through that open door, served to reveal a great stream of blood pouring down from a deep cut in his face, just under the right eye. This severe depletion doubtless rendering his resistance less determined than it would otherwise have been.

By this time (having secured Orliff in a closet below stairs) De Lon had hurried up to their assistance, and proceeded to shackle Henrique, who swore fearfully, heaping curses on them and on "That damned little fury;" by whom he of course meant Olivia, while they in turn were wondering how she had managed to wound him so severely?

"Secure those two villains in the close carriage at once, De Lon," said the doctor, "and prepare for our departure. You can drive them to prison, while we take the poor child home, dead or alive—for perhaps he has killed her."

And as he hurried on with Lenox into the room, Henrique was taken down by the policeman.

As they entered that dismal chamber, where a fearful stillness had reigned since Henrique rushed out, the sight that met them was truly appalling—for there, on the floor, in one corner of the room, lay Olivia Lacy bespattered with blood, her very lips white as those of a corpse, while the great length of her black hair (having fallen down during her struggle with Henrique) served to make that rigid, marble-like paleness more striking. For a moment those two men, free from all personal fear, stood so horror-stricken at the sight they could neither move nor speak— for the same conviction possessed them both that she was dead, murdered by that fiend in human shape; as she did not stir, and the blood looked so frightful all over her bosom and light dress, they supposed it must be flowing from some fatal wound he had inflicted, forgetting for a moment the cut in his face which had bled so profusely.

At last they lifted her senseless form on to a ragged old sofa bed—almost the only furniture in that forlorn room—and in doing so, her right hand (hidden as she lay on the floor by her thick black hair) being displaced, relaxed its rigid hold and something fell from it, striking the floor with a ringing sound like metal, and when Mr. Clifford picked it up, to their great astonishment it proved a costly Spanish stiletto of fine workmanship, the handle inlaid with gold and gems, while the delicate keen blade was now blood-stained.

Had she stabbed herself?

No, there was no wound—and as the doctor (now regaining his usual presence of mind) felt her pulse, he exclaimed, joyfully:

"She has only fainted."

And then, while they bathed her lips and face with cold water, she gradually revived, but when at last her dark eyes opened it was to gaze on them with a look of frightened wonder, for her senses were evidently wandering and unsettled by terror and intense excitement, so much so the doctor feared a violent attack of fever as the result.

Ere they drove away from that wretched house the elfish face, with its uncombed locks, was upturned to them, wearing a look of pallid terror, as the dark girl pleaded :

" For the Blessed Virgin's sake that she and her granny might not be sent to prison. She thought the gentleman and lady was going to be married, and did not know there was any harm in letting them stay awhile."

The promise was given that they should not suffer for the present offence ; but Mr. Clifford said, after seeing the supposed groom and his friend put in irons and taken off to prison, he fancied the cunning damsel and old crone would be very careful in future how they entertained wedding guests ! The ride home was long and sad, for Miss Lacy continued wild, or almost insensible by turns, from which and a certain peculiar odor about her clothes, Dr. Le Branch felt convinced that previous to her struggle with Henrique she must have been for some time under the influence of chloroform; perhaps the villain had used it during their flight to stop her screams. Nothing further could be known, however, until her mind was clear again, and we were entirely at a loss regarding the stiletto, (so opportunely in her possession,) and which she had used so bravely.

On arriving a little before midnight at Madam Armond's, they found her in a state of distracted fear about her niece, who, failing to come at the usual hour on that (Friday) evening, as was her custom, she had gone to the Catholic academy, and there learning that Miss Lacy had left

several hours before in a carriage sent by Dr. Le Branch—
supposing her aunt to be ill (as that was the message)—
Madam Armond sought the doctor, and not finding him,
feeling helpless, yet almost frantic at the thought of unknown and frightful dangers to which Olivia must be
exposed, she and many sympathizing friends had been for
hours engaged in making inquiries through the city, and
dispatching messengers in various directions to try and gain
some clue to the direction taken by the carriage in which
Olivia left—but all efforts proved fruitless, and when at
last Mr. Clifford and her old friend the doctor bore the
almost insensible girl into her presence, giving hurried
details of the danger from which they had rescued her,
Madam Armond (a handsome, regal looking woman, to
whom Olivia bore a striking resemblance) was perfectly
overcome by the horror of that peril, and the happiness
of its being partially averted and Olivia saved by a total
stranger, to whom the curious chance of supping at an
restaurant after the opera had revealed Henrique's plot.

And the stiletto,—of it she knew nothing, and was not
aware that her niece ever carried one—in fact, knew she
did not generally—another singular incident which appeared providential.

CHAPTER XXI.

WHERE OLIVIA LACY FOUND THE STILETTO.

" You are too bold !
Retire ! retire ! leave me !—LONGFELLOW.

THE severe, though not very protracted illness of Miss
Lacy prevented Mr. Clifford from seeing her for more than
a week after that dreadful night, though he went to inquire
for her daily, and soon became a favorite with Madam Armond, not only on account of the great gratitude she felt
for the inestimable benefit he had rendered, but also for the
sake of an old friendship with his father and uncle, whom
she had known years before when they were in Paris.

Now, all this time Lenox said no word about the bracelet, for the more he looked at it the more certain he felt of
its belonging to none other than Olivia, and he became
gradually possessed with a desire to present it to her when
well enough to receive him, without her being informed of
its recovery even, and therefore he refrained from mentioning it either to her aunt or the doctor, as they might wish to
please her by giving a hint about the costly trinket, over

the loss of which she must have grieved no little, and thus mar the innocently selfish pleasure he expected from the surprise and delight she must naturally evince upon seeing it suddenly restored to her.

At last they met.

In telling this story, Mr. Clifford entered into no description of Miss Lacy's appearance, save to remark,—

"Pearl is almost an image of Olivia, though slightly taller, and with less olive in her complexion."

We needed not to be told that she was beautiful, for even had Pearl resembled her less, the miniature heretofore spoken of, must have put to rest all doubt upon the subject.

And then, upon that first meeting, Lenox Clifford presented Miss Lacy with a superb bouquet of exotics, among the rich flowers of which he had wreathed the opal snake so cunningly that, as she took it from his hand, those jeweled scales quivered, and the fancy he had been nursing of how the girl's delight and astonishment were to reward him as the finder of that beautiful bauble, was fully realized, for no sooner did her eyes rest upon it than she exclaimed,—

"Oh, Mr. Clifford! where did you find my dear, lovely bracelet? What can I ever do to repay you, first of all, for saving me from that vile Henrique Lorraine, and now, for bringing back this!" and she kissed the glittering snake as it shone among those rare flowers. "Grand-papa sent it to me last autumn, on my eighteenth birthday! Oh, how many a bitter tear have I shed since losing it at the opera."

And they went on to talk of the very singular events, all leading to their acquaintance, when, in referring to the stiletto with which she had wounded Henrique in the face, Miss Lacy said,—

"The peculiar circumstances leading to my possession of it, you will find almost the queerest part of what is certainly altogether a very remarkable affair. This villain, Henrique Lorraine, who I am told belongs to quite a good family in Madrid, and came here under the pretence of studying for the priesthood, forced his acquaintance upon me at the Catholic Academy, where I have been for some time devoting myself to the languages and music, and on several occasions, when here at home with my aunt, he has sent me bouquets, and the most absurd love-letters, which coming during my absence, I could not of course return, being entirely ignorant as to where he might be found, and our servants never even saw the messenger, who, after ringing the bell, left the basket and letter in the vestibule. At last one morning, when my aunt was out, and I had just come in from driving, this impertinent man, presenting himself in person, told the servant he wished to see me a moment on particular business, when, being quite ignorant who was calling for me, and supposing it might be some of the trades people, I ordered the man to show him in—recognizing too late this same Henrique, whose attentions had for some time been annoying me almost to persecution. The moment we were alone he commenced giving utterance to the most frantic protestations of love, swearing he had given up all thought of assuming holy orders for my sake, and was determined to make me love him; when, finding all my powers of persuasion were vainly wasted in endeavors to rid myself of this troublesome visitor, I rang for the servant, and, after saying very quietly,—

"Mr. Lorraine is going—show him to the door," left the room. This conduct I thought would most certainly free me from further annoyance, but it failed to do so, for he continued to seek me in various ways, and one night, a short time before the loss of my bracelet, at a large fancy mask-ball I attended at Madam ———'s, on which occasion my costume was that of a lady belonging to the Spanish noblesse, soon after entering the room, I found myself closely followed by a Spanish hidalgo, whose short, thick-set figure reminded me of Henrique, though at first I only fancied it to be a resemblance, the thought of his really being there never occurring to me.

As the evening wore on, however, seeking the first opportunity of my being alone, he asked me to dance, in a voice so well disguised, that I assented, feeling curious to find out who the mask, by whom I had been so constantly pursued, could be. Knowing me to be acquainted with Spanish, young Lorraine had always spoken to me in that language, and while we were dancing, this mask conversed

in French, and in the voice, as I believed, of a stranger.
When the dance was over, we walked into a conservatory,
where he decoyed me by a promise to relate something
very agreeable, and finding his company rather amusing
than otherwise, I did not object, feeling that there was
something quite interesting and piquant in a little flirtation
with this mysterious personage, who, when we were there,
did not leave me long in ignorance of his name, and upon
finding myself again alone with Henrique, I would have
made a precipitate retreat.

Provoked and annoyed, I upbraided him with deceiving
me, at the same time telling this impertinent neophyte
that I believed his presence at the ball an intrusion, feeling confident he had never been invited.

Now all this was calculated to make him very angry,
but he either did not heed my animadversions, or was determined to try and gain my ear and overcome my aversion by pouring forth his protestations of love once more,
and imploring me at least to allow him the privilege of
visiting me, as it was his determination to quit the country
in any event.

I turned to leave him in the midst of this absurd rhap-
sody, and more irritated than I had been on previous occasions even, told him to desist at once and forever, as his
love was not only unrequited, but that I despised him ;
when, catching hold of my dress in a frantic manner, he

pulled me back, and snatching out a stiletto from his girdle—this causing me to cry out with alarm—said,—

"Here, kill me—don't be frightened, I am not going to murder you—stab me, I cannot, will not live without you."

"Let me go," I exclaimed, tearing myself from his grasp, "or I shall call for assistance," and as by this time we heard voices approaching, he rushed past me with a muttered curse, dropping the stiletto in his hasty retreat, which I picked up and concealed, passing out through another door into the dancing room before the persons whose voices we had heard, entered the conservatory; for I dreaded the idea of my interview with Henrique being known, feeling sure he was there without an invitation, for the purpose of seeing me, and therefore, I caught up the stiletto, fearing, if discovered, it might lead to an *exposé* of the whole affair, and determined, with my aunt's advice and assistance, to return it to him at the earliest possible opportunity. Madam Armond was not at the ball, however, as I had gone in company with some friends, and the night we went to the opera, when I lost my bracelet, there was no opportunity of speaking to her on the subject of. Henrique's interview with me; but on that Friday afternoon we all remember so well, I had the stiletto in my pocket, intending to give it into my aunt's keeping, until it could be returned to the owner. You know the result, and how, when that wicked, unscrupulous man, who kept me stupefied with chloroform during the ride, and after telling me in that dismal room I must and should be his wife, strove to throw his arms around me,—in desperate terror, I thought of the stiletto—his stiletto, then in my pocket, and drawing it out adroitly and suddenly, as he approached near enough, I stabbed him in the face, thus causing him to retreat in a fury of pain—when you came to my rescue.   Had you failed to find us—had he dared to touch me again—if unable to wound Henrique more fatally, the stiletto should have been buried in my own bosom."

It was, indeed, the most singular part of her story, that the weapon of this wicked man, almost a bauble in beauty and size, dropped in his hasty flight from Olivia's presence at a ball, for fear of detection and exposure, should thus be turned against him by her, in that trying moment when, apparently, she was so entirely in his power, knowing of none near upon whom she could call, save God, for mercy and protection.

It is often thus.   His Almighty wing overshadows us in the dark hours, and oftentimes, events attributed by short-sighted, thoughtless mortals to chance, unto trusting and believing hearts wear the halo of an answered prayer!

CHAPTER XXII.

MR. CLIFFORD'S REWARD.

"OH, Mr. Clifford, how can I ever repay you?"

Lenox remembered those words, and a few weeks afterwards, when they knew each other very well and had been much together, he reminded Olivia of them, and in a whisper told how the debt she estimated so highly might be canceled.

And it was so, even as he wished.

For Madam Armond favored his wooing, and her influence must insure the consent of Olivia's grandfather, old Mr. Lacy, who resided in Cuba, and was a planter of great wealth, to be divided between his only surviving daughter, Madam Armond, and the orphan child of his only son, who at the age of fifteen he had taken to Paris, that her education might be completed and perfected, while at the same time she could receive a mother's care and love from her aunt at the period of life when a girl stands most in need of such fostering tenderness. Mr. Clifford had been made quite independent since his father's death by a legacy from the unclo for whom he was named, and hence felt no shrinking pride in asking the hand of an heiress—which, had he been really poor, that sensitive nature of his would have chafed under, and which must have done battle fiercely with, ere it yielded to his great love. Indeed, with my knowledge of Mr. Clifford's character, I believe had he not felt independent of Olivia Lacy's expected fortune, she would never have been his wife.

Upon this part of the story he did not dwell; perhaps because his heart was now filled with another love, and all refined, sensitive natures shrink from reviving memories calculated to bring into comparison a dead with a living passion; for even though it may have been as fervent and as perfect, yet, as time steals on, memory flings a misty shade over that starry lamp, which at first a yearning affection keeps lit and trimmed in its ceaseless vigil by the grave of our buried hopes, until at last the heart, grown cold mid dreary dreamings o'er the past, weary with lingering in the shadow of a great gloom, seeks real joy amid the present; and then, flooded with a new delight, rejoicing in a new love, we shrink from turning back to liken it with the old, which must seem pale and dim by such comparison, as the dust of withered flowers blown over the roses of Spring !

Lenox Clifford and Olivia Lacy were married with the

full consent and blessing of all those who loved them, and after a brief visit to his mother in England, they left for Cuba, as one of Mr. Lacy's conditions in consenting to their union was that during his life their home should be with him. The course of their love ran on with unwonted smoothness, and a fairer home than the one to which they were welcomed, surrounded as it was by all the beauties and luxuries of a tropical clime, cannot be imagined; while old Mr. Lacy (unlike the many wealthy sires or grandsires who take a selfish, fretful pleasure in thwarting and annoying the young people whose misfortune it may be to form a part of their household) was a father not only in word, but in spirit and deed, to those who had come for his happiness and gratification as well as their own.

In somewhat less than a year after their marriage, a beautiful little daughter was born, and for a short time the young parents were supremely blest in the absorbing pleasure of this newly found happiness, which served to fill their cup of joy almost to overflowing.

> "But pleasures are like poppies spread,
> You seize the flower—its bloom is shed;
> Or, like the snow falls in the river,
> A moment white—then melts forever;
> Or, like the borealis race,
> That flit ere you can point their place;
> Or, like the rainbow's lovely form,
> Evanishing amid the storm."

For Olivia Clifford was suddenly seized with that deadly fever which has left so many infants motherless, and in a few days—spite of all that fond affection, tender care and medical skill could accomplish—the death angel entered their home of love and beauty, and passing hence, bore away the treasure whose loss left it darkly desolate.

Mr. Clifford did not dwell long either on this dreary season of bitter woe. So sacred and so long hidden, no wonder he hurried on with his story.

Human hearts are tough, and can bear heavy burdens; they are not so easily broken as poetasters and novelists would have us believe; and moreover, when plunged from off the rosy, elysian steeps of happiness down into the uttermost gulfs of misery, bravely do they battle with the black and turbid waters of despair; and though ofttimes sorely wounded, still live on. Lenox Clifford could not remain in Cuba, where everything served to recall a beautiful past, now hopelessly lamented; so committing his infant daughter—whose tender age rendered it both difficult and dangerous to remove her—to the care of Mr. Lacy and a faithful nurse, he left for New York, determined to try and dissipate his gloom amid the cares of business; and then (should he chance to reside there), in a year or two he might return and take the little Olivia to his northern home.

The child grew in strength and beauty, the delight of her old grandfather's eyes and heart, who wrote frequent accounts of her marvelous loveliness to the absent father.

A man loves his young child, as a part of the mother,

when he sees it pure and innocent upon her bosom; but should the mother die, the charm of that babe's existance for the time to him is broken—as he cannot fail (in a measure at least) to regard it as the cause of his mighty grief, the loss of his heart's idol! But when time has softened this sorrow,—when (if absent as Mr. Clifford was) he hears of his infant's beauty, that its baby lips have learned to lisp "papa," how the great, strong man yearns towards his little one,—yearns to hold it to his heart, and feel the soft, fresh cheek pressed close against his own. And thus it was, after two years, Lenox Clifford longed for his little Olivia, and was on the point of going to Cuba for the purpost of bringing hér back with him, when detained by pressing and unexpected business.

Finding it might be impossible to leave New York for several months, having some friends in the island, who would shortly return, and to whose care he felt quite sure the little girl, with her devoted nurse, might be trusted, he wrote Mr. Lacy, stating the cause of his detention, and begging he would send the child with those friends, promising at the same time, so soon as his business affairs were satisfactorily arranged, to take her back to Cuba for the winter. The letter was received, and the child was sent. But alas! for the eager expectation of that young father! While his heart was still smarting under the keen blow, which had left it so lonely when that new longing to see Olivia's child had so lately sprung up within his heart, like the first sweet violet of hope from the grave of a buried love,—the half healed heart was made to bleed afresh,—the frail bloom of reviving hope was withered, for *l'homme propose et Dieu dispose*, and that ill-fated ship in which little Olivia and her nurse had sailed with Mr. Clifford's friends, was wrecked in a frightful storm, just before day, on a reef of rocks, near the Everglades of Florida. Vainly did the anxious father watch for its coming, and unwilling to believe the terrible tidings (brought by the next vessel) that the "Southern Wave" was wrecked and all her passengers lost, Lenox Clifford still clung to the hope that some might possibly be saved, and among them his child, until at last, part of the crew from that doomed ship reached New York, having escaped in a life-boat, and from them he heard the fearful, final tidings that every one of the passengers, old and young, had perished; indeed, one of those rough old tars, wiped away a tear, as he quenched the last ray of hope in Lenox Clifford's bosom, by relating how he had vainly endeavored to save the French nurse and her beautiful little charge, when the woman's frantic cries for help, as the ship was going down, attracted his attention, and he saw her with the child lashed to part of a broken mast, striving to keep it above water.

Shouting for her to "hold on," he quickly seized the wreck again, and was about springing forward to her assistance when there came another crash, as of breaking timbers, and he saw both nurse and child swept off together by a great wave, after which they had scarcely time to clear their boat away from the wreck before the water closed over it.

What use was there in hoping on, or making further inquiries after hearing so clear and conclusive an account of his child's fate?

Mr. Lacy, overwhelmed with grief by this new loss, could not remain among scenes closely associated with Olivia and the infant he had loved so fondly for her sake; and shortly afterwards (selling out his rich possessions near Havana) he went to reside with his daughter Madam Armond, in Paris.

After the supposed loss of his child, Mr. Clifford, leaving this country, traveled for several years over Europe, and then in the East, until, weary with wandering, he went to rest with his mother and sister in England.

While there, news reached him of the failure of certain parties in New York, by whom he lost largely, and upon returning thither to try and save the balance he found scarcely enough left to live upon comfortably. After struggling on for a few more years, finding himself almost poor, and longing for change, he had suddenly determined to remove to the southern states, when my father's advertisement for a teacher caught his eye:—and so it was that Lenox Clifford came to Woodburn.

The sequel to this thrilling narrative was my Uncle

Dunbar's account of how he chanced to adopt Pearl, for such was still to be her name, her father insisting that having received it under such very remarkable circumstances, it should not be changed, not even for that of her mother.

The fisherman, McAlpine, married a Scotch woman, who had served in the Dunbar family for a long time, and hence retained always a claim upon their kindness, for they were attached to the dame. My uncle resided on a plantation in Florida, when McAlpine rescued Pearl, who was in their humble cottage on the coast two years before the Dunbars ever saw her; but about that time the old Scotchman and his wife formed a sudden fancy for removing to New Orleans, and then it was they took "their wee winsome leddy," as they called her, out to the Dunbar plantation, with a request that Miss Katy would have a care for the bairn until such time as they were settled, when the old fisherman would come for her.

Right gladly did they receive the lovely little stranger, to whom ere long they became so fondly attached, that my uncle, who, soon after the McAlpines left, sold his Florida property, and determined to remove to Elgin,—on their way thither, sought out the fisherman in New Orleans, and begged permission to adopt the child, giving her his name, and treating her in every respect as a daughter, even to making her fortune equal with Victor's.

This was a sore trial, for these humble people loved her well; but the honest, kind-hearted Scotchman hearkened not to the selfish love standing as it were between Pearl and a good fortune, and saying,—

"May the Lord Almighty bless you, sir, for this : it's far better that a gentle child be raised by gentle folks, and she's a born leddy if ever there was one. May angels keep her."

McAlpine gave up the Pearl a capricious fate had drifted unto him, to those who could afford a richer casket for so fair a treasure,—and thus it was she came at last to be the Pearl of Elgin, and now a double heiress, for, by old Mr. Lacy's will, who, when Mr. Clifford came to Woodburn, had been dead several years, she must inherit half his large estate in right of her mother—the will having never been altered—as Madam Armond's wish was that Mr. Clifford should inherit from his daughter; and directly after Mr. Lacy's death she wrote him to that effect, insisting he should claim the fortune of his child, as his by every law of right and nature; but Mr. Clifford very promptly and positively, yet most gratefully, declined to do so, for he was very proud, and feeling that all such ties, at least between himself and the Lacy's, were broken by the loss of his wife and the little Olivia, he was unwilling to accept, what, to his sensitive nature, would have appeared a gift of wealth from them.

Now, however, it was his duty to inform Madam Armond of his lost daughter's restoration, of course claiming for her Olivia's share of the estate ; and this was done at once, in a letter giving full details of Pearl's romantic history.

Mr. Clifford assured the Dunbars he had no wish to remove their darling; and even if obliged to leave the neighborhood for a time, his daughter's engagement to Cecil Clare would prevent his taking her from the home and adopted parents, so dear to her. Pearl had ever felt a peculiar reverence and love for Mr. Clifford, which now became so absorbing that she was restless when separated from him, and, after the Christmas tree, spent much of her time at Woodburn.

What wonder that such a father should be prized!

What wonder that the finding of such a Pearl should make that father almost covetous for a while of his newly found treasure.

CHAPTER XXIII.

RELATING TO SEVERAL THINGS.

TIME wore on—and a year from the time of Mr. Clifford's arrival at Woodburn, found him still there, our beloved teacher and friend—prized more and more highly as we knew him better.

It was beautiful to see the clinging, tender devotion between Pearl and her father, yet not one iota of the old, childish love for the adopted parents of her infancy had been lost, but rather mingling with this new affection, while no taint of suspicion or jealousy was ever stirred in any one of those trusting hearts, their feelings, and sympathies, blended harmoniously as the prismatic colors in a rare gem, all alike warm and beautiful, and each appearing by contrast to enhance the brightness of the other. Madam Armond had written most earnestly affectionate letters to Pearl, urging her to come and spend at least a year in Paris, but the true-hearted girl could not be tempted away (even by such an alluring invitation) from the man to whom she had pledged herself, and would only promise that perhaps, after her marriage, which would not take place for at least a year yet, that Mr. Clare might take her abroad, and then they would be most happy to visit her aunt.

Pearl was still slightly lame, but recovering rapidly.

Victor's late letters had made us all rejoice over the happy change in his mood, for they were quite cheerful, and particularly since his arrival at Florence. From this latter place I had received two, which, though still addressed to "dear little coz," were so affectionate, I stole off by myself to read, re-read, and linger over those beautiful missives.

Foolish, dreaming child! I little knew then the charm which was stealing over his existence, brightening and softening that haughty, troubled heart. Would it had been told me then—for I was beginning to dream more like a woman and less like a child !

Wizard had become so docile, under Mr. Clifford's gentle training—which neither man nor beast could resist—that I was able to ride him with safety, and had obtained Victor's consent to keep possession of the beautiful favorite until his master's return. Bang, too, was now my constant companion, Aunt Kate having needed very little coaxing before resigning him to my care; for with all her kindness of heart and warm impulses, the dear old maid felt no particular emotion of delight at beholding a great shaggy dog scampering over her handsome parlor carpets; and therefore, I fancy, she was not particularly distressed when Victor's spaniel, at my earnest request, became one of our family at Woodburn.

This constant association with the pets of my absent cousin was not calculated to wean my thoughts from dwelling on the wanderer—for little things do serve to kindle and feed a fire which, great and glorious in its burning beauty, subsides over heaps of black and bitter ashes; while the trembling vibration from a shepherd's rustic pipe may unfix an avalanche whose headlong course is marked by cold and dreary desolation!

Rachel Thorn was on a visit, just about this time, to a friend of hers—and a very nice lady, by-the-by, who knew only the sunny side of Rachel's nature—residing near the Glen, and we heard, through that most incorrigible tattler, Archey, of her being frequently at Dr. Foster's, the negro insisting upon it that they were to be married.

"Dars no kind of a doubt 'bout it, Miss Amy," he said to me, "for de crazy creeter's been kept powerful close since dat little white oman's been about, and Gabe don't get as many lickins (least-ways in day light, anyhow), for ye see dat savage doctor's afeerd of skeering his sweetheart," and Archey chuckled.

There had never been the slightest intercourse between Dr. Foster and ourselves, since his refusal to come as a physician to Woodburn, neither had we seen or heard directly from Rachel Thorn since she left us. Dr. Foster still practised at Elgin and other places in the neighborhood, but the fact of his hunting his crazy brother with a blood-hound made him so unpopular as a man, that persons generally had ceased inviting him to their entertainments, the house where Rachel Thorn was at present, being among the very few where he was received on a friendly footing.

Thus it was that matters stood, when one morning early in June, Mr. Clifford received a letter which agitated him unusually, for his cheek paled and his brow contracted while reading it; yet, after a moment's reflection over its contents, after folding it up slowly and handing it silently to my father, as he, Mr. Clifford, rose and left the room, I fancied there was less of sadness in his eyes than usual, though tears had dimmed them as he read the letter, and could not help wondering what news might be therein contained, which, while it touched his heart, had left a serene, nay, almost happy expression on his countenance.

That evening, when returning from the far end of the garden, where I had been gathering roses and jasmines for the parlor vases, a startling, yet certainly not unlovely tableau met my astonished eyes as I emerged suddenly from a dark walk fronting the summer-house—for there, amid the drooping vines, sat Mr. Clifford, with his arm—

but hold, I must not tell tales on my sister—suffice it to say, Ethel was there, too, near him, her beautiful head rather less stately in its *pose* than usual, and (though my eyes were withdrawn as quickly as possible, while I commenced singing to warn them of my proximity), it evinced rather an inclination to droop towards the neighborhood of her companion's shoulder—but maybe it was a mistake, an optical delusion—at all events when, as I turned off into another walk, Ethel called me to her,—upon joining them I found her queenly, and in a state of superb repose, as usual, though the delicate paleness of her complexion was flushed with pink, causing even her brow and bosom to glow like snow-fields beneath the reflection of boreal splendors, while in her eyes shone the light of a newly-found happiness, making its starry deeps more lustrous than ever.

And then I heard why Mr. Clifford had been so much agitated by the perusal of the late English letter, for it brought tidings of the death of his unfortunate cousin, Robert Clifford, which could not fail to cost that feeling, generous heart a pang of regret; for, though his course had been dissipated, his life utterly unprofitable, yet they were companions, playmates in boyhood, and Lenox retained too much of the old kindly feeling to hear of his cousin's death unmoved ; yet, with regret for the cause, there came a great rush of joyful emotions. He was now not only independent but wealthy enough to woo my sister without doing violence to the great pride of his nature, which ere this had prevented his seeking her hand in marriage, though it was powerless to prevent the outpouring of a love too strong to be chained in dumb obedience to a proud will; for Ethel had known, since the day of Rachel's banishment, that Mr. Clifford loved her. Fires cannot be smouldered when constantly fed, and lovers who meet daily are not apt to consume 'neath the tortures of unspoken passion.

The chain his pride had forged was riven now, for he could offer the lady of his love a home as well as a heart worthy of her; and so they were to be married soon, " very soon," Mr. Clifford said, as he must go over to England ere long, and wanted of course to take my sister as his bride.

I felt bewildered—it was so sudden! so unexpected! Then the idea of Ethel's going far away from us, of losing her as it were, overpowered me for the moment, and clinging to her I sobbed aloud, though partly for joy at her happiness.

" Perhaps father will let you go with us, little sis," she said; " nay, maybe go himself, and take Ralph to finish his education with you abroad. And then we might travel through Europe, meet Victor, too, and who knows but he would return home with you."

And she gave me a sly pinch on the arm.

Suggestions of so much pleasure proved a complete antidote to my tears, now quickly dried—and I felt very anxious to begin at once preparations for departure.

Such is the exuberant temperament of youth, which, alas! we outlive too soon—later in life tears spring not so readily, and when dried, oftentimes leave traces upon the heart bitter and burning, for the drops are like lava then, which in life's morning were mingled with the sunshine of hope, and spanned our future with an iris of expected joy!

A happy circle was assembled in the Woodburn parlor that evening—for my father had heard all, and moreover, when Mr. Clifford spoke of his newly acquired fortune, he was assured the wealth thus unfettering his pride did not gain the prize he sought, which, if sued for before, would have been as gladly granted to him as now—yet for the sake of one whose qualities of mind and heart he prized far beyond worldly wealth, my father rejoiced with Mr. Clifford in the fortune which had removed the only barrier between him and the realization of his dearest hopes.

Ethel's suggestion that we should accompany them to Europe evidently pleased my father, who said, laughingly:

"He was getting almost too old to travel so far, yet, nevertheless, would take the matter into consideration."

And then we felt just as confident of going as if he had said "yes" at once; for whenever that dear, kind, generous heart began to deliberate over matters appertaining to his children (were their preferences known to him) he was always sure to decide as they wished.

Therefore when my sister's wedding-day was fixed for the 10th of July—six weeks from that time—Ralph and myself felt quite certain of leaving with the bridal party for England, this conviction throwing us into a great state of excitement and perfect flutter of anticipated pleasure, as my brother had for some time been convinced of the fact that his existence was altogether too valuable to be expended in ceaseless pining over the disappointment of a boy's first love. It is far better to philosophize than to despond in such cases, and young hearts, in spite of what sentimental writers would have us believe, are not so easily broken as *Sévre china*. But a change—and such a change! under existing circumstances, filled the poor boy's heart with delight, and no wonder.

As to me, I cannot express the boundless joy filling me up to overflowing, while this beautiful future dawned upon me. To be Ethel's bridesmaid—to go away with her to their grand new home in England—and then, oh! crowning joy! to travel through the continent where Victor was, and would surely join us!—it was too much, and the effervescence of my delight was as impossible to keep down as it is to stop the frothing and sparkling of champagne after the wires confining the cork are fairly cut.

Mr. Clifford had been over to see Pearl directly after receiving that important letter, for she had such a near and dear claim upon him now, he would not take even the first step on the pathway to a new life without informing her;

and, though, of course, it was a bitter trial for the sweet girl so soon to lose her newly found father, yet as she had decided her own destiny by choosing to remain at Elgin—the affianced wife of Cecil Clare—what was there left but for her to rejoice with that father in his great happiness? and this she did most truly. It was a pretty sight to see them grouped together on that memorable evening,—father and daughter, with the radiant woman, who was soon to be near as she was already dear to both, yes, to both, for Pearl loved my sister too sincerely to be frightened by the prospect generally so full of terror (to young girls especially) of having a stepmother. So we were all very, very happy; and as Pearl was to be brides-maid also, there followed, of course, a grand discussion about dress, etc.

A wedding is always attended with pleasant excitement, especially to women-kind, and this one was so peculiarly interesting—the beauty of the bride elect, the unaccountable fate which brought Mr. Clifford to Woodburn, the singular romance of his finding in "Pearl Dunbar" a long lost daughter, together with this recent inheritance of wealth, converted him into a regular hero; and the old maids and gossips of N—— and its vicinity have never entirely recovered from the unusual number of tea-fights happening about that time, and where were discussed and re-discussed "the wonders of Woodburn."

Ralph had a young friend, whose aunt, being a member of this "venom club," he chanced to be present on one or

two of these memorable occasions for a time, having gone
to escort the old lady home, and through him we heard
some amiable criticisms emanating from the Tipps school.

First Speaker.—"Mrs. Linton's considered a great
beauty to be sure, but I never could see it, and she is
certainly *passé* now, but then Mr. Clifford's not particularly young either."

Second Speaker.—"Well! dear me, I only hope she'll
love him better than she did poor Arthur; he was a bright,
handsome fellow."

Third Speaker.—"And I have heard that all his dissipation was brought on (or at all events greatly increased)
by her absurd vanity and fondness for admiration."

First Speaker again.—"It's a good thing for poor Miss
Clifford that she's going to be married, for the association
of such a vain, imperious step-mother would not do her
much good."

Second Speaker (chiming in).—"Heigh-ho! and old
Percy, with that mad-cap son and smart young daughter
of his, are going abroad with the Cliffords, I am told."

First Speaker (cutting in suddenly).—"Yes, and
what a conceited little thing that Amy is! I would'nt be
a bit astonished if she were to attempt to be *literary*, for
they say she wears slip-shod shoes now and wipes pens on
her hair."

Third Speaker (snappishly).—"Well! if she isn't
obliged to write or teach before long for a support I shall

be astonished, for they live as if they were worth a mint!
and now going to Europe ! it would just serve them right
to find themselves poor one of these fine mornings; people
deserve no better that spend money as if their cellars were
gold mines.   I do declare it's outrageous ! "

The rank old venomites ! they might have bottled up
their spite for future use, had they known what was to
come, for the " wonders of Woodburn" were not ended.

Yet I fancy that stock of tea-party gossip was inexhaust-
ible, and when occasion would chance to call out such
talents, they were doubtless ever ready to concoct a dish of
scandal, like the wierd sisters boiling their cauldron of
" hell broth."   Poor old ladies ! if their tea was as strong
as their strictures their nights must have been somewhat
wakeful—their sleep nervous and disturbed.

CHAPTER XXIV.

> " Villain, thou know'st no law of God or man ;
> No heart so fierce but knows some touch of pity.—SHAKSPEARE.

IT was a sultry, summer storm,—the sun had gone down in a great sea of lurid thunder clouds, which seemed seething with heat, as the lightning broke through them, now in broad luminous flashes, and now writhing round those great dusky storm billows like monstrous serpents of fire.

Ethel, Mr. Clifford, Ralph and myself were spending the day at the parsonage; Pearl, too, was there; and now the approaching rain must delay our return until after dark. The lovers were engrossed with each other; Ralph was playing chess with Mrs. Clare, and being thus left to amuse myself, I stood idly watching the glory of that approaching tempest, with my forehead pressed against the window-pane.

On came the rain, dashing, driving, pelting, pouring in torrents upon the roof, and driven in by the wind, splashing great streams across the gallery floor. What a pleasant feeling of security and comfort it gives one to be snugly housed, and look out from a cheerful room upon such weather, and yet a tinge of sadness mingles with this feeling, inclining us to linger over past joys with a dread that such may not return, rather than dwell upon present happiness; and while gazing out absently at the vagaries of that summer storm, my mind reverted regretfully to the pleasant days gone by, when the presence of one (now far away) made Elgin and even home brighter to me—instead of exulting, as it had been of late, over the present anticipated delight of meeting him in Europe—for the one was a lost pleasure, perhaps, to be no more, the other an uncertainty of the future, which might never be—who can read the mysteries of time to come, save God?

And then, as the thought came over me that something might yet occur to prevent our going abroad, and that Victor might remain for years, perhaps marry there, I felt a choking sensation in my throat, and a great hot tear dropped down on my hand. It was brushed off hastily, and I strove to think of pleasant things; for Mrs. Clare had ordered lights, and I was ashamed, where all were happy, to be seen with traces of tears upon my face. Sometimes unaccountable fits of depression, vented in a deep sigh, or one overflowing tear, are the harbingers of grief to come, presaging a stormy time, of which these appear foreshadowing clouds.

There were deep fountains of tears in my nature—it was well—I should need them all.

More young cheeks would be furrowed, more young heads gray, if the great relief of weeping were denied to some natures!

Oh, what a flash of lightning!—so vivid the whole yard and lawn were illuminated, every object being thereby made visible as at noonday; and then such a stunning crash of thunder, that, spite my curiosity to try and catch another glimpse of the cowering figure I had seen by the lightning hurrying up the lawn—for it was a woman—turning hastily from the window, I buried my face in my hands.

After the frightful din of that storm-cannon had subsided, there was a death-like stillness for a moment throughout the room. I have frequently observed such silence following heavy bursts of thunder, even in the gayest assemblies, caused by a sudden manifestation of the mightiness of God's power, and leaving the reflection so full of awe— that one or more might have been laid low by the fury of that fiery bolt.

"It *must* have struck, and near the house, too—do go out and see if it is not one of the large trees, Cecil," said Mrs. Clare, as we all looked up into each other's faces after that moment of intense and solemn stillness.

I followed him quickly out to the gallery, remembering the woman I had seen running up towards the house, and wondering who it could be.

The lightning had struck an immense hickory tree, midway between the gate and front door, some of the shivered

splinters of which were still burning, when, attracted by
our exclamations, all the party ran out to look at it.

Then, catching sight of a dark object under the shattered
tree, I dashed down the steps and out of the yard, in spite
of the pouring rain ; for a horrid fear possessed me that
the person I had seen, whoever it might be, had been
struck, perhaps killed by the lightning.   Ethel and Mrs.
Clare, being unaware of my fears, called out to know if I
were crazy ! and bade me come out of the rain ; but on I
ran, heedless of their call, followed by Mr. Clifford and Cecil
Clare, who had also observed that some one was lying under the tree.   Our fears were not groundless, for there on
the wet grass, beside that shivered trunk, the top of the
tree having split off and fallen on the other side, lay the
prostrate form of a woman. '

I immediately recognized the bonnet and cloak, and ere
they had raised her motionless figure, I knew it was Rachel
Thorn.

" Merciful heaven ! is she dead ?" I exclaimed, as my
eyes fell upon the white, rigid face of my cousin.

" Yes," replied Mr. Clifford, " quite dead—no human
being could withstand the shaft that shivered this mighty
tree."

" Poor Rachel !" and I wept over the stricken girl as if
I had loved her, her faults for a time forgotten.   I saw
only my cousin—one with whom I had lived so many
years—and then what heart can withhold a tribute of grief

when thus brought face to face, unexpectedly, with the grim presence of death—sudden, instantaneous death. They bore her to the house, where every remedy used on similar occasions was resorted to, but all in vain—the vital spark was quenched forever.

Ethel, shocked and overwhelmed beyond expression, reproached herself for having felt unkindly towards Rachel, though surely no blame could be attached to her after the manner in which our unfortunate cousin had acted, and my sister was less vindictive in her feelings—even when she knew herself wronged—than almost any one I ever saw. We wondered why Rachel should have been out in such a storm, and still more as to what could have been the import of her mission to the parsonage?

For after quitting Woodburn she had never visited any of our friends, and though the lady she was with lived only about half a mile from the Clares, Rachel had not been there before. Her right hand was in the pocket of her dress, and upon removing it we found the fingers closely clasped around a letter, as if she had thrust it in there cautiously when overtaken by the rain, to prevent its becoming wet.

I seized the crumpled paper hastily, and glancing at the direction, hoping it might throw some light upon the object of that unaccountable visit to the parsonage—when to my astonished eyes it presented the following address:

"Mrs. Linton, Woodburn."

But the contents startled us still more, for it ran thus :

Cousin Ethel—

I know you do not like me, and no wonder, for I would have wronged you, urged on by stronger feelings than perhaps you can imagine me as possessing. Thank God ! my evil designs failed—for so utterly am I appalled by the aspect of wickedness ten-fold darker than any of my imagining, that even the memory of my own deceit toward you causes me to turn, shuddering, away from evil, and long for strength to walk in the right path.

Ethel, Dr. Foster is your bitterest, most unrelenting foe. He is meditating—nay has been, for longer than you dream of—a plot to destroy your happiness. I have known him long—yet only lately, and quite by accident, has this secret, which I would fain divulge, come into my possession.

But when, in the horror of discovering it, I threatened to reveal all to you, that black-hearted man bound me by the most sacred and awful oaths not to betray him—for if so, he would kill me were it the last act of his life, and I know Dr. Foster well enough to feel assured this was no idle threat.

One thing I beg, which may save you great wretchedness—defer your marriage for awhile. Let Mr. Clifford go to England now alone, and by the time he returns, perhaps before, some chance may reveal the secret I dare not hint at more clearly.

You may think this another scheme to separate you from Mr. Clifford ; but so help me God, I am sincere now, and have earnestly prayed for strength to save you from a great evil without perjuring myself. The letter and picture I did place in your portfolio, thinking Mr. Clifford's first impulse would be to leave you forever, after such overwhelming proof that certain statements I had made to him were correct. Yet the letter was no forgery, and the falsehood I appeared to tell was no falsehood, as you may know, alas ! too soon. Do not let uncle go to Dr. Foster about this letter, I implore you, cousin Ethel, and do not by a personal interview try to wring this secret from me— for were you to succeed, no time or distance could ever serve to hide me from his vengeance.

I am going North next week with Mrs. Davis, as governess for her children, and being miserable both in memory of the wrong I might have committed and from the bitter burden of this fearful secret, I could not go without asking your forgiveness, and that of all at Woodburn, hinting thus dimly at the truth I dare not tell.

May God bless my efforts to atone thus meagrely for evil, and save you from the vengeance of an unrelenting foe, prays your

COUSIN RACHEL.

P. S.—I shall run over this evening and ask Mrs. Clare

11*

to deliver my letter to you, dreading to send, lest Dr. Foster might in some way manage to foil me and get possession of it, for he watches me continually, and is crafty beyond belief. Pray for me, Ethel, for you are pure and good. Farewell! be warned, and follow my advice.

R. T.

Poor Rachel! what could she mean? Had she gone suddenly crazy? How vainly both my sister and myself tried to solve the mystery as we read, and re-read, that enigmatical letter, while the strange being who had traced those lines a few short hours ago, lay cold and dead before us.

What should we do? Ethel felt bound, of course, to show it to Mr. Clifford, for surely they were equally interested in fathoming its deep meaning. But defer their marriage! Suffer him to go away without her! How could she do this, even should Mr. Clifford consent? which was most improbable. And how could Dr. Foster do them any possible harm? Surely Rachel's evident dread of that fierce man must have caused her to overrate his power. Thus it was we reasoned together, having taken advantage of Mrs. Clare's temporary absence from the room to peruse this warning letter, at last concluding to say nothing about it, even to Mr. Clifford, until the following day, save that it was a few lines of penitent farewell from Rachel which she had intended asking Mrs. Clare to deliver to my sister.   Mrs. Davis, who was really attached to Rachel—as my father had been—having seen only the brighter side of her character, was truly grieved at this most awful event, and from her that very night we heard some few interesting particulars regarding our poor cousin, who it appears had been very low spirited for a fortnight past, at the same time taking a curious aversion to Dr. Foster, which was unaccountable; as for the first week or two after Rachel's arrival in the neighborhood they were frequently together—so much so, indeed, that Mrs. Davis fancied they must be lovers; but from Rachel's recent dislike to him, was led to believe the Doctor had made himself disagreeable and been discarded.

The afternoon of that fatal day she had been writing, and coming down from her chamber after sundown, told Mrs. D. that she would run over to the parsonage with a note, which she wished Mrs. Clare to deliver, and though warned by her friend of the coming storm as almost sure to overtake her, the unhappy girl persisted in going, and said she felt certain it would not rain before her return.

Such is fate!

And Rachel met hers in trying to atone for past enmity and bitterness by doing the woman she had envied, hated, and sought to wrong, a kindness.

Two days afterwards, the very sad funeral of Rachel Thorn took place, and we saw her laid in the family bury-ing-ground at Woodburn; wishing she had lived to endear herself to those who would fain have loved her long ago, and regretting, as we always do so vainly over the dead, no matter what may have been their faults—that we had not judged her less harshly, and that she had not lived to shine forth in the new light breaking upon her, just before it was quenched forever.

Perhaps 'twas better thus. She had prayed in penitence to be forgiven, and "there is joy in heaven over one sinner that repenteth." So God called her away, ere yet greater temptation might arise, and lead her footsteps again wandering from the narrow pathway "leading to eternal life."

Mr. Clifford was bewildered and troubled by that mysterious letter; yet could not imagine a probability of Dr. Foster's enmity to Ethel, emanating from the spite of a discarded lover, being replete with danger, as Rachel represented.

He said the poor girl's fancy was evidently distempered by dread of this man,—from some cause unknown to us,—she must have overrated his ability to injure them; and feeling sure his watchful love could guard Ethel from Foster's wrath, he almost ridiculed the idea of postponing their marriage.

Go to England without her! Oh, it must not, could not be—and he earnestly implored my sister to dismiss that part of the letter, at least, from her thoughts—and she strove to obey him, though from a dejected, worried look she wore at times, we knew this mysterious communication, coming, as it were, from the dead, weighed upon her as a presentiment of coming evil.

Yet still the wedding preparations went on, for the 16th of July was now only three weeks distant.

Rachel Thorn's letter had never been mentioned to my father, save as one of regrets for the past and farewell, because we feared the dark hints of Dr. Foster's vengeance might alarm him unnecessarily, or if based on reality, he would be powerless to avert a danger to which there was no tangible clue.

So sudden, fearful, and unexpected a death was, of course, felt as a shock in our little community—it is always thus that such events affect a small and intimate neighborhood; and the thunder-clouds of after storms looked darker and more full of danger to those who came, as it were, under the immediate influence of Rachel's mournful fate.

Days glided by, wedding dresses were made, wedding presents ordered; for thus it is, and thus must ever be, that joys and sorrows follow each other over the same thresholds, and when happiness appears almost within our grasp, we turn not aside from pursuing it, though the path be chequered with darkness, and ofttimes seek to win and wear a panoply of earthly bliss, where even yet the shadow of death is lingering.

CHAPTER XXV.

THE ROOM WITH PRISON WINDOWS.

Upon that wild and haggard face
The warm light left no cheerful trace
Of gladness—God's own sunshine there,
Seemed lost in darkness and despair !

SHORTLY after Rachel's death, Ethel and myself had occasion one evening—after spending the day at Elgin—to ride over to the cottage of a poor widow—a *protégé* of my sisters—formerly the wife of a gardener employed at Woodburn, where she had lived with her husband for several years. Her humble home now was on a remote portion of the Elgin plantation, and just back of the Glen, being only divided from Dr. Foster's garden fence by a lane so narrow, that one standing in the cottage porch or door might recognize persons in or about the Glen mansion. We had never been to see Mrs. Slone until now, since Dr. Foster's arrival in the neighborhood, and though the poor dame was quite sick and had sent for us to come and minister to her wants—she dwelt so little upon her suffer-ing—which always is a particularly pleasant subject for ailing females of the lower class to expend their eloquence upon, and was so inclined to gossip about the doings and sayings over the way, that I was half tempted to believe she wanted to see us simply because she coveted the pleasure of initiating us into the mysteries of the Glen!

"I hope the neuralgia in your head is better, Mrs. Slone," said Ethel as we seated ourselves near the invalid, who was propped up with pillows in a great wicker chair, near the front window, where her vigilant eyes were ever eagerly on the watch, no doubt, for new wonders on her neighbor's premises.

"Why, yes, I haven't been quite so poorly of late," she replied, "but I'm made most awful narvous of nights by the baying of that awful fierce brute across the way. It makes a body feel in the night as if there must be a corpse about to hear such a dreadful howling, and sometimes I think that wicked doctor keeps dead people in his office to cut up, and I can't sleep for fearing that maybe he'll go and dig up my poor old man, who you know is buried in the far corner of the Elgin burying-ground."

I saw a beam of mirth and mischief in Ethel's eye as glancing at me she answered:

"Oh, I don't think that's the least likely, Mrs. Slone, for you know doctors only want for subjects those who have died recently, and your husband (if I mistake not) has been dead three years."

"Well, sure enough now, I never thought of that,"

chimed in the sick woman, "but you know, mam, ailing folks will be narvous like, and then there's such wicked doings forever going on over there that I've felt scared like, and 'specially of nights, ever since that awful man moved to the Glen."

"Why what harm do you think Dr. Foster can possibly do to you, Mrs. Slone," I said, with a sly look at my sister.

"Nobody can tell what a wicked man, who has dealings with the Evil One, may do at any moment, miss," she replied quickly, "a man that keeps his crazy brother shut up on bread and water, and then when he gets out sometimes —for the madman's dreadful strong—hunts him with that horrid bloodhound 'Wolf;' they say the beast tears his flesh too, when he catches the poor suffering creature ; and oh! then, miss, Dr. Foster beats Gabe almost to death every time he lets the crazy man out; this I know, for I can hear the licks, and the poor nigger's cries for mercy, both plain enough; gracious! how glad I should be if Gabe would turn on his savage master some day and kill him!"

"Don't wish that," said Ethel, "for then the unfortunate negro would be hung, and some other roughly treated . in his place ! try and not think so much about these things, it does no good—and if your neighbor is so very wicked, he will doubtless be punished in God's own time. I hope this medicine will be of service to you, Mrs. Slone, and the jelly and fruit may be a pleasant variety to your every day diet. Come, Amy, we must be going."

I arose at Ethel's bidding; but the poor woman, laying her hand gently on my sister's arm, said, in a pleading voice :

" Do, please, stop a few minutes, mam, for I must tell you something I accidentally overheard, which makes me think (from some cause or other) that Foster is a bitter enemy of yours, and means to do you evil if he can; this is why I sent for you to come, and have been trying to get a chance to speak out about it ever since you got here, but I'm slow and stupid."

Ethel turned so white at these words, I feared she would faint, and said (almost angrily) to Mrs. Slone :

" We don't care what Dr. Foster says—and he can't harm us—so please don't repeat his spiteful sayings. Come away, sis." But Ethel reseated herself, and rebuked my quick manner by saying :

" Amy, she means kindly, and if what Dr. Foster said in her hearing concerns me, it is surely right I should know it."

" Yes, miss," rejoined the widow, " for you know how much I think of you all, and especially Miss Ethel, who has been like an angel to me; and when I heard that awful man say what he did, it made me sick with fear; and the reason of my wishing to tell it, was thinking she might balk his wickedness. You remember the evening that poor

young lady, your cousin, Miss Thorn, was struck by
lightning—well, two or three days before, she came down
to the Glen—the fact is she was there often, and seemed
so thick with Dr. Foster, that people said they was engaged to be married, and I could'nt help thinking so 'till
that day, when he spoke so dreadful savage to her I knew
it must be a mistake.   I was sitting here knitting, when I
saw Miss Thorn and the doctor walking down through the
garden to the back gate just opposite, so as I didn't want
them to see me, I pulled down the white curtain, still
keeping my seat by the window; and soon I heard their
voices at the gate, where through a break in the curtain I
could see them standing talking together, she on this side
in the lane, and he leaning with his arms on the gate glar-
ing at her like a wild-cat as he said, in reply to some
remark of her's, which I could not hear : ' Go, and tell
Ethel Linton if you dare, Rachel, it shall not foil my
vengeance; and as for you I will. only let you live long
enough to regret having made an effort to thwart me.'
Then the poor girl buried her face in her hands, weeping
bitterly, as she exclaimed, ' Oh ! God forgive me, but I
never dreamed of such wickedness; what shall I do ? '
' A curse on your hypocritical penitence,' said Foster
fiercely, ' you would have sold your soul to gain the love
of that insolent English tutor ; but since the scheme you
laid to draw him off from Ethel failed, that most pious soul
of yours must needs shudder, because I don't drop on my

knees and pray for blessings to rain down on the woman I hate for blasting my happiness; but she shall suffer despite your threat to warn her. Be gone now. Never set your foot here again, and remember you are watched by me, no matter where you are, or what you do.' Saying which he turned back to the house, and the young lady, still weeping, drew down her veil, and walked slowly along the lane towards Mrs. Davis's, where, if you remember, she was then staying. I don't know, dear lady, whether this bad man has it in his power to harm you, yet still could not rest until I told you of his vile threats, which were overheard so unexpectedly and quite accidentally I assure you."

Poor woman! she might have left the window at once, and thus avoided this accidental eaves-dropping; but people who overhear generally find an excuse for so doing, and perhaps others less ignorant of the proprieties of life than Mrs. Slone, might, under similar circumstances, have remained behind the curtain and heard all, as she had done; therefore, we could not blame her for listening, and though agitated by the conversation she repeated, especially my sister, who looked miserable, we thanked her for her kind intentions—while, at the same time, with a kind of desperate defiance, I tried to ridicule the idea of Dr. Foster's having power to injure Ethel. "And Miss Thorn's not the only woman that's been driven from the Glen," continued the loquacious invalid, "for I've seen another, whose black eyes blazed with fury, making her white haggard face look awfully fierce, when with curses—more bitter than those heaped on your cousin, Foster bade her 'begone, and trouble him no more.' They say he was the ruin of that woman in his early youth, and I doubt it not, for the desperate hardness of her look now tells a tale of love, wrong, and hatred!"

As we were about to get into the carriage, Archey, who held the door, said, "Miss Effie, Miss Amy, dus you see dat dar window up in de east end ob de Glen House, with iron bars 'crost it?" And while speaking, his eyes rolled up towards the attic window indicated. "Well, dat's de prison wha Dr. Foster keeps his crazy brudder, and dar him now, a clinchin and beatin de bars. Gosh! but I pities Gabe!"

Involuntarily our eyes had turned with his; and there, sure enough, wild and ragged, with lean fingers twisted through the pitiless bars, gazing vacantly upon the bright prospect without, while the glorious sunshine lit up his haggard face with mocking splendor, stood the poor maniac. But for a moment we saw him thus, and then, hurrying into the carriage, drove quickly home. Heaven knows, we both pitied that wretched prisoner, for being in the power of so cruel and hard-hearted a tyrant and prayed God to have mercy upon him. Pale and silent we were during the ride, for though I strove to dismiss the dread which had settled on Ethel's mind since the receipt of Rachel's letter, and must now grow darker, my own heart was scarcely less heavy than hers; for the mystery of that man's hate and threats of vengeance, made my beloved sister's future, like the path of one lost amid quicksands, in whose treacherous depths he may sink suddenly, and when feeling past all danger, helpless and overwhelmed!

CHAPTER XXVI.

FOREBODINGS.

IT was a strange picture, but so wondrously beautiful that I held my breath, and paused involuntarily midway of my sister's apartment, to gaze upon it. The wedding dress, veil, jewels, etc., had arrived that day, and just before dark, Ethel, having tried them on, was waiting for me to come in and see her. The lamps, though ordered, had not yet been brought up, and hence it happened, upon entering, I beheld the lovely tableau referred to above.

Through the open shutters a full flood of summer moonlight was streaming, and there, close by the window, perfectly refulgent beneath the warm splendor of that July moon, stood my sister, toying with a superb emerald bracelet, in form of a serpent, with opal eyes and diamond crest —in workmanship almost the counterpart to the one (belonging now to Pearl,) picked up by Mr. Clifford at the opera-house iu Paris, and which he had matched, as nearly as possible, in New York, as a wedding gift for Ethel.

The moonlight gave a queer, mystical gleam to the green, glittering scales of that jeweled snake, as it quivered between her delicate white fingers, and my fantastic dream of the broken bridge, where Mr. Clifford crossed and tore the wreathing viper from her bare white arm, came up in singular contrast to the fairy scene before me. Perhaps the very sad expression of Ethel's face, just as I entered, may have recalled the memory of that frightful dream—for she did look almost despondent, as if the shadow of a coming sorrow were hovering over her then, and there veiled, yet not hid by the beauty of that summer night.

A moment thus I paused to gaze upon her, for ladies in bridal array are generally seen beneath the glare of artificial light; and hence this silvery halo invested Ethel with an almost superhuman loveliness. Then stealing up to her I whispered:

"Oh! my own dear sister, why do you look so mournful? I know full well you are perfectly happy in your love, and all things seem combining to render your prospects fair, very fair; besides, you will not even know the pain of leaving those you love at home, for we are going with you. Then why this sadness? Is Rachel Thorn's letter still weighing upon you?"

"Yes, it is," she replied. "I know not why, but it haunts me more and more as the time for our marriage approaches; and since putting on my bridal dress a foreboding of evil to come, from which I shrink, shuddering, appears settling upon me like an unseen vampire; and this phantom of fear has been as it were hovering over my existence ever since the reading of that fatal letter (the truth of which Mrs. Slone's story so fully confirmed); and now—though God knows how reluctant I should be to have it so—I almost wish our wedding had been postponed, and that Lenox were going to England alone! Yet, this would have been a great trial to us both, and if nothing happens to prevent—and what can prevent our marriage now save death?—I shall laugh at these fears as groundless; so let's dismiss the subject. And now tell me how you like my bridal dress?"

"Perfect," I answered; "you look peerless, my own sis; so do try and cheer up for Mr. Clifford's sake. Poor Rachel! I have not a doubt that Dr. Foster made her believe he was going to blow up the whole bridal party, by aid of some villanous gunpowder plot, *à la* Guy Fawkes, or an infernal machine, *à la diable*, of home manufacture."

Ethel smiled, nay almost laughed, at my ridiculous conceit regarding Dr. Foster's vengeance, and then, after reflecting a moment, she rejoined:

"What could Rachel have meant by declaring the letter she put into my portfolio to be no forgery? If so, (and we cannot doubt this earnest assurance) Basil must have given it to her for me, and perhaps the picture too, years ago, when he was (or pretended to be) so crazily in love with me ; and she, knowing his suit to be hopeless, may have thought best not to deliver them—for Rachel was very bright and discerning—until, when striving to separate Mr. Clifford and myself, remembering they were in her possession, the poor girl determined to make use of both to serve a purpose; and yet one might suppose, according to Archey's story, that she received the letter and miniature from Dr. Foster. Can he be a friend of Basil Thorn's ? And Amy, what could have caused Rachel to scream and act in such a queer way that morning at the parsonage, when she went in with the soap-dish to Dr. Foster while he was washing his hands? The whole affair bewilders me beyond expression, and one might think our unfortunate cousin was at times demented, yet the more I reflect upon her letter the more convinced am I that the poor repentant girl must have had strong motives for writing as she did, and some substantial foundation for the warning she gave me."

Here I interrupted her, saying :

" I thought we were to dismiss the subject, sis ? Please do, for it is worse than useless to speculate regarding matters so perfectly vague. Come, let me take off your things so we may be ready for tea."

She turned away from the window, and while assisting

in changing her dress I chatted gaily on other topics, until
Ethel's mood, if not cheerful, was at least less desponding
when we joined the family circle at tea time.

Ralph and myself, in talking over Archey's stories
about Rachel Thorn and Dr. Foster, had come to the conclusion, long ago, that a negro's distempered fancies regarding the woman he hated, and the man he feared so excessively, were scarcely worth speculating upon. Ralph said
he believed, firmly, that Archey thought Dr. Foster had
sold his soul to the evil one, and having entered with Rachel
into some diabolical league, this renowned tattler would not
have been astonished at any moment to see one, or both of
them, disappear in a cloud of brimstone and fire! We
laughed heartily over this exaggerated idea, but after
events proved that the negro did not overestimate the Doctor's capacity for wickedness.

On the sixth of July—four days previous to the wedding—as Bang and myself were taking a walk towards the
negro quarters, where I was going with some nice things
for Mammy—who had been sick—in passing down the
lane, I heard Archey's voice in loud discussion with some
one in the barn lot, which, from his own account, having
been the scene of his *espionage* over Dr. Foster and Rachel
Thorn, was evidently a favorite resort of that notable
young African, and where it appears on the present occasion he chose to entertain his company—for (upon peeping
through the hedge) I saw seated near him, on an old horse-

trough, a gigantic negro, who, from Archey's description of "Gabe," I at once supposed to be that identical personage, and part of their conversation (which I overheard in passing very slowly, for my curiosity was on the *qui vive* to know why a servant from the Glen should visit Woodburn,) confirmed this supposition into a certainty.

"What business is it of your ugly cantankerous master's when Miss Effie's gwying to get married? He's not a gwying to be axed, I ken tell him dat, to none of de weddins or jollyfyins in our family, and you can jis go and tell him so if you like; but I know you an't gwying to do no sitch a ting, for big as you is, you're a darned sight more afeerd of him den me," and Archey chuckled.

"I know it ain't nun of his business," replied Gabe; "but he told me if I did'nt find out when dat weddin is to be, and when you'r folks is gwying away, dat he'd lock me up in de prison room wid dat crazy brudder of his; and Archey, I'd rader die den be fastened up dar—so, for de Lord's sake, tell me if you know."

"Well," responded Archey, "I wouldn't like to see no respectable nigger treated like dat, and, as he's not to be axed no how, why I don't mind telling you; de weddin is to be next Tuesday, and de next week follerin dat, dey is all gwying—oh, ebber so far!—away ober de great sea, de Lord knows whar!—may be to de mountins ob de moon, I believes dat's de name of de place."

At which piece of information I could not help laugh-

ing, in spite of the uncomfortable feeling created by Dr.
Foster's anxiety to know my sister's plans, yet as we had
heard that the Glen was to be sold, and its present master
intended removing, perhaps his idea after all was simply to
know when we left, in order to go at the same time and in
the same direction, thus annoying us by his presence as
much as possible; at all events I would try to think so,
and on no account mention the subject to Ethel.

Upon my return from mammy's house, Archey was sitting on the barn fence, who, so soon as he saw me coming,
dropped down quickly into the lane, and with one of his
shuffling bows, said,—

"Bless you, Miss Amy, who you. tink been here, axin
all kinds ob questions bout our family-fares, but dat big
nigger Gabe, what takes keer of de crazy creeter, but he
didn't get much off ob me, kase, I believes, miss, as how
his master's got dealins wid de debble—axing your pardon,
miss—and if he chooses to, kin blow us up all to bits, in
no time—but when de poor darkey said dat child of Beel-
zebub would put him in wid de wild man, if he didn't find
out when de weddin is to be, I made no bones ob telling
him dat much, kase de doctor's not to be axed no how,
so I thought it wouldn't matter, and hope I aint dun no
harm."

"Oh, no, Archey, we certainly cannot object to the day
of my sister's wedding being known, especially now, when
it is so near; yet it is surely no concern of Dr. Foster's,

who I believe with you to be a very bad man, and if Gabe comes here on any more such errands, don't fail to let me know it, that's all."

"Fore de Lord, I will, Miss Amy. He knows I'd radder hab dat wicked doctor, and his crazy brudder, and dat big bully nigger—doe I feels sorry for Gabe, I does—roasted alive on de debbil's own red-hot spit, den have one hair of yours, or your sister's blessed heads hurt, or any ob de rest of our family—I would, in fac, Miss Amy," and Archey bowed low as he shuffled off.

I walked away, laughing with a kind of unquiet, disturbed amusement, for Gabe's mission troubled me, in spite of all the efforts I made by silent reasoning to convince myself that it was not worthy of a thought.

Sitting down on the front steps, after my return to the house, with Bang's great shaggy head upon my lap, I began to sum up the evidence thus far collected regarding Foster's proposed vengeance, wondering if there existed any real foundation for his schemes, and if anything could possibly happen now to prevent our going abroad; and if so, when Victor was likely to return, for in writing he never alluded to coming home. The dog was looking wistfully in my face with his large soft eyes as I whispered, "Where's Vic, Bang?" He wagged his tail, seeming almost to understand me. I took a mournful pleasure in talking to this intelligent, faithful creature about his absent master, and particularly so as I shrank from mentioning Victor's name thus tenderly to any one, even to Ethel, who, in everything else, possessed my unbounded confidence.

"We miss him, don't we, Bang?" and again there was a low whine, as of assent, while the great bushy tail wagged approvingly. A sudden sensation of sadness then overcame me, as on that evening when I watched the thunder-storm, whose voice had come as a trumpet of doom to poor Rachel Thorn—bringing tears this time, so thick and fast, that Bang snuffed and shook his head, as the great drops rained down upon his nose.

Again the shadow of a coming sorrow was upon me, as it had been then,—the same that hovered over Ethel, when she stood with the summer moonlight glorifying, spiritualizing her beauty, idealizing the very dress and gems she wore, until they shone with a mystical splendor 'neath its mellow beams.

This peculiar presentiment was to me like the deep, sultry calm which, in hot climates, presages a tempest, but when or how it was to burst, we knew not—and still hoped the cloud might pass away; it was well, for what would we be without hope, in a world where shadows checker life's pathway with so much darkness? And where does hope point us for comfort, but to Heaven?

CHAPTER XXVII.

THE WEDDING.

THEY were married. I had watched Ethel's cheek
flush and pale alternately, as the solemn words were so im-
pressively uttered by Cecil Clare, which bound her forever
to the man of her choice, the one so truly and perfectly
beloved.

The shadow left upon her by Rachel Thorn's letter and
Dame Slone's story had never passed away, and once or
twice during the ceremony the color died out so entirely
from my sister's lovely face, that I thought she must
faint, but when Mr. Clare raised his hands solemnly
and the newly-married pair bent their heads low for the
benediction, that cold, suppressed dread appeared to pass,
and the tear trembling in her eyes, as I whispered, " God

bless you, my own darling sister," fell, when Pearl looked up with her beaming smile into Ethel's face, and uttered softly but distinctly, the sweet word " mother."

It was the very perfection of a wedding; no event for years had created such a sensation, and not only were the *élite* of our town and neighborhood assembled at Woodburn that night, but many friends from a distance; for the romantic circumstances of Mr. Clifford's history, particularly his residence in our family as a tutor, and the discovery thereby of a long lost daughter, excited a wonderful curiosity in all those who heard it, to witness the *dénoucment* of so remarkable and interesting a story.

Pearl stood up with my brother, as first bridesmaid, and my attendant groomsman was a friend of Mr. Clifford's from New York, who had come on for the occasion, and whose name was Clarence Morton.

Having neither taste nor inclination for long descriptions of dresses, and how different people looked, suffice it to say that even Miss Tabitha Tipps in her bitterest, most unrelenting mood, could scarcely have found a vulnerable point of attack, either in the dress, appearance, or deportment of the peerless bride and handsome groom; for though that worthy spinster and her notorious clique were in the habit, to be sure, of seeing and hearing things beyond the ken of less gifted individuals, we think their inventive malice would have been sorely tried then and there to find ground for ill-natured remarks, but as none of the " venom club " were among those wedding guests, scarcely a doubt can be entertained that they made spicy hash of the bridal party at one of their cozy tea-fights !

Lenox Clifford wore the expressively happy and contented look of one who has gained a great prize, yet not unmingled with a certain proud serenity of demeanor indicating that he fully appreciated, and therefore was not undeserving of such happiness. I have already drawn a picture of Ethel in her bridal dress beneath the summer moonlight, and while looking perhaps less *spirituelle*, she undoubtedly appeared more radiant in that same array under the warm and rosy glow of wax candles; and yet, I fancied that a shadow of the shade, saddening and subduing her beauty then, still lingered, even after the agitation of the ceremony was past; however, brides are wont to be pensive, and my sister's happiness was a fact too well established for any one, save myself, or perhaps Mr. Clifford, to observe this tint of gloom cast by a dread of coming evil— one single dash of darkness upon a picture redolent with light. It was on me too—in my heart and brain a haunting presence—and spite of the brightness, mirth, and beauty of the scene I felt a nervous undefinable dread, connected with Rachel's warning letter, Dr. Foster, Wolf, Gabe, and the madman, which would not be banished, filling me up " from top to toe " with direst apprehension that the doctor, or one of his grim attendants, or perhaps poor Rachel's ghost, would appear suddenly in the midst of that " goodly companie "—and once or twice, when standing near the window, I felt a sharp shudder of fear as a glancing shadow across the lawn, or balcony made me gaze out anxiously with a kind of morbid fascination and expectancy, for the actual appearance of one or the other, and perhaps all of that dreaded living trio, or my dead cousin's shadowy figure, with spectral finger held out in warning towards the Glen. When the human mind is thus possessed with horrors, it is wonderful how keenly susceptible the imagination becomes, and how like an inquisitor it summons us continually to be tortured on a rack of endless fears!

Once, as I started quickly from the open window, upon hearing some trivial noise, Mr. Morton (my attendant groomsman) laughingly asked me,—

" If I believed in ghosts? " To which I made the jesting rejoinder :—

" That southern girls, with African nurses, were not unfrequently a little imbued with superstition, but never having as yet been favored by a ghostly visitor, I could not exactly profess myself a believer in spiritual manifestations!

Saying which, I led the way into an illuminated conservatory, and began speaking of our anticipated visit abroad, asking if he had ever been to Europe?

" No," but he spoke of going, and might possibly join our party, as his father and sister were now traveling in Italy, and very anxious for him to meet them there.

"By the by," said Mr. Morton carelessly, "I wonder if the Mr. Dunbar, of whom my sister Eva writes so enthusiastically, is any relation to your Dunbars—I mean the family by whom Mr. Clifford's daughter was adopted?"

It is wonderful what control women (nay girls even, with that intuitive tact, which is a part of female nature, dawning in them,) can put upon their feelings when, ever so unexpectedly, an accidental remark chances to touch or even jar rudely a hidden chord of tenderness!

I felt my heart give a great bound, followed by that choking pain in the throat and chest so often caused by strong emotion, and yet idly tapping my fan against the slender trunk of a date palm, and glancing up at its feathery top, I replied :—

"Quite likely; I have a cousin traveling abroad. Did your sister happen to mention his first name?"

"Yes, I think she did, and that it commenced with,—hum—let me see—well, really, I have forgotten," said Mr. Morton hesitatingly.

"Was it Victor?" I asked quickly, "and has your sister known him long?"

"Ah! that is it, Victor Dunbar, (it is queer I did not remember at once,) for they met at Florence, and she has mentioned him frequently in writing for three months. In replying to her last, I could not help hinting at the possibility that a certain young lady's heart of my acquaintance might be in rather a precarious situation, and," he laughingly continued, "'it is not impossible either that Mr. Dunbar may become enchanted with my bewitching little sister, for though brothers are, not generally regarded as impartial judges of their sister's attractions, yet, as Eva is so far away, I may say without flattery that she is both beautiful and fascinating. She is very clever too, and has most winning and coquettish ways, though not a coquette I am happy to say, for a woman who plays with human hearts for pastime could never command from a brother the love and respect I feel for Eva. .

"There now! Miss Percy, you have broken that beautiful fan. I could not help trembling for it, and rather anticipated its fate some time ago. You struck it too roughly for such a delicate little thing," and stooping down, he picked up the shattered fragments of pearl, which had fallen at the foot of the palm tree.

For, scarcely aware of my agitation, while Mr. Morton ran on gayly describing the fascinations of his sister, I had struck the dainty carving of my fan so fiercely against the tree as to shiver it. I felt my color rise, and my rebellious lip—which had a most perverse inclination to curl up when I was either piqued or annoyed at anything—assumed a slightly scornful expression, when, as he handed me the broken toy, after replying quickly :

" Ah, thank you, it is of no consequence," I went on to

remark, in a much more excited manner than the occasion warranted :—

"My cousin's *affaires de cœur* must indeed be of slight consequence, and are not apt to be the cause of much suffering, if even your fascinating sister can charm him now, for he was supposed to be in love with another lady when he left America."

"Ah, indeed," replied my companion, raising his eyes to mine with an astonished look of inquiry.

And in a moment it flashed across my mind that what I had said, taken in connection with my very excited manner, was just enough to convey the impression to Mr. Morton that I might have fancied myself the object of Victor's attachment. So with an eager desire to undo this impression, even at the risk of betraying confidence, I said smilingly, or rather trying to smile (for my mood was no happy one) :—

"Yes, but I ought not to be severe upon cousin Vic for recovering, as it was only a boyish fancy for Miss Clifford. You know her romantic history, Mr. Morton, and this must be quite *entre nous*, for she is now engaged to our young pastor, Cecil Clare," and I mentioned the subject rather inadvertently. "It is truly no great wonder that Victor should have loved, even from his boyhood, the Pearl of Elgin ; yet time and distance are often known to change the love of young hearts, though it is not always so."

And feeling my lip begin to quiver now, (instead of curl) I changed the subject, after expressing the hope that we might have the pleasure of meeting his sister in Europe, and turned again into the drawing-room.

The guests had all gone. My sister's brilliant wedding, which for weeks past had been the theme of wondering conversation throughout the neighborhood, was over. Dr. Foster had not yet appeared to carry out his scheme of vengeance, whatever it might be, and the shadow lessened on Ethel's brow as the evening wore away joyously to its close.

At two o'clock, beneath the waning moon, before the open window of my chamber, I sat gazing out upon the lawn, absently, drearily—not with the fear of seeing Dr. Foster, or Gabe with his bloodhound, or the lunatic—they were now far enough from my thoughts—and the bewildering picture of beauty, conjured up by my imagination in the person of Eva Morton, shone out a haunting and tormenting presence, smiling at me through the warm moonlight, gliding amid the trees on the lawn, floating dreamily through the very atmosphere of my room, like a bright, persecuting phantom, mocking me continually.

Clarence Morton had spoken jestingly—then why was I so troubled?

Because Victor had never mentioned Miss Morton either in his letters to me or others, so far as I knew, and my jealous heart was goaded by this silence regarding one whom it now appeared he had known for months.

The attractive feature of European travel, which had been so pleasantly beguiling my fancy of late with an imaginative panorama of beauty and delight, appeared now receding, paling, dissolving, into a dim and cloudy obscurity of distance and gloom; for the scenes through which I had pictured myself as wandering with Victor, gaining new and pleasant ideas from his instructive and interesting remarks, dreaming ever that the glowing skies of Italy would look warmer and brighter, and the glaciers of Switzerland grander, more magnificent, if we gazed at them together, all wore a different aspect since the absorbing idea haunted me that Eva Morton had thrown a spell of enchantment over my wayward cousin, more potent even than his early love for Pearl; and that in foreign lands (though I was in years almost, and feeling quite, a woman) he would still pet and care for me only as " little coz."

Alas ! for the silly child who had dreamed too long. Alas ! for that painful waking !

CHAPTER XXVIII.

DR. FOSTER'S "CRAZY BROTHER!"

A sense of calm security attends
  On happiness—
Fear flies before the beaming face of joy;
And then, when sudden shafts of sorrow fall,
We sink beneath them, hopeless and oppressed,
As those who in the balmy realms of sleep,
The grim gaunt king of terrors sometimes meet,
Who, unrelenting, wakes them but to see
The lamp of life, beneath his icy breath,
Flicker—and then go out!

THE time of our departure had been fixed for a fortnight after the wedding; but as my father proposed remaining abroad a year, and perhaps longer, we found the packing and arrangements consequent upon so protracted an absence could not be accomplished comfortably in that time; and hence the first week in August found us still at Woodburn, so far ready, however, that the 8th was fixed for our departure.

Lulled into a perfect sense of security as the days glided by in undisturbed happiness, the shadow of Rachel's warning had passed gradually from Ethel's brow, leaving it as sunny as ever, and as perfectly the throne of happiness as earthly brows appear.

Mr. Morton had been a frequent visitor at Woodburn since the wedding, until his departure, and before leaving, his mind appeared made up to go abroad with us. I liked him in spite of the disagreeable intelligence he had so innocently and carelessly imparted regarding my cousin; for, without being positively handsome, he was attractive, with a rather peculiar disposition, a noble, manly nature, and not altogether unlike Victor, especially in a certain degree of eccentricity. I was too blue and out of sorts just then, to care much about strangers, even as agreeable as Mr. Morton; and perhaps it may have been my perfect indifference to said individual which made him perversely determine to interest me, and if he succeeded, so far at least that I did not dislike him when we parted, nay, might even have tolerated his society longer had it been necessary, he at all events gained a victory under the circumstances. Yet when he left, there was a degree of relief in not being obliged to entertain him every day, and consequently caring very little whether Mr. Morton went with us to Europe or not, I went on listlessly about my packing and assisting Ethel, but so pale, dispirited and unlike myself, that even Mr. Clifford noticed it, my father felt sure I was sick, and my sister at last one day said abruptly :—

" What is the matter with you, Amy?" Which question I evaded answering, sincerely, by saying,—

"I was not well, and felt a wee bit blue at leaving home and many friends for such a length of time."

How utterly insignificant the half imaginative sorrows, which young people almost nurse into being with sighs and tears, appear, when brought into contrast with a stunning, overwhelming grief, startling and gigantic in its proportions, whose unlooked for appearance causes the puling, sickly, morbid diseases of our fancy to vanish before a grim reality, as different as those terrible tragedies which wring our hearts in the great drama of human life, from the mimic horrors in theatres, over which, carried away by imagination, we often weep.

I was out in the front hall, packing a trunk of books for Ethel,—we were to leave the next morning, and piles of baggage cumbered the gallery. Down on my knees, absorbed in the work before me, I was just in the act of wrapping a superb copy of Shakspeare in soft paper, when there was a rush through the front door, and Archey appeared to my astonished eyes, looking ashy, as negroes frequently do when greatly alarmed—his eyes staring and lips apart, as if attempting to speak, while trembling, evidently in speechless terror. I shall never forget the boy's appearance, and dropping the volume in my hand, I started quickly up, exclaiming,—

"Archey, what is the matter? Tell me, has anything happened to my father? Why don't you speak?" And I shook him, in my alarm, roughly by the shoulder.

"Lord God of massy, Miss Amy, I's been trying to speak and couldn't—for who you tink is cummin up de road to Woodburn, in a carriage, but Dr. Foster's big nigger Gabe and de crazy creeter—it's as true as gospel, for I see'd um myself, and run in (like de debble was arter me) to tell you—fact is, I'd rather see him den de wild man. Oh, Lord, what is dey cummin here for? Dar—don't you see de carriage jis drivin frough the front gate, miss?"

And Archey's ashy face grew a shade paler as I ran towards the front door, filled, as he had been at first, with voiceless horror, for no word escaped me in reply to the terrified negro's communication.

My father was out on the plantation, Mr. Clfford and Ralph in town, Ethel lying down up stairs; and hence I stood alone, waiting breathlessly for a verification of Archey's incredible report regarding the occupants of that approaching carriage, with a cold dread on my heart, while yet I strove to ridicule my own timidity, by asking mentally the question, "What can Gabe and the maniac have to do with us?"

The nearer roll of wheels caused Archey (emboldened by my presence) to steal past me out on to the front gallery, just as the carriage drew up, and there, sure enough, through the open window, I beheld the huge head of Gabe, while opposite to him, and gazing out, not with the wild expression we had seen upon his haggard face, in the woods, when hunted and full of terror he had suffered my sister to hide him in the hollow tree—but with the vacant, subdued look of an idiot, sat the maniac. With the desperation of excessive, though vague and undefined fear, I called out in an excited tone to the driver,

" Who sent you here, and what do you want ?"

The man lifted his hat respectfully, saying,

" I am only a hack driver from town, miss, hired by Dr. Foster to bring the crazy gentleman and his attendant over here from the Glen, which the doctor has sold. This is all I know, miss, he only said,

· " The crazy gentleman will stay at Mr. Percy's until my return," and paid me for the job, so I did as he ordered, but Gabe has a letter for Mr. Percy.

Saying which, he jumped down and opened the door quickly, as a sign for the negro to get out, who immediately did so, and walking up to me with visible trepidation in his manner, and glancing anxiously at Archey, held out a letter addressed to my father, whose absence obliged me, of course, at once, under the circumstances, to open it, without a moment's hesitation.

So, snatching it hastily from the negro (scarcely conscious of what I did), walking back a few steps into the passage, I tore this mysterious missive open, unaware at the time, that a note fell from it on the floor; and then, turning with nervous restlessness to the front door—cold and shuddering with dread in that warm, southern summer air—my eyes ran rapidly over the following :

" UNCLE PERCY—

" I take the liberty of transferring to your care—as it is well such charitable offices should be divided—a connection of yours, who for years you have supposed to be dead. I thought so, too, when the paper containing a notice of his death was forwarded to you ; but he who was left for dead revived after that heavy trance, a hopeless maniac, of whom I took charge, determining to use him as an instrument of vengeance against you, for driving me into exile, and your haughty daughter, for spurning me from her as she did to marry this same Arthur Linton ; and it is hardly necessary to add, that her late scorn towards me, under the assumed name of " Dr. Foster," was not calculated to soften my heart particularly.

My vengeance is complete ! for the existence of Arthur Linton renders Ethel's late marriage with Mr. Clifford unlawful, and I wish her much joy with her two husbands !

" If you doubt the identity of this maniac with your son-in-law, his wife will recognize him, if not by the letters, picture of herself, etc., in his trunk, at least by a peculiar mark tattooed on his right arm, which was there when they were married. Should such proof be unsatisfactory, write to ' Bland & Co., San Francisco Cal.' for a confirmation of my statement regarding Arthur Linton's almost fatal illness, if he was not afterwards placed in an asylum by a relation, and if that same relation did not subsequently remove said Arthur from the asylum, and take him to the Southern states?

"You refused to heed that last letter, warning you and Ethel that there was *madness* in the Linton family, in fact, that his (Arthur's) mother died insane.

"No wonder you failed to recognize me, as flesh, hair-dye, beard, and riches, go far towards disguising one who left you slight, fair-haired, closely shaven, and poor! I am revenged, and now again as completely though differently disguised, beyond your reach.

"BASIL THORN."

With eye-balls burning as if scalded by the dreadful words I read—terrified and overpowered by the inhuman wickedness of this fiendish plot, I stood like one paralyzed, staring vacantly at the carriage, with the letter still clutched in my trembling hand, when Archey, touching me respectfully on the arm, whispered:

"Miss Amy, look dar," and rolled his eyes up as if to some one standing behind me.

When at the same moment, a shriek rang out so startlingly full of heart-rending concentrated agony, I comprehended instantly that the whole truth was known to Ethel, though being unaware of the note which had slipped from my father's letter, I was totally at a loss as to how it had been revealed to her; and writhing under the torture inflicted upon that dear one, almost as if the blow so withering to her happiness had fallen on my own heart, though shocked, bewildered, and feeling for a moment as if my feet were rooted to the spot, I turned round—electrified by my sister's piercing cry—but too late to save her from falling heavily to the floor.

There are moments when—though mind and senses are overpowered by some fearful and unexpected blow—yet where a stringent necessity compels us to act, we appear possessed with supernatural strength to do so, and thus it was tearless and with automaton-like precision, I went through the duties devolving upon me after the never to be forgotten horrors of this frightful scene.

After having Ethel carried in that deadly swoon by Mammy and Lucy to her own chamber, and leaving her in their care for a few moments, I dispatched a messenger for my father, and then telling Archey and Gabe to remove the crazy gentleman to the library, where they must remain to guard him for the present, I dismissed the hackman without a word of explanation, for the awful truth must soon be known to all, and hence any effort at deception, or even glossing the matter over to this stranger, would have proved unavailing. After he had left, I returned to my sister, who (spite of unceasing efforts to arouse her) still remained cold and rigid in that death-like swoon.

As I passed through the hall on my way up stairs, the note, dropped from Basil Thorn's letter to my father—which Ethel, coming quietly down stairs, had picked up, and (seeing it addressed to herself) read, unobserved by me, as I stood oppressed with wretchedness in the front door—was again lying on the floor, having fallen from her hand when that wild shriek smote my ear—thus then it was the truth so appalling had been revealed to the victim of an unrelenting hate, which knew no mercy.

Intensely cruel in their sarcastic malignity, those few withering words were worthy of the fierce black heart from which they sprung. The note ran thus:

"ETHEL LINTON:

"I leave you a memento in the person of your first love—a charming addition, the madman, Arthur Linton, will make to your *cortège* through Europe—serving to remind you of the vengeance of   BASIL THORN."

My beautiful, beloved sister! how wretched must be her waking from that state of insensibility! My father, too, how would he bear this overwhelming sorrow hurled down upon us so unexpectedly—a crushing avalanche of grief?

And Mr. Clifford! who had strength and courage enough to meet him as the bearer of such frightful news.

My heart appeared to stand still with wretchedness and dismay, as one after another those torturing questions rushed through my mind, and looking back since to that time of helpless suspense—when alone, with the servants, I watched Ethel's tardy restoration to life—her consciousness of the reality, thank God! for that fearful present was gone—overpowered by a sense of misery and terror beyond description,—I wonder and must ever wonder why it was I did not either swoon too, or go mad.

13

CHAPTER XXIX.

Oft the dizzy heights of pleasure
Overlook some gulf of woe,
Dark and wild ; yet who can measure
Deeps thus hidden far below?

I CANNOT bear to live again, even in memory, the
wretchedness of that dreary, hopeless time, (for hopeless
it did appear) and the impress of suffering then left upon
our hearts—even those that were young and buoyant—has
never been entirely effaced by after years of happiness.

Though adorned by wreathing vines and flowers, and
brightened by the sunlight, yet do scars left there by burning lava remain upon the mountain side—and so oftentimes does scathing and unexpected sorrow leave scars upon
the human heart! My father, whose fine constitution and
cheerful temperament had kept him so free from that
despondency and want of interest in life which not unfrequently contributes towards making people old before their
time, was so crushed by this one fell blow, that a few hours
effected the work years had failed to accomplish. Grief
could not affect his hair, for it had been white almost from

his youth, or perhaps if those thick locks had chanced to be yet unbleached, it would not have planted so many, and such deep furrows upon that beloved face.

And Mr. Clifford—it devolved upon me to break the frightful truth to him, for so completely was my father stricken down that for many hours he sat speechless with his head bowed down upon his hands, silently motioning off any one who approached for the purpose of trying to rouse him.

Oh! what a fearful plunge it was for Lenox Clifford—from the sunny heights of perfect human happiness into the very blackest, deepest gulf of despair! Language fails even to convey a faint idea of such misery, therefore will I let the dark cloud which then settled upon Woodburn, cover as a veil the wretchedness too sacred and too deep for description.

Every effort was made by my Uncle Dunbar and other kind friends to disprove that Arthur Linton and the maniac (heretofore supposed to be Dr. Foster's brother) were one and the same person, for they still cherished a lingering hope that Basil Thorn invented this story and used the poor lunatic as an instrument for his vengeance, when in reality Arthur was dead as we had supposed years ago. But alas! every effort, far from disproving, went on to prove the certainty that this fiendish scheme was based on a reality, and not risked as a venture of reckless malice. Ethel's picture and letters were in the trunk—true it is, they might have been placed there; the peculiar figures were found tattooed upon his arm—this might have been done to be sure in imitation of those alluded to by Basil Thorn; but when the poor maniac was shorn of his long, uncombed hair, his matted beard shaved off, and genteel clothes substituted for the unsightly rags he wore, the striking likeness he bore to a miniature of Arthur taken just after my sister's marriage, could not be disputed, for though gaunt, haggard and changed in many respects, the features were there, though so altered in expression—and then every answered letter from California (and there were many written to various parties there) went further and further to confirm the dreadful truth whose certainty we had felt, yet tried to discredit, from the first.

Every effort to discover the hiding place of Basil Thorn proved utterly ineffectual; he had vanished like an evil spirit, leaving no trace, and I was half inclined to believe with Archey—who proved the only one (save his unfortunate sister Rachel) fully appreciating that dark man's capacity for wickedness—that he had vanished in a sulphurous cloud after accomplishing his diabolical purpose.

Arrangements were made immediately for sending poor Arthur to a most excellent asylum in the State, where we were quite sure everything would be done possible to alleviate the weary monotony of his negative existence.

His departure from Woodburn was a great relief to us all, removing as it were from our midst the immediate presence of a reality terrible enough when contemplated at a distance.

Ethel's deep swoon was succeeded by a brain fever so severe that for a month her life trembled on such uncertain tenure, we feared even each delicate change from sleeping to waking, or waking to sleeping, might put out the vital spark. While fearing for her life, however, we could scarcely help feeling grateful that delirium rendered her oblivious, for a time at least, of the blighting misery which had fallen so heavily upon her heart. Twice we thought she was passing away, and then I felt it would be better to think of my precious sister as dwelling among the angels than watch her waking to the realization of a torturing weight of agony, to be borne on perhaps through a long and dreary term of years.

God orders all things in wisdom, however, and he willed that in this terrible struggle between life and death Ethel's fine constitution should gain the victory, and on waking from a long deep sleep (which was pronounced by her physician as the crisis of the disease) we knew at once from the expression of her eyes, that reason had resumed its sway—and so perfectly did she remember the shock received from that fearful note as Mr. Clifford bent over her, waiting in breathless anxiety for her first words, she whispered :

"It is the will of God, dearest; we must submit. We did not mean to do wrong, and perhaps may yet be blessed.

You will go to England without me, Lenox. Oh! why did I not heed the warning of Rachel's letter?"

And then we saw with thankful hearts a tear roll down her wan, emaciated cheek, for it came as a harbinger of relief to that tense and long pent-up sorrow. My father had, without the least difficulty, procured a divorce for Ethel from Arthur Linton; but when she was told of it, and urged to go through with another marriage ceremony, that their union, in the eyes of the law at least, might be valid, my sister gently, but firmly, refused, saying she could never live with Mr. Clifford as a wife during the life of Arthur Linton, and therefore to go through the marriage form again would only be useless and unnecessary torture. So at her earnest request, Mr. Clifford went to England, leaving his mourning wife—for we could not help feeling she was as much so indeed as if Arthur had been dead—to our care.

Ralph went with him to remain abroad for the completion of his education, and it has ever been a source of pleasure to me that his bright young spirit was saved the misery of dwelling longer under the shadow of that dark cloud.

Mr. Clifford's last words to my father were—

"You will write constantly of the precious treasure I leave with you, trusting (even in the midst of so much wretchedness) to the mercy and goodness of God, and if there should come a time when you can summon me to return, do not delay."

"I will not, Clifford," almost sobbed my father; "and the Almighty, in whom we trust, grant the summons may come to you at no very distant period."

Oh! the tedious misery of that long, weary, wretched time. Years, even of ordinary common-place comfort and happiness, would have appeared shorter than the six months of that dreary fall and winter, when our darling Ethel lay stricken and pining, the very shadow of her former self. For after Lenox Clifford's departure, she became so ill again we thought she must die, and when I watched her, so pure, so good, so beautiful, lingering so long (as it were) on the very threshold of the portals of death—yet patient and uncomplaining beneath that heavy burden of suffering and unhappiness—my rebellious heart dared to murmur at the will of heaven, arguing against the wisdom of that decree, which, in calling Rachel Thorn away summarily and without suffering, had left the innocent victim of her perfidy to linger on in torture.

For, though Rachel did repent, yet was it too late to save Ethel. Being then so much under the influence of her wicked brother she feared to betray his inhuman malice at first encouraged for the furtherance of her own schemes. Had she at once (upon discovering in the pretended Dr. Foster her long absent brother) revealed the fact to us instead of leaguing with him, or even when Arthur Linton's existence was revealed, had she possessed courage enough to come at once and tell the whole either to Ethel or my father, she could, nay would, have been protected from Basil's fury—and then, oh! what wretchedness had been saved us all.

Thus it is ever we see "through a glass, darkly;" but when that cloudy time had past, long afterwards, when I knew retribution had overtaken the guilty, and joy was dawning once more upon those who had bowed in humble submission to kiss the rod of affliction, then I too felt humbled, and, shuddering at those rebellious thoughts of long ago, sought forgiveness for my presumptuous repining. Justice and mercy from above go hand in hand—for " whom the Lord loveth He chasteneth " to prove their trust in Him, while those who have sinned, and sincerely repent them of the evil—yet are not strong enough to endure either great suffering or temptation—He calls away in mercy, ere the glorious light of repentance, full and perfect enough now to save that trembling soul, be dimmed or quenched perhaps by grief and pain—as it might have been with poor Rachel Thorn. God doeth all things well and in wisdom.

Pearl was so devoted to Ethel that almost every day found her at Woodburn, tending, with unceasing devotion, the pale, fragile, angelic. looking being whom she ever persisted, with refined tenderness, in calling "mother."

All that human love could suggest was done to win my

sister back to live as one of us again—and all that tender hearts can devise we resorted to, as gentle means of interesting her in the every day events of life ; but alas ! in vain. She listened when we read or sang, took the flowers listlessly we brought, and was very grateful; for we read the affection and gratitude of Ethel's heart in her large, expressive eyes, whose light was deeper and more heavenly since she had suffered so severely; but never once, from the reading of Basil's wicked note, and during all that dreary autumn and winter, did even the shadow of a smile flit over those pallid lips, and neither by word or action did she indicate the slightest interest in any earthly thing save by expressions of love for us, and eager watching for Mr. Clifford's letters.

Aunt Kate was ever faithful, and I often saw the tears roll down her furrowed cheeks when gazing upon our patient sufferer, whose eyes which erst had looked up to the old lady so full of affection and mirth, were now so veiled by sadness that not a ray of their old light shone forth.

One day when I was straightening the perverse cap, which through storm or shine, joy or sorrow, still retained the same obstinate inclination for crawling to the back of our dear Aunty's head, she actually sobbed out—

"Oh, Amy, how that reminds me of the dear, winsome darling who now lies there pale and quiet. She was so fond of fixing my crooked cap, and joking me about it. I wonder if we shall ever see her smile again?"

Uncle Dunbar had ceased almost to quiz or joke, and even the presence of itinerant ailing deacons, and bilious schoolmasters, with their mush, gruel and black tea, at Elgin, failed to arouse his hospitable interest as formerly; and I don't believe he pulled off his wig in frolic for months.

Aunt Kate had written Victor a full account of Ethel's terrible trial, and his letters to me afterwards were full of affectionate sympathy for us all—but never once did he mention the name of Eva Morton.

And so the months wore drearily away at Elgin and at Woodburn. I saw the crisp leaves of autumn drift through the open window over Ethel's couch, where she rested, gazing listlessly out on the warm, hazy splendor of an Indian summer sunset—that very same window where she had stood a vision of beauty crowned with the July moonlight—and there again I stood watching the cold, dismal rain and sleet of January pelting against the glass, and wondering if there was as little of joy in the darkly veiled future as my gloomy fancy pictured of sunshine hidden beneath those dense and leaden clouds?

CHAPTER XXX.

THE LIGHT BREAKS.

He who orders storm and tempest,
Also sweeps the clouds away,
And has willed the deepest darkness,
Just before the dawn of day!

SIX months had gone by since Mr. Clifford left Woodburn, when one morning early in March, while sorting out the letters Archey had just brought from town, I felt my heart beat faster as my eye fell upon one bearing the postmark of the town in whose asylum poor Arthur had been placed, and where (though known to be in a hopeless state of idiotic imbecility) everything that humanity could suggest was done for his comfort and relief.

For, not trusting to those who kept the asylum, a physician was employed by my father to see him at intervals; and once a month, faithful Michael McAlpine went over to see that he was properly attended and not allowed to suffer for bodily comforts. Therefore, as Michael had but recently returned, this letter startled me, and placing it at once in my father's hand, I stood watching eagerly while he opened it. No sooner had his eye glanced rapidly over the contents, than ejaculating fervently—

"Thank God," he handed me the letter, and saying—

"Poor Linton is gone, our suffering Ethel may yet live to be happy," sat down at his desk, and began writing hurriedly.

Then, with an overpowering sense of gratitude and penitence for my rebellious moods, I dropped down on my knees beside the old arm-chair from which my father had just risen, and poured out a heart-felt prayer of thanksgiving to Him who looked with pity upon beings so innocent in their erring—doing all that was possible to atone for the wrong, by childlike submission to his heavenly decree—and now, with the ocean between them, were waiting patiently until such time as God should see fit to remove the burden of this mighty sorrow.

And now that time had come!

My father's letter to Mr. Clifford—the glad missive summoning him to return—was written, and on its way to the mail, when we went up stairs, eager to break the glad tidings to Ethel, and yet fearing the effect, even of such pleasurable excitement, upon her delicate frame.

When we entered, Pearl was standing at the head of my sister's lounge, passing the comb gently through her long bright hair, which, swept entirely back from her white forehead, rolled over the pillow in great shining masses, and fell with its heavy length upon the carpet. Pearl motioned us to be silent—for Ethel's eyes were closed, and she appeared sleeping—so we sat down quietly to await her waking."

It was a most lovely picture! the contrast of their beauty, at all times striking, was now particularly so, for the glow of health upon the creole girl's cheek caused the marble pallor of her companion's to look still more unearthly in its fairness—while the purple blackness of Pearl's tresses seemed intensified by the rippling mass of glistening hair she was combing. Presently, the first shadow of a smile we had seen there for months, hovered over the sleeper's lips, and then, as those long lashes were slowly lifted (unaware of our presence), she murmured—

"Oh, Pearl, I have had such a sweet dream! I thought your father was here, and that we were all so happy—what a pity I awoke just now, it is very sad to arouse from blessed dreams to a wretched reality:"

Then, turning her head wearily on the pillow, she saw us, and observing my father's altered expression, said quickly—

"What has happened, father, to make you look almost happy?"

"I am happy, my darling child, because your dream, let us trust, will be ere long realized, for the letter bidding Clifford return is on its way to England."

She knew all now, and as tears unbound a tense grief, she buried her face in the pillow. Oh, what a relief that fit of weeping was to one whose sensitive nature felt, as it were, the burden of a great sin lifted from her soul! At last, becoming calm, she said,

"Father, how long will it be before Lenox can arrive? I shall so pine now to have our marriage made lawful in the sight of God."

And a mysterious, sacred chord then thrilled within her heart, for the first tinge of color we had seen upon my sister's face, since that fatal evening, when the shaft of Basil Thorn's horrible vengeance struck her low, now suffused it, mounting even to her brow, creating a glow beneath its perfect pallor, like a faint blush of pink, a dim glow after sunset shining through the transparent whiteness of pearly clouds. We all observed this flush, and our hearts thrilled responsive to hers, for we knew the tender secret of her bosom, and my father replied,

"He can be here in six weeks, by returning in the vessel which will probably take over my letter—at all events, we know he will not lose a moment—so my stricken bird must cheer up, and try to look more like her own bright self by the time our exile returns," and kissing her tenderly, he left the room.

"What do you think is our last news from Victor?" said my uncle Dunbar, while shaking hands with me that afternoon, as he came up the front door steps where I happened to be standing, "you can't guess."

"Nothing bad, I trust, uncle—is he going to be married?"

And the calmness with which these words were uttered, astonished the foolish dreamer, who was at last forced to realize the certainty of a final waking from these cherished delusions, which, though not entirely unexpected, was hard to bear.

"Ha! you have guessed well, or were you in his confidence? He never even mentioned Miss Morton's name in writing to me, until now—the scamp—when he goes on abruptly to say, they have been traveling together for months, that she is the most fascinating creature in the world, and, in short, begs my consent to their immediate marriage—

"But bless me, Amy, how pale you look—is Ethel worse, or have you had any bad tidings from Clifford? I was so busy thinking and talking about Victor, as to forget for a moment how much you all have to trouble you here—shame on me for it," and he patted me kindly on the cheek.

With an effort to be calm, I told him of Arthur's death, at the same time opening the library door where I knew he would find my father, and I longed to be alone, for my heart was full of contending emotions. Rejoicing most fervently with my beloved sister, that the dark cloud was sweeping away from her existence, while the certainty of an event, whose anticipation even, had caused the rosy flush of hope to fade from my romantic future, fell upon my heart sadly, coldly, like snow upon violets, covering them up with a dreary white shroud—and yet the violets do not die, for when warm winds blow again, melting that chilly veil, lo! those sweet spring flowers uplift once more their modest blue eyes, joyously to meet the returning sunlight.

A delicate structure had it been, that enchanted palace of my girlish dreams—such juvenile efforts at aerial architecture are apt to topple over for want of a firm foundation, and those who indulge a taste for building them, resemble children who blow out shining bubbles in the sunshine, adding breath after breath to make them larger and brighter, 'till suddenly the glittering wonders burst and leave them pining over the loss of things so fair and so unreal.

After leaving my uncle in the library, I seized my hat and mantle, and followed by Bang, ran off to the garden.

How dreary the summer-house looked to me now! with dead leaves still drifting in through the gnarled vines by a stormy March wind—no jasmine flowers were there, no vestiges of summer glory—for the trees were just beginning to bud, and the green of the clinging, sombre ivy had a mournful look in that chilly air, beneath that leaden sky —where grey clouds looked stationary, as if gathered there to imprison the blue beyond, and as if they never intended to pass away.

I was silly enough to wish the dog could understand and appreciate my sorrow, and as he looked up wistfully into my face—whose expression just about that time I feel convinced, must have been exceedingly forlorn—I could not help whispering to him—

"Oh, Bang, if you only knew!—"

But dogs are not romantic, and my shaggy companion, with a most unfeeling, reckless indifference of the fatal consequences which might occur to me from Miss Eva Morton's becoming Mrs. Victor Dunbar, began to jump up and bark violently at a dignified grey grimalkin who came gliding stealthily down the side of the summer-house on her return from an unsuccessful expedition in search of certain little brown wrens, which were in the habit of haunting that same rustic bower, summer and winter, as constantly as myself, evidently heeding my presence as little as if I, too, were a wren.

These wee things were very wide awake, however, and though pussy often laid in wait, meditating the destruction of the feathered innocents, I never saw any feathers flying about as marks of her destructive abilities, and moreover, in her descent, she always looked lank and hungry, particularly so, I thought, that dismal March afternoon, and I was glad of it, for the amiability of her mood was not improved thereby, and as Mr. Bang jumped up at her when fairly within his reach, she gave his sleek nose such a succession of sharp scratches, that turning from her ingloriously vanquished and howling most woefully, he rushed to me for comfort.

But I was in no humor for comforting even a dog, and pushing him off roughly, with a kind of bitter satisfaction, that a fine large male dog should be thus signally defeated by a common sized female cat, and feeling rather a contempt for said specimen of the canine race under the circumstances, I exclaimed,

" Begone, ungrateful beast, you barked at the cat when told of my sorrows, and she scratched your unsympathizing nose—I am glad of it—Bang, you are a coward !" and struck with the absurdity of the scene, I startled the brown wrens by bursting into a queer fit of hysterical laughter, for the old spirit of defiant merriment was strong in me yet, and though of late so overwhelmed by gloom, it would occasionally struggle to the surface, mocking my sad thoughts like some gay frolicking child, shouting for joy among a company of mourners.

CHAPTER XXXI.

A BLIGHTED MAY-FLOWER.

As a spring snow-flake, frail and fair,
Melting away upon the air,
A waif of heaven—unstained by earth,
Lost in the moment of its birth !

On the 1st of May an infant's feeble wail was heard at
Woodburn—plaintive and trembling it died away; and
then, by that very same window where Ethel had stood
before me in her bridal attire, while a shade of coming
sorrow hovered over her in the moonlight, where the
crisped leaves of autumn had whirled in over the couch on
which she lay mourning and suffering, and where I had
watched the heavy, dismal clouds of January like a black
mask upon the smiling face of heaven—even as the shadow
of that great sorrow then obscuring the light of joy within.
our home—there on the same spot I stood again, weeping
over the little white-robed form of Ethel's dead baby.

Pale, dewy rosebuds and lilies of the valley were clasped
in its tiny hands and grouped gracefully upon the breast
and around the cold, delicately beautiful face of that silent

little one whose sinless spirit had passed away without a taint of earth. I could scarcely help feeling grateful, even while mourning, that God had claimed my sister's lovely boy as one of his own bright angels, for though Mr. Clifford had returned a week before its birth, when their marriage was made lawful the very next day in presence of all at Woodburn and Elgin, yet by a censorious world, in after years, a slur perhaps might have been cast upon the birth of that fair child, and hence 'twas better thus.

Touching and beautiful was the tender love with which both Ethel and Lenox Clifford clung to and yearned over that little waif of heaven. Grateful that the cloud of late lowering over their path, darkening both past and future, had been swept away, leaving them united and blest, yet humbly, hopefully sorrowing over the grave of their child, whose eternity of delight in a far off celestial home could never be dimmed by the shadow which might have darkened its earthly existence.

Down in the Woodburn cemetery, overshadowed by a clump of myrtles, there is a little grave ever guarded by a snow-white dove of finest marble, and covered in spring time with sweet violets and daisies—meet emblem of an ephemeral May-day existence!

Months of sorrow and anxiety had changed Mr. Clifford, for there were lines on his brow and a few white hairs shining amid those waving brown locks when he returned from England; but as my sister began to recover, when her tears had ceased to flow in their first bitterness over that sunny little mound among the myrtles, those care-worn lines lessened and the gray hairs did not increase.

Utterly vain still proved every attempt to trace out the hiding place of Basil Thorn, though no possible means were left untried by which he might be arrested and brought to justice—for even apart from my father's power to convict him for forgery, the feeling excited universally by his base and malignant vengeance against Ethel was so strong, that many persons thought if discovered he would be hung up by a mob.

I felt perfectly satisfied that if not found and punished then, he would never escape a just retribution even in this world, for " vengeance is mine," saith the Lord.   What a triumphant leer shone in Archey's eye when (upon meeting me one day after the terrible *dénouement* which so speedily followed his panic of terror when I was packing books in the hall) he said—

" Golly, Miss Amy, but did'nt I tell you dat Dr. Foster was a real son ob de debble ?   Fore de Lord, but I'd like mightily to have a chance of hashin his ugly carcass up in master's cotton-gin," and the negro grinned with ·almost savage ferocity.

Gabe had been sent back to the Glen where he belonged, and which, instead of being sold as we had heard, was simply claimed by the person from whom the pretended Dr

Foster had bought it, for he had made but one very small payment on the property, after enjoying the benefit of an unusually large crop, when suddenly declaring himself unable to pay for the place, he gave it up, having accomplished the dark purpose which brought him there, and flitted away amid the ghastly gloom of his own wickedness, even as "Hans of Iceland, the demon of the North," is described by Victor Hugo, as vanishing instantaneously, mysteriously, his beastly claws still recking with the blood of human victims, down a perpendicular height, or within the unexplored windings of a mountain cave.

Ralph was charmed with his college life in England, and now his cheerful letters were full of anticipated delight at the prospect of seeing us ere very long at Clifton, the beautiful place to which Mr. Clifford was so anxious Ethel should accompany him, and over which Ralph was in raptures, having visited it before going to college.

My sister's health, however, continued so delicate during several months as to unfit her for undergoing the fatigues of a long journey, which, therefore, had to be postponed until after Pearl's marriage, now fixed for September—and the anticipation of our presence upon that occasion was a great source of happiness to all at Elgin, especially the lovely bride elect.

I must not forget to mention here that Clarence Morton concluded not to go abroad, in spite of the very great desire he had expressed to meet his father and sister there, and the delight he would have in going with Mr. Clifford. Yet was Mr. Clifford suffered to depart without his friend Clarence, who, oddly enough, when the time was again mentioned for our departure, wrote to my brother-in-law that he would join us in New York.

Mr. Morton's letters frequently alluded to his sister's happy engagement to Victor Dunbar, as I knew from hearing Mr. Clifford read them aloud to Ethel, but she never mentioned the subject to me, for with a woman's clever acuteness, having read long ago the secret of my girlish heart, she respected it too much to chafe, either by serious reference or careless joke, the sensitive wound, which, though generally healed by time in juvenile hearts, is yet very apt to leave a scar, as gashes in the bark of a tender sapling, though failing to destroy its life, or even strength, for full of vigorous sap, it grows up to be a tree of the forest—yet in after years, upon the matured trunk, may be found corrugated scars left by early wounds upon the delicate rind.

And so the days and weeks glided by, and so the summer wore away at Woodburn.

The starry myrtle blossoms had fallen on the grave of little Percy Clifford, where the sod was greener and the tufts of violets and daisies more luxuriant than elsewhere, because it was so carefully and constantly tended, and within that clump of myrtles from day to day, all summer long, there sang a mocking bird, whose notes were so thrillingly sweet, especially when the moon was full and bright, that my sister loved to linger there drinking in the musical tones of its wondrous melody—for she said they were like messages of peace and love from the spirit of her angel child.

CHAPTER XXXII.

HOW THE PEARL OF ELGIN SHONE IN AN AUTUMN SUNSET.

PEARL CLIFFORD and Cecil Clare were married in the elegant little Gothic neighborhood church, near Elgin, the ceremony being performed by the Bishop just at sunset on the 10th of September. Aunt Kate insisted on having a grand entertainment, and Pearl was determined to be married at the altar—so, as night church weddings are not convenient in the country, they compromised—the hour of sunset being chosen for their nuptials, at which only relations and intimate friends were present, and a large party invited to Elgin later, when the yard was illuminated and all festive preparations carried out on a grand scale.

The golden glow of declining day stealing in through violet and crimson glass with that mellow richness so peculiar to autumn sunsets in southern climes—the venerable appearance of the Bishop, together with the youth of the lovers and extreme loveliness of the bride—all contributed

14

towards rendering that wedding the most touchingly beautiful and at the same time holy sight I ever witnessed.

Madam Armond had sent Pearl's dress, veil, etc., as bridal gifts from Paris, and they assuredly did no little credit to her taste, being composed of the most delicate lace imaginable, and over the veil, in place of flowers, was clasped a bandeau of rare and costly pearls, so suitable to her name, and forming such a charming contrast to the glowing charms of her Creole beauty.

So thrilling was the effect of that scene on the spectators that when they knelt for the benediction there was scarcely a dry eye amid the company there assembled. It was rather remarkable that the gayest, nay, I might almost say the wildest, girl in our neighborhood—for she undoubtedly was so until after the fall from her horse two years before —should marry Cecil Clare, and this very fact, together with the gentle, restraining influence his love and blessed, cheerful teaching of religion had exerted over her, added to the singularly striking and picturesque splendor of that solemn ceremony.

Mr. Clifford was visibly affected when called upon to give away the lovely daughter he had so lately found, and yet it was not a dismal wedding where people drew down their faces as if called upon to look as much as possible like chief mourners at a funeral. Nothing of the kind. So much beauty and holiness combined to thrill a tender chord in feeling natures, causing almost a pleasant emotion of sadness, one which we enjoy, and love to remember in after times.

I must not forget to mention here a most touching scene occurring just after the ceremony. Michael McAlpine had been sent down to New Orleans for his father, as Pearl was most anxious to see the old man and have him present at her wedding, which suggestion was warmly entered into by all at Elgin and Woodburn. He came, and being present with his son in church, was the first (after her immediate family) whom Mr. Clifford led up to congratulate the lovely bride.

With humble gallantry, and true feeling, the honest old Scotchman dropped down on one knee, and raising the little white hand, whereon now shone Pearl's wedding-ring, to his lips, said earnestly—

" God bless my bonnie bairn," and then to Mr. Clifford, as he—McAlpine—rose and turned away: " I always knew she was a born leddy, sir—aye, just as well when I picked her up out of the tumbling brine and called her ' my pearl,' as at this moment, when my old eyes are blessed with a sight of the lassie then so wee, and now grown up to look as grand and bonnie as a queen. Nae wonder ye look sa happy and proud, sir, wi' sic a winsome wife and daughter."

My father being anxious to leave Woodburn in charge of a trustworthy person—after old McAlpine came— Mr. Clifford suggested him as most suitable, and with the consent of the Dunbars it was arranged that Michael should remain there with his father until our return from Europe.

The wedding party at Elgin was a decided success, and Aunt Kate proportionably exultant. My sister looked almost like herself again while there—for they left before the late guests arrived—the memory of that fair little sleeper beneath the myrtles, being too fresh for those grieved though grateful hearts to participate yet in scenes of mirth.

A sort of proud resolution had taken possession of me since the fall of my air-castles which did more towards transforming the child into the woman than years of happy experience could have effected, and when the subject of Victor's engagement to the fascinating Miss Morton was freely discussed at Pearl's wedding, I listened and smiled, and even joined in these conversations; yet my heart was heavy. For while these sweet young dreams faded away, I clung to them as they receded, striving sometimes to forget the reality, and revel once more in the ideal; but fancies of impossible happiness are rather tantalizing than consoling, and as time wore on, ceasing to encourage them, I tried to feel old, and look on my ruined hopes as the result of childish folly.

Aunt Kate was in her element amid wedding festivities on that 10th of September, and just as excited, or perhaps a wee bit fussy—as the dearest, best Scotch spinster might naturally be upon such an occasion. I never saw her look so well, for in arranging her cap, which was a present from my sister, especially contrived for that occasion, of soft lace and lilac ribbon—Ethel protesting against the queer propensity aunty's caps had generally evinced for crawling to the remote part of her head—laughingly told the old lady she would make it impossible for this one to follow the example of its predecessors, by pinning it on, and then begged as a favor that she would not pull at it, for if so, instead of coming gradually from the back of her head to the proper position for dignified caps, as usually followed after sundry vigorous jerks, that this one would probably land on the end of her nose, before the end of the evening. Aunty Kate promised well, but towards supper time, I saw the new head-gear receive several alarming tugs, and but for Ethel's cute plan of securing it with hair pins, the soft gray curls she had taken such pains to arrange to the best advantage, would inevitably have disappeared entirely under their overtopping of lace and ribbon.

Uncle Dunbar was well pleased also as the dispenser of hospitality to such a " goodly companie," though Pearl said jokingly that papa was miserable, not at the prospect of losing her, but because there were not half a dozen sickly parsons in the house, with their gruel, broth, and black tea, instead of a healthy set, capable of digesting salads and ice-cream ; he laughed, but not unmindful of the one bilious stoop-shouldered individual who happened to be so-

journing there at present—just before supper, in passing
me, as he hurried out of the drawing-room—kind, unselfish Uncle Dunbar ! with that quizzical wink so peculiar to
him, said—

"I'm going into the kitchen to order some mush and a
cup of tea for poor Ogden—a fine wedding feast ! suppose
we join him, Amy—he's gone up stairs—can't stand late
suppers—a good fellow, but unfortunately with a bad di-
gestion, and everybody, you see, to-night, forgets he is
dieting, except myself—and away went that most hospitable of hosts, who could never resist a joke, even at the ex-
pense of his own hobbies.   The next day Cecil Clare and
his bride were to go home, the parsonage having been
beautifully fitted up for the reception of its new mistress—
and being now as dainty a cottage as could well be imagined.
 I think Aunt Kate would have grieved more at the
prospect of Pearl's bright presence passing away from the
home of her childhood—even though it was to linger yet
so near—but for the twitter of excitement she was thrown
into by Victor's determination to return with his charming
Eva to Elgin.   They were to be married at Paris towards
the end of September, return to Elgin for the winter, and
probably revisit Europe the following spring—so, as we
would hardly arrive in England before their departure
from France for America, there appeared but little chance
of our meeting at present—which was a great relief to
me !   What a change ! — to feel relieved at the pros-

pect of not meeting one who had been so much in my thoughts, and from whom the idea of a prolonged absence had, but a short time before, made all things appear so dreary! Far better thus, than feel the stinging mortification of hearing Victor call me " little coz" in the presence of his beautiful wife, anything but that now—and, moreover, it was scarcely possible for me to love Eva yet, as I should wish to love his wife. Women's hearts are not generally as pliable as wax or potter's clay, to be moulded into shapes to suit occasions—whatever hypochondriac, morose old bachelors may say to the contrary, and mine was less yielding than most hearts to circumstances—if pulled one way against its inclinations, being most perversely inclined to go in an opposite direction. Perhaps the time might come, when some potent influence was destined, with subtile power, superior to its own, to conquer the perversity of my wilful nature—but that time was not yet. For though delighting in the happiness of my sister and Pearl—spite of all my efforts to banish it—there rested, like a deadly shadow of the Upas tree within my heart, the bitter, regretful thought, that such bliss was not, and never could be mine! How paltry and absurd such fancies appear as we look back upon them through a long vista of years, whose experience has taught us that the passion, *par excellence*, of one's life, is not generally the first.

CHAPTER XXXIII.

THE PEDDLER.

A FEW days after the wedding, as I sat in my room, making preparations for departure, Lucy came rushing in, greatly excited and evidently pleased, for with a broad grin, she exclaimed—

"Oh, Miss Amy, dar's a peddler down stairs in de back porch, wid a great pack of such pretty things, do, please mam, come down and look at dem, won't you? Dar's sich a monstus splendid calico, wid red spots all over it, I'd like if you'll be so kind as to get it for me—do, please, Miss, for I'll take sich good care of your birds, and Bang, too, till you comes back."

She was a faithful creature, and this appealing touch about my pets was irresistible, so I went down, and there, sure enough, was the peddler, with his pack of wonders displayed to the admiring gaze of a whole host of darkeys, big and little, who stood with staring eyes and open mouths, as wonder-stricken as Aladdin when he beheld the glories of the magician's cavern, or as children might be dazzled and amazed by the glittering splendors of an eastern bazaar, for this simple-hearted people, delighting in bright colors, never tire of beholding the varied stores of these itinerant merchants.

The peddler was a fat man, with stooping shoulders, green goggles, and gray hair, which, in its bushy, unnatural appearance, rather resembled a wig. I purchased the dress so coveted by Lucy, and while selecting a few articles for the other house-servants, found myself singularly and disagreeably impressed by the man's manner and appearance, and once, as he looked up quickly at Ethel, who came running out to buy a skein of sewing silk, a queer fancy came over me, that, spite of the gray bush on his head and those disguising goggles, there was a resemblance between this strolling vagrant and the pretended Dr. Foster, though, of course, I did not venture a hint even regarding this idea of mine to my sister, who could never hear the name of that black-hearted man. without great emotion, and expressed herself, as yet, in dread of some further demonstration of his unsated vengeance, should he chance to hear of Arthur's death. Ethel went off, however, without bestowing more than a glance on the stranger, at which I felt relieved, and while watching the peddler as he waddled off, bent down beneath the load of his pack, I ridiculed myself mentally for the absurdity of such thoughts; yet at the same time feeling oppressed and disturbed, as after the receipt of Rachel's letter, and—without any definite cause, save the shadowy likeness I had conjured up between this gray-haired vender of dry goods and Dr. Foster,—I found the queer figure receding down the front avenue, connected in my mind with Basil Thorn, the wild man, Gabe, and the blood-hound, and full of dreary thoughts, turned into the house, nervous and anxious, I scarcely knew why, wishing Mr. Clifford were at home, and wondering if the peddler would meet him on his way from the parsonage. Just as I crossed the threshold of the door, Archey shuffled round the corner of the house, saying—

"Wait a minit, please, miss, I'se got some ting to tell you."

"Say on quickly, then, for I am weary and want to go in," I replied, remembering that Archey was not among the dusky group gathered around the peddler, and wondering what he could have been about to miss such an interesting exhibition.

"You see dat crceter wid a pack, miss, what's jis gone out ob de gate—well! Gabe told me dis mornin dat he was down to de Glen yesterday, and who you tink Gabe says he is?"

And Archey, rolling his eyes around furtively from right to left, and as if in dread of being overheard, putting his hands up cautiously to his mouth, as he stepped up on the gallery, whispered—

"Dr. Foster."

I started, and felt myself paling at the mention of that detested name, yet instantly chiding myself for credulity, said quickly,

"What could put such a thing into Gabe's head?"

"Why, miss, kase he's always been so skeered for de doctor, he says he'd know him in Jericho, spite of his white wig and green spectacles. Gabe tells me he's sartin dat son of Satin is come back here, jis to see how much mischief he hab done, and (if he gets a far chance) to do more, but maybe he won't go waddling round here long, for Gabe hates him powerful, and Gosh! but I pities de peddler if dat nigger gets alone wid him in de woods, for you see, Gabe looked savage as a wild-cat when he says, ' I never lets on as how I knows him, but maybe it will be so dat I can remind him of our 'quantance 'fore he goes.' Je-ru-sa-lem! but wouldn't I like to be squattin down in a old holler stump, and see what dat great black giant would do to de stranger-man, if dey happens to meet in a lonesome place—for wedder he is de doctor or not, its all one, for Gabe tink so, he do—and folks dat peddles tings round can't spec, miss, you know, to keep niggers in such a skeer as fine doctors dat owns plantations!"

"You and Gabe are crazy, and if you don't stop talking so absurdly, should anything happen to the poor old peddler, you'll both be hung, so take my advice and hold your foolish tongues; and Archey, this evening, at six o'clock, saddle Wizard, and prepare to attend me over to Elgin, for I have a head-ache, and want to ride it off."

The boy bowed and disappeared, while I went in the house to torment myself with imaginary horrors until evening. Miserable for fear Gabe's suspicions might prove correct, yet not daring to hint such a thing to Ethel, or even my father, from dread of alarming or annoying them unnecessarily, I determined to relieve my mind in a measure, at all events, by telling my suspicions, and also what I had just heard, to uncle Dunbar.

My heart leaped with delight when Lenox Clifford came home safe and sound from the parsonage, for I had wrought myself up into a perfect frenzy of dread, by imagining him strangled or stabbed, and then flung into a dark way-side pool by the peddler, and forthwith, as stimulants to my morbid fancy, every hideous murder of which I had ever either heard or read, stood marshaled before me in ghastly array. Before sundown on that same evening, having succeeded partially in banishing these tormenting fears by a rapid ride, I found myself discussing the matter with Aunt Kate and Uncle Dunbar, on the balcony at Elgin.

"If it is Basil Thorn," I said, "there is no knowing what fiendish motive brings him here again disguised, and indeed believing that no crime is too enormous, either for him to conceive or execute, I cannot help feeling a dread of something awful, and am particularly anxious about Mr. Clifford's personal safety—what shall we do ?"

Who could answer ?

They were puzzled, and apprehensive too—and yet upon the mere say-so of a negro, what earthly ground was there for arresting the peddler ?

The dusk of autumn twilight crept on slowly as I yet lingered talking at Elgin, and when at last I called for Archey and my horse, they said it was too late for me to ride home alone with a servant, and insisted upon sending for Michael McAlpine to accompany me, to which I most readily consented ; for, though not very timid, the idea of riding home through the dark woods at that hour, with no more chivalrous attendant than Archey to protect me—perhaps from the murderous hands of the grizzly vagrant—was not cheering.

" Mr. Michael ain't here, sir ; he went out to hunt up Miss Pearl's filly soon arter dinner, and he's not got back," said Archey, who was sent by my uncle to summon young McAlpine.

" Well, well, sit down, he will be here directly, and if not soon enough to go home with you, why then, (if you won't let me accompany you, Miss Amy, though I could do so without the least trouble) why just write a note by the negro and stay all night."

So we began again discussing the then all absorbing

theme of whether there was any real possibility of Basil Thorn (*alias* Dr. Foster) circulating again through the neighborhood under a hoary wig and green goggles?

Presently there was a slam of the front gate, and some one on horseback rode furiously up the avenue.

" Why there's Michael now ! What on earth brings him this way in such a hurry? Hal-loo! Michael, what's the matter ?. Has Frolic broken her neck ?"

But the laugh accompanying this question was checked at the sight of McAlpine's pallid face, who had come up to the balcony evidently the bearer of startling news, and in extreme terror I cried out :

" Has anything happened at Woodburn ? Where is my father—Mr. Clifford—have you seen them, Michael ?"

" Oh, don't be frightened, Miss, it's all right there, no doubt; but something dreadful has happened, though to no one we care about. A man, sir," turning to my uncle, "has been murdered between the Glen and town, which I was the first to discover while hunting for Mrs. Clare's little filly out in a lonesome piece of woods, and it was such an awful sight, sir, I did not tarry a moment, but rode over in breathless haste to tell you and see what is best to be done."

" Murdered !" we all exclaimed almost in a breath. " Oh ! how dreadful !"

" Tell us all about it, Michael, my boy; who is it, and

where and how did you happen to find the body?" said my uncle.

" Well," he replied, " the shadows were growing deeper in the woods, for evening was creeping on, as I circled the little thicket of holly, thorn and beech about a mile beyond the Glen towards town, hoping to find Miss Pearl's pony, when my horse reared back so suddenly as almost to throw me from the saddle, at the same time snorting violently as if in great terror. I threw myself down instantly from the frightened beast, and was advancing towards a dark object in the thicket, when the ringing bay of a blood-hound caused me to start back with horror—for at the same moment my foot sank in an oozy puddle, from which this fierce creature, crouched so low that I could scarcely see him for the tangled vines and brush-wood, was lap-ping—not water, as I at first supposed—but blood !

" I felt faint with terror and disgust, for my feet were saturated with it; and there, half-hidden in that dense copse, with his ghastly face upturned to the sky, while red streams were flowing from his throat and a wound over his heart, lay the body of a thick set, heavy man, whose bare head—though it looked as if shaved, not bald—was dabbled with blood, and a gray wig, probably torn off in that deadly struggle, I found lying at a little distance from the body, and near a heavy pack of goods—which induced me to believe that the murdered man is no other than a peddler who for several days past has been wandering through the neighborhood. Queerly enough, too, the goods were untouched, thus proving that this awful deed was not committed for the purpose of robbing the unfortunate stranger. I am no coward, Mr. Dunbar; but the awful sight of that gory corpse, and the fierce brute drinking blood, made me so sick with horror I had scarcely strength enough to mount my horse and ride home, but when fairly off I gave him the rein and left that dismal wood behind as soon as possible.".

We all listened with breathless attention to Michael's dreadful story, and when he ceased speaking I remarked aside to my uncle—

"If Archey's gossip about the peddler had any foundation of truth, there could be little doubt as to who had committed this crime." But he instantly checked me, saying:

"Let the law find out, and prosecute the murderer, my child. It is a grave and awful charge for one human being to bring against another; and particularly when all you or I know is founded upon the idle tattle of a negro—just enough, perhaps, to bring an innocent person to unjust punishment, a far greater evil than permitting the guilty one even to go unpunished."

I felt the truth and justice of this rebuke, and never afterwards hinted at what Archey had said, save to those who were as careful in guarding the secret as myself.

This murder made a great sensation throughout our quiet neighborhood, and indeed the whole country—not only on account of the deep mystery by which it was enveloped, but because ere long a report became whispered about that the murdered man was none other than Dr. Foster, *alias* Basil Thorn, in a new disguise, which came not only from the servants but from the overseer at the Glen who had been there while the pretended Foster owned it, and said he recognized his former employer not in the living, but the dead peddler, when bereft of his disguise, in spite of that shaven head and the disfiguring wounds upon his face and throat. My father, who also saw the body, felt no doubt upon the subject, and we were all humbled and overpowered by such unmistakable evidences of the just retribution of an offended God. Had that dreadful man been permitted to live (even a few days longer) who can tell what fatal turn his vengeance might have taken? Perhaps then, too, there might have been a murder, and a far fairer corpse, with soft brown hair and marble brow, found lying cold and dreary in some dismal, lonely spot, and a broken-hearted mourner left pining hopelessly within our home! God be praised for averting the possibility of such unspeakable wretchedness—the very imagining of which caused our darling Ethel, when informed of Basil Thorn's fate, to cling, weeping, around her husband's neck, as she whispered—

"He never came here again save for a dark purpose, and I shudder at the thought of what it might have been."

The fact that "Wolf," the blood-hound, of whom Gabe

had charge, was found reveling in a gory meal beside the body, gave rise to a suspicion that he might be the guilty party; but as he was proved to have been in the field at work during the whole of that day, even up to the very hour when Michael discovered the body, and as the dog's chain was broken, there existed no testimony to back this suspicion, and therefore after being for awhile kept in close custody, examined and cross-examined, the great black giant was released. He was sullen when questioned, saying he did not kill the man, but (suspecting him to be Foster) had an opportunity offered would have done so, for he was the worst man that ever lived, and deserved to be killed.

Nothing was ever known of what Archey had said to me, and after the deed, that most discreet Ethiopian, either from fear of getting into trouble himself or through friend-ship for Gabe, considered silence his best policy, and re-mained forever mute upon the subject; but the roll of his eye, accompanied by a low chuckle, as he said—

"What I tell you, Miss?"—pointing towards the Glen when first I saw him after the murder, convinced me what he thought; but placing my finger upon my lips I passed on, and Archey was smart enough to take that silent hint.

All efforts to detect the guilty person were unavailing at that time; but here let me mention, before dismissing the subject finally, years afterwards the ravings of a dying woman, at N——, revealed, in herself, the murderer of

Basil Thorn. She was known to us as a young and pretty girl, though poor, and a seamstress—having worked for Ethel before her first marriage—and afterwards we heard she had become worthless and abandoned to habits of intemperance. Among this poor creature's clothes were found letters from young Thorn, addressing her as his wife, and others (bearing a later date) in which he denied, with curses, that she had any claim upon him, and swearing their marriage to have been a mockery. She was, doubtless, the haggard woman described by Mrs. Slone to Ethel and myself as having been repeatedly driven away by Foster from the Glen, and at last, stung to desperation by his neglect and curses—no doubt penetrating the disguise under which he came, like a "thing of evil," that second time among us—this fierce avenger, inflamed to madness by strong drink, laid in wait for and murdered her destroyer!

Oh! the hardened and frightful wickedness of that man's course! How can such escape punishment here, and greater condemnation hereafter?

CHAPTER XXXIV.

AN UNEXPECTED MEETING.

'Tis sad to leave our childhood's sunny home,
For the sweet spells of love which bind us there
Rude contact with the world will sometimes break,
And when we come again, a shade of care,
Or new found joy, perchance, may make it seem less fair.

SHORTLY after the events related in the preceding chapter we left Woodburn, and I never realized how dear to my heart was this beautiful home of my childhood until through a mist of blinding tears it faded from my view. The anticipated novelty of traveling through foreign lands even could not overcome my regret at parting with so many dear asscciations, and also our beloved friends at Elgin and the parsonage, especially Pearl, who was as a sister to both Ethel and myself, and scarcely less dear to us than we were to each other; yet it was a source of great consolation that we left her so happy and so fully absorbed with her new duties of wife and housekeeper, and I am rather inclined to believe Cecil Clare had it entirely within his power to console the Pearl of Elgin for our departure.

I shall not dwell upon our journey. Suffice it to say

that Mr. Morton made it convenient to join us in New York. Before we reached Liverpool I knew the reason of his anxiety to make one of our party, and also why his acceptance of Mr. Clifford's invitation to accompany us to "Clifton"—my brother-in-law's beautiful place in ——shire—was conditional, being to the effect "that he would be most happy to do so, but it must depend on circumstances." This contingency, whatever it was, resulted unfavorably for Mr. Clifford's wishes, as he left us at London and went to travel on the continent.

We did not meet Victor and Eva Dunbar, as, after their marriage, they sailed from Havre for America, and a few weeks subsequent to our arrival at Clifton we received letters from Aunt Kate and Pearl expatiating upon the charms of Victor's bride. Then, for the first time, the regretful sadness heretofore haunting my heart with Woodburn memories, and at times possessing me with a perverse desire to return, faded away—for the great fear which had oppressed me of meeting those two happy beings abroad was lifted, and since they were now so near my sunny southern home the thought of remaining away from it for an indefinite period became less distasteful to me. Indeed there was a positive satisfaction in calculating the wide distance separating me from Woodburn, and in dwelling upon the certainty that no possible chance, for a very long time, could bring us in contact with Victor and his wife.

Clifton, my sister's new English home, was a grand old

place, and if present happiness can atone for past misery, they were compensated for even the bitter wretchedness resulting from Basil Thorn's malignant vengeance—for though it had left a shadow on Ethel's life too heavily fraught with gloom to pass entirely away, yet was that shadow brightened now by a perfect sunshine of earthly bliss. The three months we passed with them at Clifton, during part of the time Ralph was also there—has left a memory of that sweet and peaceful happiness whose reality calmed my feverish and tormenting regrets over the vanished dreams of early girlhood.

In January we all went to Paris, Mr. Clifford and Ethel at last acceding to our earnest request that they would travel with us over the continent. What young person can resist the fascinations of Paris? I was amazed, bewildered at the endless variety of wonders presented to me there, and proposed that our "tour through Europe" should begin and end in this emporium of magnificence. Mr. Clifford introduced us to Madam Armond, who was a most charming old lady with soft gray curls and courtly manners. She appreciated Ethel fully, quite to my satisfaction even, which is saying a great deal, for the intense admiration and affection I awarded my peerless sister made me exceedingly exacting as to the esteem she was held in by others. We found it almost impossible to satisfy Madam Armond's curiosity regarding Pearl, who was so dear to her aunt for her mother's sake, though as yet personally unknown. The old lady said her most earnest prayer was that she might live long enough to bless Olivia's child—for Olivia had been unto her as a beloved daughter.

In reverting to Mr. Clifford's early history she told us that Henrique and Orliff having worked for years among the chain-gang and then been released, were afterwards convicted of other monstrous crimes and sentenced to transportation, when, on the very night before the sentence was to be carried into execution, Henrique dashed himself to pieces in trying to escape through his prison window by means of a rope made of the bed-clothes torn into strips, which, proving too weak for his weight, broke, precipitating him down from a great height on to the stone pavement, where he was picked up shortly afterwards by the night-watch, a lifeless mass. Orliff was transported for life, and Madam A. knew nothing further regarding his fate.

I must now pass rapidly over the time until our arrival at Florence, where I took it into my silly little head to plunge recklessly—not into the Arno—but into that dismal swamp of despondency elegantly entitled "the blues." Why so? Because it happened to be the spot where two people (now far away, and entirely unconscious of causing me the slightest unhappiness,) had chanced to meet and fall in love with each other, greatly to my discomfiture—and, in spite of my respect for the decalogue, be it here confessed that I was occasionally in the habit of coveting the happiness found by those same envied lovers at Florence;

and hence it came to pass that I, Amy Percy, on a certain evening towards the middle of February, 1845, stood on the banks of the Arno watching the sunset clouds pale and the yellow moon come up, feeling very forlorn and most egotistically sorry for myself. Weary with climbing about a ruined villa near by, (where the rest of my party still lingered) having no fancy for being dusted by mouldy curtains, or festooned with cobwebs from toiling through deserted halls and dim old picture galleries, despoiled perhaps of the chief artistic gems which constituted their bygone glory, I had stolen off to brood drearily over a past in whose lost joys—rather selfishly to be sure—I felt far more interested.

I really do enjoy looking at beautiful or curious things in frequented places, but this mania possessing most people, to go rummaging through deserted old mansions, be they ever so grand, is rather beyond my comprehensive love for, or appreciation of the mystic and marvelous. The dusty arras, with its dismal rustling, in chambers said by tradition to have been years ago inhabited, perhaps for one night, by a celebrity (which may or may not be true), never presented any particular charm for me—neither am I fond of cultivating the ghostly fascinations of a gloomy apartment, wherein story says a diabolical murder has been committed long ago, and where dark looking stains on the floor are pointed out as blood, which all the floods of all the oceans could not remove—though perhaps there was never either mop, scrubbing brush or soap introduced within those haunted, or rather supposed to be haunted walls.

Now it is far more likely that such mysterious spots resulted from the upsetting of a subtile hair-dye by some shaky old bachelor, in by-gone centuries, or the breaking of a bottle of vinegar rouge by an antiquated beauty, while vainly endeavoring, through the sorceries of art, to replace the vanished freshness and glory of her youth, than that they were produced by the murderous knife of a jealous husband or lover! At all events I am very sceptical regarding such marvelous tales, unless authenticated by history; and it was my habit, when deserted castles or villas were being explored, after submitting myself to be dragged about for a time greatly against my inclination, to steal off and enjoy the out-door world of beauty, as on the present occasion when lingering at twilight on the banks of the Arno. Suddenly I was startled by the splashing sound of oars, and almost at the same moment, a very small skiff ran in to shore just below where I stood. My first impulse was to turn and retrace my steps towards the villa, but before I could possibly effect my retreat, a gentleman bounded up the bank, who was apparently astonished no little at the sight of a solitary damsel in that unfrequented place—for the bank prevented his seeing me until, to the surprise of both parties, Amy Percy and Clarence Morton stood again, and most unexpectedly, face to face.

"This is not altogether accidental," he said, as I greeted him cordially and expressed my astonishment at seeing him there, " I was in the city when your party came, but only heard of their arrival this evening, and being informed of your intention to explore the ruins in this direction, could not resist the temptation of following, yet have found you somewhat sooner than I expected—why are you here alone, and where are the Cliffords and your father ?"

These questions were soon answered, and feeling quite cheered by his presence, I had little difficulty in freeing myself from the blues; for notwithstanding the fact of my perverse refusal to encourage Mr. Morton's accompanying us to Clifton—be it known to thee, oh gentle reader, that Mr. Clifford's friend was very far from being a disagreeable person, on the contrary, exceedingly cultivated, with fine natural powers of mind and great originality, he was a most charming companion, and as the old subject upon which we had failed to agree when crossing the ocean was for the present left at rest, I found myself delighted with Clarence Morton's piquant conversation, and the moonlit river, and the dreamy light of that Italian sky appeared absolutely more attractive in their beauty now, than when gazed on by me a short time before through a sombre vista of morbid melancholy.

The exploring party were all surprised and happy at meeting my companion, and so we returned to the city, all well pleased, and one, namely myself, feeling, from causes unknown or at least undefined at that time, far less forlorn than when I left it. The next morning Ethel asked me very timidly if I had any objection to Mr. Morton's joining our party until his departure for the East. He had begged of Mr. Clifford to find out, if I objected, and hinted very humbly that the forbidden subject should not be revived. I turned red, felt half provoked and replied,

"Mr. Morton has a right to travel when and where he pleases, without asking my permission. How absurd to ask me."

At this little outbreak my sister laughed and went off, I presume to inform the gentleman that no embargo was laid by a certain young lady upon his traveling with Mr. Clifford, as nothing further was said about the matter, and Mr. Morton remained one of our party for the next seven or eight months. We visited all the most interesting portions of Europe, and though almost constantly with the gentleman during this period, let me remark, *en passant*, I was not tired of him, no, not in the least, and rather glad than otherwise when he agreed to return with us and spend a few weeks at Clifton, entirely *en ami*—unselfish Morton!—to Lenox Clifford, who was not obliged to exhaust his eloquence in persuading this same pattern of disinterested friendship to sojourn with him most willingly!

And lo! he lingered amid the beguiling beauties of that fine old English home—for Clarence Morton was a lover of nature—and hence, how could he fail to appreciate lawns, parks, gardens, of such rare perfection? Until at last the gentleman who was to be his *compagnon du voyage* through the East, wrote to know what had become of this loiterer. Now I do verily believe he was not just then so zealous in his desire to reach the holy city as Godfrey de Bouillon or the intrepid Rinaldo, who dared and won so much in those glorious days of crusading chivalry! There was a charming little lake at Clifton, and beside its limpid deeps Mr. Morton was very fond of wandering, in company with an American lassie whose disposition he chose to admire, having seen her upon the occasion of their first acquaintance shatter a little pearl fan rather spitefully against the trunk of a palm tree; and there is not the slightest doubt this deluded individual, with a most egregious, unpardonable want of taste, would have preferred lingering in the society of said damsel by the fairy lake, to plunging headlong into the Jordan or refreshing himself with a morning bath in the pitchy waves of the Dead Sea!

However he had promised to go, and promises with such men are sacred; so one cool, gray, misty day towards the close of October, he left us, looking desperate and forlorn, a handsome likeness of the "knight of the rueful countenance."

I wonder if the "spiteful" young lady was sorry to see him go? Nobody asked her; but there were two or three bright drops on the beautiful white tea rosebud he had given her at parting, and when she put it in one of his favorite books to press, they trickled out and moistened the dainty pages. I wonder if they were dew-drops? Certain it is she could not help thinking it odd how agreeably Clarence Morton had effected the change from a discarded lover to a most charming friend, and furthermore these reflections ended in that perverse little heart of her's wishing, most perversely, to know if he loved her yet? Alas! he was gone now, and I think there would have been more drops on the rosebud had she dreamed how many years would pass and how many sad changes take place before they met again. Such is life with its endless chances and uncertainties.

In November my father took Ralph and myself to Paris for the winter and spring, that we might be perfected in the French language before returning to America. This six months was a bright, pleasant epoch in my life, and yet during the time I fell back somewhat into a habit of building air-castles again, though with far more maturity of architectural taste and experience, and with even a surer foundation I thought than the little withered rosebud which so often distracted my thoughts from the fascinating pages of Victor Hugo and Racine.

In June we returned to Clifton, where Mr. Clifford and Ethel were supremely happy in the possession of a lovely boy, the glowing, healthy image of their little lost Percy, and bearing also his name. On our arrival from the continent he was three months old, and as fair a child as ever blessed the love of two such doting parents. And so when the autumn leaves were once more falling at Clifton, we left them—absorbed in this newly-found joy—to go back once more to our far-off home at Woodburn, where they promised to visit us in the course of a year.

Before we reached America, Victor and Eva Dunbar had left Elgin for her father's home in Maryland, and so again it chanced we did not meet, which was a source of regret, for then I felt a wish to know and love my cousin Victor's wife. How strange it seemed to be at home again, and how pleasant—yet I felt so old, being almost twenty; and then missing Ethel and Mr. Clifford made a sad void in our family circle — long was it ere we became accustomed, and never entirely reconciled, to their absence.

The Clares were very happy—Pearl as lovely as ever, and quite matronly with a sweet little Ethel in her arms. Aunt Kate's cap was as far back on her head as when it gave her fingers the slip in their spasmodic efforts to pull it forward when we parted two years before. In joy or grief it was ever given to backsliding, while its wearer remained the same dear, kind, faithful Aunty.

Uncle Dunbar still rejoiced in the dispensation of an insatiable hospitality, and mush, gruel, broth and black tea were, as usual, in high repute at the Elgin board, which Mr. Ogden and others of the same dyspeptic fraternity were wont to illuminate, as formerly, with their bilious presence.

And here let me drop the curtain over several years, to lift it again after many changes had altered the aspect of things both at Elgin and Woodburn.

CHAPTER XXXV.

AGAIN AT WOODBURN.

AGAIN upon the gallery at Woodburn there was a group assembled on a day as fair as that with which this story opened, when we were so merrily discussing Mr. Clifford's expected arrival.

The sun was warm and bright, the air again redolent with fragrance of myrtle, rose and jasmine—the birds singing as joyously as if the shadow of a mighty sorrow had not of late fallen upon the threshold of that beloved home. The group was changed. My sister Ethel again appeared, scarcely less beautiful than when she sat almost on the same spot nearly ten years before, laughing at Ralph's ideal picture of our dreaded English tutor—but a deep shade of sadness rested on her lovely brow, while the close mourning of her dress—as did mine also—betokened that our loss had been recent and heavy. There were golden spring flowers there again, for a beautiful little girl was twining garlands of laburnums from the same old tree, with which she proceeded to decorate a venerable dog resting half asleep and wholly patient by her side on the front steps. Poor Bang! he was too old and lazy now to torment the cat, and must submit in his turn to be thus delicately tormented.

Alas! the wreaths of my childhood were withered long ago, and that beloved head of silvery tresses which it had been then my delight to crown, was now lying low beneath the willows. No wonder Woodburn looked gloomy to us in spite of its many attractions—even arrayed thus in the full glory of spring-time freshness! Ah! none can realize our loss save those who have looked their last on such a father! Ralph, too, was gone—not dead, but married, and living far away in Virginia.

Mr. Clifford was with us, looking the very picture of a fond proud parent, as he stood out on the lawn, watching his son Percy, now five years old, who shouted aloud with joy from the back of a beautiful little Texas pony, which he had ventured to mount for the first time, and was holding on, not only to the bridle, but to the animal's long thick mane, delighted and yet half afraid, as Archey the second—being a worthy descendant of that most notable African—led the docile thing up and down the carriage walk. It was a pretty sight! the handsome child, with his bright, expressive face and long brown curls, laughing and shouting to the young Ethiopian, whose sleek black skin and woolly head appeared in fine contrast to his little master's aristocratic beauty, as he, the darkey, grinned and chuckled—which last accompaniment he undoubtedly came by most honestly—evidently enjoying and participating in Percy's delight. And here it may not be out of place to remark regarding our tattling acquaintance, Archey the elder, that he continued still high in favor at Woodburn— being rather more dignified and somewhat less inclined to gossip, since becoming the respectable father of a family, whereof the dusky little urchin leading Percy Clifford's pony, was the eldest hope; let us trust my faithful Lucy, who had the honor of being Archey's better half, while teaching her offspring the virtues of their sire, will also warn them against the evils of eaves-dropping.

Aunt Kate was now with us, and also in close mourning —for dear good Uncle Dunbar had been called away a year before my father, and Elgin was shut up, as aunty could not remain there alone, and the Clares were abroad. She sat in the place occupied by Rachel Thorn at the opening of this story, looking placid, yet older and sadder than when first introduced to the reader—even her cap had settled down now, for it was of white crape, and too close in its pattern to fly backwards as formerly. The old lady's chief happiness was in Pearl and her children, for whom she was at present knitting soft white stockings, in anticipation of their return the following autumn. She was still devoted to Victor and Eva, but almost despaired of seeing them sometimes, or the lovely little daughter regarding whom they wrote such glowing accounts; for though their nominal home was in New York, yet, preferring Europe, they had been abroad now for two years. Though generally regular in writing to Aunt Kate, many months had elapsed lately without her receiving a letter, which caused her kind anxious heart much pain, and she often expressed herself as very uneasy about the wanderers. Ethel and Mr. Clifford had been summoned to come over when our beloved father's health commenced failing, and fortunately arrived two months before his death.

"Tarrage tummin, mamma," lisped little Amy, as she toddled up to the door, having left old Bang enveloped in garlands to run out where her father stood for more flowers, "tummin now, most fru de front date."

And she pointed with her chubby little finger in the direction indicated, where, sure enough, we saw a close carriage rolling up towards the house, and my mind involuntarily flew back to that wretched, never-to-be-forgotten time, when Archey rushed in to announce the coming of Basil Thorn's freight of vengeance to Woodburn. There was but a moment, however, to indulge this gloomy retrospect, for the carriage soon drew up before the door, and our astonishment may be better imagined than described, when Clarence Morton sprang out, holding in his arms a frail, fair, golden-haired girl, about four years of age, who clung to him nervously, and hid her face confidingly upon his shoulder.

After his return from that journey to the East, undertaken so reluctantly, Clarence—unaware, doubtless, of the tender manner in which a certain spiteful young lady had preserved that parting rose-bud—went off to India, and engaged in business there. We corresponded occasionally, as friends—for he proudly refrained from alluding to a subject, once forbidden, and from which the interdict had had never been removed, neither had he been in the slightest degree encouraged to plead for its removal. We were equally proud, and I liked him all the better for meeting my haughty spirit as it deserved to be met, while I sometimes found myself wondering how the male species, under such circumstances, could be so determined in their obstinacy. Unreasonable girl!

His letters were eagerly watched for, and as a long time had elapsed since my heart was gladdened by one of these foreign missives, I feared, perchance, some evil had befallen my far-off friend, and never realized the fullness of this anxiety until it was suddenly relieved, and I found myself again in his presence after a separation of years.

His story was soon told, and sad enough we found it. Victor and Eva, being apprized of his intention to leave India at a certain time, made their arrangements to quit Germany, where they had been for several months, and meet him in England, from whence they would all return to

America forthwith. But alas for human foresight! They met with unavoidable detention at a small town in Germany, where—unknown to them—a deadly fever had been raging, by which, soon after their arrival, Victor was stricken down, and became so alarmingly ill that Eva wrote a frantic letter to her brother in England, imploring him to hurry on at once and join them.

Two weeks elapsed ere the letter was received, and though Clarence lost no time in seeking his beloved sister, full of fear, yet hoping for the best, he found her a widow raving in delirium. For awhile he trusted it might be the result of grief and unceasing watching: but ah! too soon were there unmistakable signs of the same fearful malady, whose malignity had stricken down her idolized husband, and in mercy smote her also. That fond brother could not stay the destroyer's hand; and suddenly, in the freshness and vigor of youth, were these two loving ones cut off together, leaving their little Eva doubly an orphan. I say the blow was dealt in mercy to that mourning widow, Eva Dunbar's love for her husband being of that absorbing kind which cannot brook the loss of its idol, and earth without Victor to her would have been a desert—life a blank.

She loved her child for it was his; but maternal affection was secondary to that one overmastering passion, and the little Eva could not have consoled such crushing grief, or revived, by her dependent, clinging love, one germ of hope in her mother's wretched heart, had she lived on despairing after that withering blow.

Clarence Morton's mother was dead, and having no near female relation to whose care he was willing to confide the child, knowing at the same time Aunt Kate's devotion to Victor, he at once determined that she should take charge, for him, of little Eva, while his by adoption she was and must ever be.

Victor Dunbar's child! I could not realize it! For we had never met since he left Elgin after his mad attack on Cecil Clare. And he was dead! I should never see him again—the idol of my early girlhood—yet only remembered now with the fond, affectionate regret of a sister.

The fair wee stranger was soon at home with Percy and Amy as playmates, and such a winning being did she prove, we all put up petitions to be the keeper of so lovely a charge; but Aunt Kate contended in a very determined manner that she would never resign the care of her darling Victor's baby to any one save Clarence Morton's wife.

Thus it was that matters stood when an answer came from Ralph to a letter in which I had strongly urged him to purchase Woodburn. It belonged to me. I could not live there alone, and such was my attachment for the dear old place that spite Mr. Clifford's and Ethel's earnest desire to have me go back with them and live at Clifton, I could not make up my mind to let the home of my childhood pass into stranger hands, which must have been the case had I left it permanently—and hence my desire that Ralph should be the purchaser, for then I might remain there at least part of the time.

My brother's letter was full of affection, wishing he could buy Woodburn, but it was impossible, as his wife would be miserable away from her family and friends, and urging me, if determined to be an old maid,—for I was twenty-five—by all means to invite some still more anti-quated spinster—Aunt Kate for instance, or Miss Tabitha Tipps, if anxious to cultivate gossip in my old age—to come and dwell there with me in peaceful, dignified retire-ment. He thought the sweet, balmy atmosphere of Wood-burn would improve Miss Tabitha's temper. But—joking aside—he hoped I would not sell the old place; better rent for awhile (if anxious to go abroad) or leave it in charge of Michael McAlpine, for there was a possibility yet of my marrying—more wonderful things than that had happened. Spinsters more venerable than myself had been known to commit similar indiscretions, etc., etc.

It was like Ralph—so completely in his merry, rattle-te-bang style, that spite our sadness, it brought such pleasant memories of our dear light-hearted brother that we were cheered and amused by this missive so full of the dash and fun with which he used to keep the house alive in by-gone days—the morning hours of our fair, unclouded youth. Then half in laughter, half in tears, I told Aunt Kate she must stay with me, for Pearl had husband and children while I felt all alone.   And so at last it was arranged that we should keep old maids' hall together at Woodburn.

Poor, confiding old lady !   The next chapter will disclose how faithless I proved to this compact—with what ruthless ingratitude I repaid her unselfish devotion !

CHAPTER XXXVI.

In vain we battle with our fate,
 To alter its decree
That might have changed it, comes too late,
 What God ordains will be.

WEEKS elapsed, and still Clarence Morton lingered at Woodburn. Nor was this to be wondered at so long as my brother-in-law remained, of whom he was very fond. Oh! Lenox Clifford, I wonder if you entertain a full appreciation of this disinterested friendship? Little Eva was much attached to me, for children are easily won by kindness, and I petted her even more than Ethel's babies. A poor little orphan child! she needed all the affection and tenderness we had to spare.

One sweet evening in June—the very anniversary of that fragrant ride through a certain magnolia grove ten years before—I was standing with Eva in the conservatory, beneath the same date-palm against which my fan had been shivered on Ethel's wedding night, when the amiability of my mood was not increased by the intelligence conveyed to me most unsuspectingly by Clarence Morton.

There were scarlet geraniums blooming on a shelf far above our heads which Eva wanted—how human it is, even from infancy, to covet things beyond our reach—and begged me to get them for her. So, catching up the child, I stepped on to the lowest shelf and held her towards the flowers, saying :

"There, now cousin Amy's baby can get them' herself."

"Me ove tussey Amy, but me is Uncy Tarance's baby ; he tey me shan't be anybody's baby but his," and the little witch laughed as I snatched her back and said :

"But won't you be Amy's baby if she gives you such pretty flowers and loves you so? Then suppose I won't let you have them ?"

"Uncy Tarance oves me too, and he divs me every cing I want, and me tan't help it if oo won't div me de red fowers, for me promised to be his ittie Eva always ; but, peasey, tussey Amy, let. me dit de pitty red sings," and she kissed me coaxingly.

"You shall have them, my dainty bird. Amy loves you dearly, if you won't be her baby," I replied, tossing the child up again towards those scarlet clusters, when a full low voice whispered in my ear—

"She shall be yours too, Amy, if you will it so. Say, tell me, shall I have two treasures instead of one ? For nine years have I loved you, and something less cold in your manner of late rekindles a ray of the hope quenched out so long ago.   Say, shall Eva be our baby?"

I almost dropped the child when first he spoke; for, believing myself alone with her, his voice startled me.   In a moment or two she had plucked the geraniums, and putting her down with cheeks almost as deeply flushed as those scarlet blossoms I said :

"There, deary, run and show them to Aunty Kate." She toddled off laughing, and looking back at us said :

"Uncy Tarance, tussey Amy tied to make me her baby, but I toud'nt do dat," and the wee fairy disappeared.

Then, while I stood bewildered, overpowered by a new, delicious sense of happiness, my head was drawn down gently to its own true resting place, as he whispered again in that rich, deep voice—

"Nine years!—yet it was worth waiting so long, darling, for such a wife!"

And so it came to pass that Woodburn was not sold; neither did it become an abiding place for old maids— though Aunt Kate, more faithful to her agreement than I had been to mine, spent half her time only at Elgin with the Clares, giving us the other half, always maintaining a jealous and special care over the child she never did entirely resign even to Clarence Morton's wife.

Years have gone by since then.   There are bright young faces lighting up our home—gay, glad young voices echoing through the groves and garden of Woodburn.   Loving and united, strangers would not think that the eldest and fairest of that fair band is our adopted daughter, our own Eva Dunbar.

I hear her sweet voice now singing to my other children out in the jasmine bower, for it is summer—and even as I write, the spicy breath of those old box borders comes drifting through the casement, the same I loved so as a joyous child, a dreaming girl, giving forth ever, beneath sunshine or rime, the same aromatic, evergreen odor—a fragrance fresh, pure and unchanging—meet emblem of that immortal hope which alone has power to render the fruition of our earthly joy complete.

THE END.

Ready April 15th.

DANGERFIELD'S REST.

OR

BEFORE THE STORM.

A Novel of American Life and Manners. One volume, large 12mo. Price, $1.50.

This is the production of a polished and experienced pen, qualified by much travel, experience and literary practice in other walks of literature, to attempt an elaborate description of American Life, Politics, Letters and Factions, whose clashing led us to the Great Rebellion.

It will be especially attractive to those who believe in the indestructibility of the Union, and to those who desire to see the American people rise through their present ordeal to a higher standard in morals and manners.

Ready April 20th.

WOODBURN.

A Novel by Rosa Vertner Jeffrey, author of "Poems by Rosa." One volume, 12mo. Price, $1.50.

From the Louisville Journal.

A NEW ATTRACTION IN THE LITERARY WORLD.—A NOVEL FROM THE PEN OF MRS. ROSA VERTNER JEFFREY.—A novel entitled "WOODBURN," by Mrs. Rosa Vertner Jeffrey, who under the *nom de plume* of "ROSA" has achieved so bright a reputation as a poetess, is forthcoming from the press of Sheldon & Company, New York City. Where its scene is laid, or what its plot is, or who is its hero or heroine, are points upon which the public as yet have received no inkling; but those who are acquainted with the genius and taste of the fair authoress must feel assured, that, in respect to the scene and plot as well as in all other respects, the production will be brimful of charm. . Her legion of admirers feel a world of curiosity respecting the work but no solicitude. · They confide implicitly, as they well may, in her rare and beautiful powers.

We predict for "WOODBURN" a very rapid and extended sale.

MARION HARLAND'S WORKS.

Uniform editions of the works of this favorite authoress are now ready.

ALONE. 1 volume. 12mo. Price $1.50.

HIDDEN PATH. 1 volume. 12mo. Price $1.50.

MOSS SIDE. 1 volume. 12mo. Price $1.50.

NEMESIS. 1 volume. 12mo. Price $1.50.

MIRIAM. 1 volume. 12mo. Price $1.50.

HUSKS. 1 volume. 12mo. Price $1 50.

NOTICES OF "NEMESIS."

" It is a story of surpassing excellence—its scene laid in the sunny South, about half a century ago ; its characters limned with a master's hand ; its sketches graphic and thrilling, and its conclusion very effective. Such a work is beyond criticism, and needs no praise."—*Troy American.*

" In all the characteristics of a powerful novel it will compare favorably with the best productions of a season that has produced some of the most successful books that have appeared for a long time."—*Courier and Enquirer.*

" ' Nemesis ' is, by far, the best American novel published for very many years.—*Philadelphia Press.*

" It is worthy of note that the former works of this authoress have been republished in England, France, and Germany—indeed, no other American female writer has the honor of a republication in the Leipzig issues of Alphonse Durr, which embraces Bryant, Longfellow, Hawthorne, and Prescott."—*N. Y. Home Journal.*

" Marion Harland, by intrinsic power of character, drawing and descriptive facility, holds the public with increasing fascination."—*Washington Statesman.*

NEW BOOKS THIS FALL.

PETER CARRADINE,

OR

THE MARTINDALE PASTORAL.

By Caroline Chesebro'.

One vol. 12mo. $1.50.

BROKEN COLUMNS.

A Novel of great power and interest.

One vol. 12mo. $1.50.

(From Peter Bayne, Author of " Christian Life," " Essays," etc. etc.)

" I have complied with your request, and read " Broken Columns" *carefully*
I do not hesitate to pronounce it, in my judgment, superior to " Adam Bede "
The plot is admirable, and the execution is a singular nearness to perfection.
You must not hesitate to publish it.   I am confident when it is read and
known it will have an extensive sale."

HUSKS.

By Marion Harland.

Author of " Alone," " Hidden Path," " Moss Side," " Nemesis," and
" Miriam."

One vol 12mo. $1.50.

CHRISTMAS STORIES.

By Charles Dickens.

An elegant edition on tinted paper, small quarto size, illustrated from
designs by F. O. C. Darley.

One vol. 4to.

SHELDON & COMPANY, Publishers,
335 *Broadway, New York.*